THE LADY OF DEERPARK

THE LADY OF
DEERPARK

———◆———

BY

SEUMAS O'KELLY

Library of Congress Number: 96-060146
ISBN: 1-885983-14-x

Design and composition by Wilsted & Taylor

Printed in the U.S.A.

TO
S. O'S

Contents

PART ONE

MARY HEFFERNAN

CHAPTER ONE

I

PAUL JENNINGS, the President wants you."
I tossed out an ace, put on my coat, left the ball
alley, and found the President awaiting me in his
parlour. He laid a kindly hand on my shoulder; in the
other he held a recently opened telegram. He seated me
on a chair near the table. And while I sat there the news
was broken to me of the family calamity. My father had
died rather suddenly. I could speak no word, no tears
came to me. A blinding sense of sorrow and a curious
elation struggled in my mind for mastery.

A little later as I flew up the stairs to the dormitory
this strange elation got the upper hand. Although I was
half-way through my last term I could have cried out a
thanksgiving that I was to escape from that school, for I
hated it—hated it with that hidden sickening unreason-
ing hatred which sometimes makes miserable a young
life. I was about to get away from it all, and death was a
remote thing to my mind. I fired my miserable belong-
ings into the trunk with joy.

Two evenings later I was back in the solitude of the hills, sitting alone with my mother, all our friends having gone away after the funeral.

She looked at me a little sadly and said, "I wonder, Paul, how you will fill his place?"

I knew that the serious side of life had begun for me. My father had been agent of the Heffernan property. Along the highway, like a jagged memory, straggled the demesne wall, eloquent in its gaps and breaches. About a mile down the road was an entrance gate covered with lichen. A drive, overhung by elm and chestnut trees, bordered by shrubberies, swept from it to a solid square flat-roofed mansion of dressed limestone. A flight of steps, a portico supported by granite pillars, gave the entrance dignity. For background there was a lavish sweep of the hills. This mansion was the home and the cradle of the Heffernans, and it is known to the world by the name of Deerpark.

The Heffernans were of hot blood, root and branch. When one heir to the estate dropped another more impossible than himself stepped into his shoes, and from start to finish it was a story of spending, of gambling, of running through the property.

The womenfolk of Deerpark were set up in splendid bone. They were stately of carriage, good to look upon. As far as the family property was concerned, they were well intentioned. They did what they could to keep the male Heffernans straight, and in this they failed. Some of them had their hearts broken in the process, and in course of time they were all ruined or exiled and the estate fell into a most parlous condition.

II

I can only distinctly recollect once seeing a male member of the family. He was standing at a window as I passed, and the impression that remains with me is of a nervous-looking gentleman, very florid in the face, and the most round shape that I have ever beheld: a round body, a little round paunch, round shoulders, round, bird-like eyes, a half-opened, round mouth, a round dimple on each cheek, a small round head, and a round bald patch, as geometrical as a tonsure, gleaming on his crown over the yellow hair. He was really a prisoner in the house. The law was such at the time that if he ventured forth between sunrise and sunset his round body would be seized upon and he would be rolled into prison in satisfaction of the family debts. Consequently a number of very ugly characters constantly hovered around the place, vultures watching their prey. The doors and lower windows of the house were barricaded, the demoralized servants became a heroic bodyguard for their master and sworn devotees of his cellars.

One day Mr. William Heffernan got down on his knees in his room before a heavy chest and pulled out a bottom drawer. His round hands rummaged through the chaos of its contents: there were old letters, bills,

Christmas cards, cheques marked "refer to drawer," twine, a hammer, discarded cravats, pill-boxes, part of the tusk of an elephant, blessed wax candles, ribbons, camphor, and several silver and bronze military medals conferred on various members of the family for deeds done in campaigns against inferior races in the East. And at the bottom of the drawer his hand at last closed about what he sought. He drew up an old pistol and a tin box of cartridges. Mr. William Heffernan dusted the pistol, handled it, looked doubtful of it, then rose. He put in a cartridge, cocked the pistol, threw up his window, and looked down into the Deerpark lawn. The only living thing there was a tiger cat picking its way along the walk almost directly under the window. Mr. William Heffernan smiled, put out the pistol with a drop of the hand which expressed decision, took aim, fired. The cat sprang into the air, somersaulted, showing a flash of its white belly, fell back, lay tense on the gravel. Mr. William Heffernan smiled and drew in his round head.

"Not so bad," he said. "Nine lives in one crack." He was so pleased that he polished the pistol with some of the military ribbons, made a round ball of them and shied them back to the drawer, his smile cheerful. He put another cartridge in the pistol and laid it beside an envelope on the table. He wheeled an armchair to the fire, seated himself, luxuriously smoked a cigar. When finished he stretched himself, yawned, went to a mirror, oiled and brushed his hair, dusted his clothes, put on a clean collar, a showy necktie. He lay down on a sofa, drawing the tails of his coat under him so that there should be no unseemly creases, jerked down his waist-coat, felt his necktie, and with the palms of his hands smoothed upwards the crescent eyebrows. He reached out for the pistol, raised it daintily in his hand, his little finger hooked upwards like a very polite lady raising her teacup. The barrel of the pistol shifted about his meagre brow, feeling for the direct centre, for Mr. Heffernan was precise. It stopped at the dent immediately above the nose, there was a pause while his tongue moistened his lips, then the trigger was pulled.

The faithful men-servants in the kitchen at the back of the house downstairs were seated about the fire, pewter noggins in their hands, talking about the good old times. The butler, Martin Fox, lay asleep in a settle-bed by the wall. The hours passed. The noggins were replenished, the men grew more pensive about the good old days. The butler woke up, yawned, looked about him, rose. He stumbled over a hound stretched asleep on the floor, shuffled out of the kitchen, along the hall, and mounted the staircase. The hand on the banister which helped his upward progress was shaky. He blinked a good deal, swayed now and again; the sleep in the settle had not been altogether a success.

The butler belched some wind from his stomach as he opened Mr. William Heffernan's door. His uncertain gaze at last rested on the figure reclining on the sofa. He crossed the room, looked down at his master for some time, made the sign of the Cross, and ambled to the open window, out of which his body leaned. He saw the tiger cat sneaking into the shrubbery, but beyond the shrubbery he addressed a possible audience lurking behind the trees.

"Gentlemen," said the butler, "you may now all go to hell, and may the devil roast you there." He spoke with very great vehemence, spat from his fiery breath, and drew down the window. It was the only public speech he had ever delivered.

As he turned back to the room the white envelope on the dark-red mahogany table arrested his attention. He went over, took it up, and read with difficulty: "To my faithful butler, Martin Fox, with compliments from William Heffernan." He opened the envelope and drew out a cheque. His rheumy eyes ranged along the document. According to its proclamation it made payable to him the sum of £500. It was duly signed by William Heffernan. Through the sodden brain of Martin Fox there shot one superb beam of ravishing joy in the fortune acquired. Lucidity and a dull numbness supervened. He put the cheque in his pocket, shuffled to the sofa again and swayed over the quiet figure there.

"No matter, Mister William," he said. "If it's no good itself, maybe that's not your fault. Your intentions were good, Mister William—your intentions were good."

He rose on his toes and heels as he spoke, and suddenly the knowledge that something wet and sticky sopped under his slippers sobered him at a stroke. He turned and trotted to the door. At the door he looked back. Dark wet marks on the carpet recorded his flight from the sofa. With a little cry he kicked off the bloody slippers, and in his stocking feet ambled down the stairs, whining in a low cry of pain as he went.

III

I remember this occurrence mostly because I saw a carriage drive up to the door that same night and a girl hurry out of it. This girl was a sister to Mr. William Heffernan, and the only one of the family then left living in this part of the hemisphere, and I remember, too, that my father spoke of her as "the other prisoner," because she had been hidden away in some remote part of the country. There was a scuffle on the doorsteps when she alighted, blows were struck between the servants and the sheriff's men, and my heart fluttered with the terror which comes to one who for the first time hears the rough angry voices of passionate men breaking into curses and imprecations. They struggled around the figure of the solitary girl: she was smuggled into the house in a fainting condition, and once more the watchdogs found themselves at their old occupation—all doors and windows, which they dared not force, secured against them. The body of Mr William Heffernan was quietly removed at night and committed without any undue ceremony to the family vault in the churchyard of Gorrybeg, down the road.

The lady who had driven up to Deerpark under these circumstances was Miss Mary Heffernan. She assumed ownership of the place and made great efforts to pull the estate together, but it was mortgaged beyond her power of redemption, and in the course of time passed into the grip of the Court of Chancery. The grass was let to neighbouring farmers right up to the hall-door. She had no beast of her own that stood upon four feet, if I except a mare that was too old to go between the shafts.

With what she received from the Court of Chancery she was able to hide herself away from the world. A servant, a widow, one Mrs. Briscoe, who had seen a great deal of the rollicking of the family, looked after her wants. Miss Heffernan never stirred out of Deerpark. She was still under a mortal terror of lurking enemies behind the trees, and no amount of persuasion would induce her to venture forth.

The house itself fell into a condition of the greatest dilapidation. The great bulk of the rooms were stripped of every stick of furniture. The paint and the paper had begun to peel off the walls in long shreds, tapestries were rotting under the cornices, plastering had fallen from patches of the ceiling and lay untouched in little heaps on the floors. The very panelling was crumbling away, and I have always had the most extreme loathing for rats because of the manner in which I saw them coursing about the rooms of Deerpark and heard them squealing and fighting behind the wainscoting. In the lower passages and corridors there was a thick damp vapour, the walls wept eternally. Miss Heffernan could not afford to keep fires going except in the few rooms at the end of the right angle of the house in which she lived and into which she had stacked such property, personal and valuable, as had been held back from the bailiffs. If ever anybody was entrenched in the last ditch, that person was surely Miss Mary Heffernan.

Next to her horror of the now imaginary enemies outside, she had one other haunting fear. She stood in terror of the thought that some day the only living relative she had in the world, one George Heffernan, a nephew, a son of the late Mr. William Heffernan, would turn up. He had been taken to Australia when a boy, and was really heir to the property. It was in his name, as a minor, that the Court of Chancery administered the estate. If this heir should ever turn up we all know from family history that he would fire the last miserable shot in the Deerpark locker. His very name held such terror for the lady of Deerpark that it was never even mentioned to her.

CHAPTER TWO

I

WHEN I was hurried home from school, about the year 1894, to succeed my father in the agency of the Deerpark property, I discovered that my position was little more than a nominal one. The estate was hopeless: there did not seem the remotest chance of getting it out of Chancery, and Miss Heffernan was living in the house in the manner I have related. My friends often said to me that I was wasting my time, and should be looking after some business other than a bankrupt estate; but truth to tell, I had not the heart to desert the last of the Heffernan race. We often cling to a family like that in this part of the country, partly, I think, through a strong sense of unreasonable loyalty and partly through love of a more than ordinarily shaky speculation. And for me there was something more in the position than could be considered within the ambit of business; the agency and management of the Deerpark estate were traditional in my family. I never reasoned the thing out with myself, but I had subconsciously the feeling that if I were to desert Miss Heffernan because she was in her last ditch in Deerpark I would be a disgrace to my name, a traitor to my traditions. I was allowed sufficient by the Court to follow my traditions and idle the hours away.

II

Every morning it was my custom to call upon Miss Heffernan. Should I fail to do so I knew she would be greatly agitated. For in her eyes I was the most important of men, being high priest of the Deerpark property. Miss Heffernan believed in that property as she believed in nothing else in this world or the next. It was for the sake of the estate that she refused to see defeat, to acknowledge any degradation; it was for the sake of the estate that she sustained the family pride, kept up all the possible pomp of her position. Not once did the misery of her surroundings ever touch her dignity.

She would receive me in her sitting room, seated at the head of the table, a pathetic pile of dosed ledgers, old rent rolls, and some yellow parchment documents in front of her. She would extend a long arm and a lean hand to me, which I would politely touch and make the best bow I could manage. We would seat ourselves, one each side of the documents, symbols of the dead estate, and Miss Heffernan would speak about that property as an exiled queen, old in sorrow, young in years, might speak of her lost kingdom to a Prime Minister whose very name was obliterated from the memory of her subjects. We expressed much the same opinions every day in the year; the sentences were thrown up on the beach of our discussions as pebbles, rounded and polished and worn with long rolling, are cast up by the eternal tides of the sea. But to the mind of Miss Heffernan these pebbles were beautiful, precious, a necessity; if they ceased to roll her life would become rank, arid. Desolation would overwhelm her.

Once in a while a letter would come from the Court of Chancery, and for Miss Heffernan this was always an occasion for tremendous excitement, not to say emotion; she would become as agitated as the exiled queen who received some message from the lost kingdom of an intrigue to bring about a restoration. I have seen her hands tremble as she took up such a letter to read for the sixth time. Each time she read it she would discover some new interpretation, and her ingenuity in reading fresh meanings into very explicit and familiar legal announcements was really something to admire. When she showed signs of a flagging imagination—when all possible colours of pebbles had been cast on the sands—

I would venture to politely but firmly disagree with her. My disagreements had always the same effect; it was as if a great wash of the waves had called down all the pebbles into the abyss, never to give them up again. Her excitement would give way to tokens of absolute physical prostration.

On the table was a great mellow gong, and on all such crises Miss Heffernan would strike that gong, and in response Mrs. Briscoe would come bustling into the room.

"Briscoe," Miss Heffernan would say, "fetch my salts. This letter from the Lord Chancellor on the affairs of the estate has much upset me. I feel quite faint."

I would make some appropriate observation, usually that she should not allow business preoccupations to worry her overmuch. Briscoe would fetch the smelling salts. I remember that bottle as vividly as if it were the first gift, precious beyond expression in the realm of childhood, handed down from a Christmas tree. It was a large yellow bottle with a faded paper cover—intimate to my sight now as then. I never knew that magic bottle to fail Miss Heffernan in these critical moments of her business preoccupations. She would remove the glass stopper with the air of a sorceress going through some mystic rite. Leaning back on her chair she would breathe at that bottle as if she were performing an act of sacred devotion. And from that moment her recovery was assured. The salts in the bottle were as dead as the estate,

but to see Miss Heffernan inhale the revivifying noth-
ingness it held and instantly to recover her strength—to
behold this ritual and this miracle was to behold one of
the realities of life which we are pleased to call illusions.

In all these matters Mrs. Briscoe and myself humoured Miss Heffernan; we were like a very respectful
audience which beholds little "business" in a tragi-
comedy which has grown mellow through familiarity.
We were faithful to the last of the race. Between Mrs.
Briscoe and myself there was the link of the devotees
who kneel at the same wayside shrine. Mrs. Briscoe had
begun with a tender sympathy for one in dire distress,
she continued through a sense of loyalty and as a matter
of curious speculation—at which point our devotions
became amalgamated—there developed for both of us a
remote gospel of duty, we were touched with a little of
the dogged zeal of the fanatic, and we grew into the life
as people grow into and come to accept as almost imperative any set of the most extraordinary circumstances.
Indeed, sometimes Mrs. Briscoe and myself had our
own hours about the importance of the Deerpark estate;
there were moments when we unconsciously crossed
the little frontier separating the land of the Actual from
the land of the Vision, the little frontier where the
guards of Reality and the guards of Fantasy sometimes
go to sleep. If our quaint life were to continue I suppose
Mrs. Briscoe and myself would eventually acquire cour-

age enough to make adventures which would bring us as much joy and as great magic in the Deerpark property as Miss Heffernan experienced herself.

III

It was about at this period of my life that an event occurred which I must touch upon because it has its place in the strange events destined to take place in the house called Deerpark.

I was crossing the fields near Kilbeg, a gun under my arm, one day in the early summer, my object being the destruction of crows which were doing much damage to my mother's crops. I remember that day as all men remember such days. I was stalking the crows by a tall hedge when suddenly the voice of a young girl broke into song the other side of it. For quite a minute or two I was not very much concerned with the song. Then suddenly I stood quite still and listened. The singer was not very intent on her song, and I knew she was unaware of her audience. The song—some old love ballad—was sung in snatches, carelessly, half forgetfully. A line would be gone through, there would be a pause, another few bars, a long pause, then an entire verse in a complete abandonment to the song. As a vocal effort it was tantalizing. But it would be quite impossible for me to explain the effect of that song on me. I was scarcely breathing: the pauses between the song snatches were extraordinary; I would have my mind made up that the voice would never be heard again, and that I had never heard it at all, when it would burst fresher and more exquisite than ever on the breeze. The dark bulk of the hedge was quite close to me, thick as a wall, except for a space where the lack of foliage made a vacant space around the root stumps. These root stumps bulged up through clay, broken twigs, decayed leaves, like swollen knuckles. The sun was playing upon them. On the bright side of that space was the singer, whoever she was. The notes were fresh as youth, elusive as a waking thought.

As I stood quietly on the dark side of the hedge I had a sensation that was at first almost affrighting. I was like a man who wades into the sea and suddenly finds a ground swell lifting him off his feet. Something quite as mysterious was now breaking in upon my life. I stood there quite still until I was satisfied that the singer had forgotten her song, then I turned back on my footsteps, making for an opening in the hedge that I had only a few minutes previously gone by quite casually. I approached it now with the feeling of one who is about to look into the Unknown. The grass was rank, tall, clumpy, wet with the rain of the night before, along by the hedge and my boots swished eagerly through it, the thick square toes spattered with the petals of yellow buttercups. A blackbird, with a shriek of protest, flew out of the hedge, a cow moved leisurely out of my way, the not unpleasant smell of the beast assailing my nostrils as I went by. Then the opening in the hedge shone brightly before me and I leapt through it on to a yellow heap of earth in the next field, a yellow heap of earth beaten flat by the hooves of animals.

The sun was flooding the field before me. The grass was the vivid green of a rich pastureland well cropped. But it was the brightness of the picture that I was mostly conscious of. And on a little green mound on that field was seated a young girl, her lap full of the daisies she had gathered and from which she was making a long chain by stringing them together. The simplicity of the vision swept over me in an emotion of pure joy. The young girl turned her head and looked at me. I laughed when the young girl turned her head and looked at me—just threw back my head and laughed gaily. I was no longer a being obeying any sort of logical direction, no longer was I at the behest of harsh Reason. Something wholly unexpected in the emotion of life had come to me. I had left a world, a sphere, a cycle, behind me the moment I had sprung out of that opening in the hedge and stood on the heap of yellow earth. My heart had learnt a new cunning. I was part of the mad riot of life upon the earth. I was one with the wild hare who dances upon the moor when the vibrating earth carries to him the music of the pattering feet of a little doe on the sod. I was companion of the bird whose spring hour is made lyrical by the flash of a wing in the hedge. I obeyed the same impulse, responded to the universal instinct. I danced across the sunny space of the grass to the young girl, still laughing as I went.

She arose as I approached, the alarm of a new and a precious experience on her face. A shower of loose daisies fell from her lap. They strew the grass between us like a blessing. I stood looking at the black hair that flowed down on either side of her head, at the straight black brows, the little veins of colour that were delicate in the direct shaft of sunlight playing upon her cheeks. The eyes were downcast, fixed upon the chain of daisies which she had preserved and swung in her hands. I laid my hand on her shoulder lightly.

"What is your name, little girl?" I asked.

"Betty Carolan," she said. The words were softly but not bashfully spoken; there was a mysterious faint dark passion in the voice that was akin to the hair, the eyebrows, the name. The lids fluttered over the eyes, then the eyes themselves were raised to mine, clearly, openly, expressive of a decision.

"And your name?" she inquired, the same disturbing vibration in the voice, the lips a little apart as she awaited the reply.

"Paul Jennings," I said. A sudden sense of all my shortcomings almost overwhelmed me. The name appeared inadequate; it seemed to call up all my limitations and scatter them like the daisies lying at her feet on the grass.

But the steady look of the young girl's eyes slowly melted into a smile; that smile seemed to absolve all my shortcomings, to make of them things eternal in the epic of life.

"Paul Jennings," she repeated, as if trying over words that came out to her from some strange world.

That was all, then. . . . But an hour later the little dark songbird was quivering in my arms.

CHAPTER THREE

I

A NEW interest warmed my life after this episode. I had my secret. I was of account in the world. The summer months were vivid with splendid adventures over the hills.

But even at this time I could not find it in me to neglect Miss Heffernan's business.

One morning in the ensuing winter I beat my way to Deerpark, whistling, as is my custom when making good tracks along a frosty road. Mrs. Briscoe had no sooner opened the door than I suspected something untoward had come to pass. Her eyes were red from recent weeping, unkempt wisps of hair were hanging about her ears. The face, always so serene, had an expression of woe.

"Dear, dear," she said, her hands making a gesture of despair, "the mistress has got such an upset!"

"What happened?" I asked.

"A letter came this morning," said Mrs. Briscoe. She looked at me and added, "Bearing upon it the Australian postmark."

I walked into the hall and we stood there, a shaken little confraternity. "She fainted dead in my arms the moment she saw the picture of the kangaroo on the stamp," said Mrs. Briscoe.

"George Heffernan is coming home," I said, and the words rang in the hall with a dull boom. "He'll wreck us in twenty-four hours. He's been ranching and will come home spoiling for glory."

Mrs. Briscoe was so moved that she raised her apron to her eyes. "He could not be so cruel," she said.

"He's a Heffernan," I retorted. An avalanche of memories crushed behind the harsh words.

With that the gong sounded upstairs. The clang came down through the empty house in waves of vibrating pleading. It was like the voice of doom.

"Fetch the smelling salts, Briscoe," I said, and we both mounted the broad staircase, the smell of dampness reeking in the air, making our way through an atmosphere as thick as a London fog. I knocked at Miss Heffernan's door, then opened it.

She was like a figure of Tragedy seated at the head of the table, a brilliant Indian shawl, or wrap, one of the preserved family treasures, about her shoulders, the colour of her face ghastly by contrast, the dosed ledgers, the old rent rolls, the yellow parchments, the symbols of the vanished dominions, before her. A hand rested limply on the rail of the chair, there was a half-dazed look in her eyes. "She requires a tonic this time," I thought as I walked down the long room.

She had not the energy to go through the usual ceremony with her Prime Minister, and I sat down when I had made a little obeisance. Her hand strayed blindly over the account books until it found an open letter, which she raised without a word. I felt very much for her distress, so much that I could not think of anything appropriate and conventional enough to say. The Prime Minister was cut adrift from his platitudes.

"Mr. Jennings," she said rather quietly, "I'm so glad to see you. I wanted your help."

"You've had serious news Mrs. Briscoe tells me," I ventured.

She inclined her pallid face over the brilliant Eastern shawl. "I have had serious news, indeed," she admitted.

"From Australia?" I ventured again, mentioning the danger spot on the globe with some trepidation.

"From Australia," she acknowledged and sighed. Miss Heffernan turned her head away and wiped something from her eye with a handkerchief. If it was a tear I could not help thinking that it was a very solitary tear and removed in a very polite sort of manner.

"Ah, well-a-day!" she sighed. "Poor George!"

I was encouraged by this evidence of an acceptance of

the inevitable on the part of Miss Heffernan. Some conventional old-world philosophy was standing to her.

"When do you expect him?" I asked with more brisk-
ness.

If Miss Heffernan required a tonic—and indeed she
did—I supplied it by my brisk question. Her tall, somewhat angular frame was galvanized into life at once. A
shock had gone through her body with electrical effect.
She looked as if she were about to call out—to call out in
genuine terror—controlled herself after a struggle, and
then groped a little blindly to the side of the table. I was
much amazed, not to say alarmed. I had an idea that
Miss Heffernan would suddenly collapse over the side
of the table. I was entirely helpless, could not think of
anything effective that I might do. I had been so much
accustomed to conventional interviews in that room
that a departure from them left me quite useless. My
eyes wandered aimlessly about until they caught sight
of that friendly gong on the table. It was part of the ritual of the place. I raised the drum-stick and struck the
gong a resounding thump. Mrs. Briscoe rushed in with
the great yellow bottle. Miss Heffernan groped back to
her chair, the bottle was applied.

I was filled with terror lest it should fail on this unusual occasion. My feelings were like those of one who
gazes at a daring feat on the trapese, tense with a morbid
fascination and dreading some slip which might end in
tragedy. The restoration was not so rapid as ordinarily,

but gradually Miss Heffernan recovered herself. When she turned to me again her expression was one of mild reproof, a brave smile struggling through a cloud of sadness.

"You are so injudicious," she chided me gently. Then, falling more into her old attitude, she announced quite distinctly, "I am not expecting George. Poor George has died."

I was so sincerely relieved to hear the news that I said, "Dead? George Heffernan dead? Thank God!"

I had no sooner, in the honest gush of my relief, said the words than I realized that I was disgracing myself as a diplomatist. I recovered myself so quickly, however, that with a brazen effrontery altogether politic I said in a loud insincere tone, "Dead? How sad! I am very sorry to hear it, Miss Heffernan, very sorry, indeed."

After a moment's hesitation Miss Heffernan helped me out by pretending she had only heard the observation of insincere regret.

"Yes, indeed, poor George!" she said. "It was so sudden." Then in a murmur, her eyes gazing somewhat absently out of a window, she added, "I am the very last now."

A silence followed, a silence which seemed to settle down on the room. The pathos of her words struck me. All that was left of the Heffernans sat there in her weird room, a frightened thing, sensitive and nervous, living in a land of illusions, bundled away while still in her comparative youth from the sight of the world in an angle of the once stirring family home, a straight, tall, narrow figure, as splendid in bone as any woman of the Heffernans who had ever lived, wrapped in a shawl worked in colours of brown and gold and green—an owl brooding in a half dark place wearing the wings of some magnificent tropical butterfly.

II

Miss Heffernan was speaking in an undertone for some time before I realized what she was saying. . . . "But I had always great faith in my brothers, and, you know, George was the son of my brother William. So very like my dear father was William, and everybody was struck with the resemblance between father and Sir Maurice Heffernan, the seventh baronet. You could not help noticing the likeness even in their portraits, which are there behind the chest in the far corner of the room. . . . I had faith in my brothers always, and I had, above all, faith in William's son. I knew that as the last of the male line George would not fail me, that he would redeem the family name. It would be so unlike a Heffernan not to do so at the very last. George has not failed me. . . . I would not have blamed him, indeed, if he had altogether forgotten me, but all his thoughts must have come back to this home of his at the very last. His re-

membrance must have been so affectionate, so intimate.
Is it not a very lonely thing to live in Australia, Mr.
Jennings?"

"Life in the Bush, I believe, is very lonely."

"Well, George lived a great deal in the Bush, especially in the beginning. It must be such a wonderful
place! He never married. He was as much alone as myself. And now all this fortune! I suppose I shall have a
great deal of business to think of since so much money is
involved. . . . It was his last wish that the estate should
be redeemed. I am so glad they told me that. What do
you think I had better do first, Mr. Jennings?"

"Has George left you money, Miss Heffernan?" I
asked, incredulity in my voice in spite of myself.

"Oh, yes. That is what I have been just telling you!
Quite a large fortune."

I was a little stupefied at hearing that a male Heffernan—and the last of them—had died leaving money instead of fresh work for a Court of Equity.

"Read the letter for yourself, Mr. Jennings," she said.

My eyes fell on a printed memorandum from the
firm of Henshaw and Davidson, solicitors, Sydney.
The typewritten document announced, with regret,
the death of their client, Mr. George Heffernan, who
had, shortly before his demise, executed a will now in
the possession of Messrs Henshaw and Davidson. The
terms of the will were short and simple, naming his
aunt, Miss Mary Heffernan, gentlewoman, of Deer-

park, county Galway, Ireland, sole legatee. The estate, which involved a very considerable property, was at present under investigation, and a more detailed statement would follow in due course; certain sales of sheep stations in New South Wales were in the meantime being carried out according to their late client's instructions, and the realization of the sales, together with a list of the bonds, securities and shares concerned, would be furnished as soon as possible to the legatee. Messrs. Henshaw and Davidson would, meanwhile, like to hear from Miss Heffernan, or her solicitors, and to consider such instructions as she might deem advisable. The late Mr. Heffernan had, shortly before his death, instructed them to convey his affections to Miss Heffernan, and to express the wish that she would continue in the possession of Deerpark and revive the family estate there, a project which the testator had himself in contemplation when he was taken ill.

III

Miss Heffernan continued to gaze absently through the window, and when I had done reading the letter from Sydney I looked about the weird room. It was as disorderly and yet as orderly as some great auction mart preceding a big sale of antiques; but the antiques here were not the remnants of scores of broken homes, of dead romances, of rising and fallen fortunes, of family flights. They were all of the one heart throb, the collection of a family which had bred treasure-seekers from generation to generation. That grand medley of personal family property lay stacked along by the walls, piled in the corners, heaved up on shelves, sticking out of overflowing presses: curios and relics, pieces of rare furniture, primitive war weapons from the East, unknown things of fantastic shape sewn roughly into faded calico covers, great solid iron-bound chests piled one upon the other, which I often imagined belonged to sailors who had turned pirates on the high seas, wonderful treasure trove no doubt secreted within them. Here was the shape of a harp in a shroud, leaning against it were the enormous antlers of an elk. A stuffed Irish wolf-hound stood nobly on the upturned bottom of a primitive canoe which had sailed down God only knows what African forest river. Pictures of generations of Heffernans lay stacked in their frames against the walls, a grand procession of splendid gentlemen whose very memories were thus brought into obloquy. Coats of armour lay about, one complete warrior with his helmet stuck against the wall, his chest rounded up to a wooden shield with the cuts of arrows still visible upon it, his short thick limbs lost in the skin of a tiger, his stout arm resting on the prostrate form of a bronze Venus as if he had stricken her down in a moment of jealous rage.

There Miss Heffernan sat now, the presiding goddess over all this concentrated antiquity, her eyes shining with a new light from out the green pallor of her face, her hands absently hitching the brilliant shawl, its shimmering movements as startling as the flutterings of the magnificent wings of the tropical butterfly. Under the influence of this moment of reverie my own mind began to wander, too . . . I was recalled by the drumming of Miss Heffernan's fingers on the table. The dream was over! The new era had already begun!

"What do you think I had better do first, Mr. Jennings?" she asked.

I collected my scattered wits. "This letter has first of all to be acknowledged," I said, handing her back the document from Messrs. Henshaw and Davidson. "Then, of course, you must see a solicitor—some man of standing—and instruct him to act for you in the subsequent negotiations."

"That occurred to me," said Miss Heffernan. "I should place the whole matter in his hands, you think?"

"Yes; there is nothing else for it."

"Should I see a bank man?" she asked timidly.

"Not just at the moment," I said. She looked crestfallen.

"You will find, Miss Heffernan," I said, "after you have seen your solicitor and he has fixed things up with the authorities in Australia, that all other sorts of people whom you may require—and many more whom you won't require—will come along of their own accord."

"It looks genuine, does it not, Mr. Jennings?" she said, touching the letter.

"Yes, it looks all right and genuine," I said. "And it is wonderfully good news, Miss Heffernan. I am glad to be the first to offer congratulations."

She inclined her head in acknowledgment, the shawl shimmered, a shower of brown and gold and green looking as if it tumbled down the cascade of her shoulder.

"Of course you can arrange about the solicitor and all that?" she said.

"Certainly," I replied. The Prime Minister was receiving his portfolio.

Mrs. Briscoe opened the door and announced, "Miss Silver has called. She will see you in your own room, miss."

"Thanks, Briscoe. I shall see her presently."

I was thunderstruck at this. A visitor in Deerpark! Unheard of! I expect Miss Heffernan noticed some of the amazement in my face. Her own fingers were trembling as she returned the Sydney letter to its envelope.

"I sent for her this morning—after I had read the letter—after I had recovered," Miss Heffernan said with nervousness.

"Who is she?" I asked.

"The dressmaker—the dressmaker from the village," Miss Heffernan said.

I had clean forgotten the corner-stone of civilization! I rose at once and took my departure.

CHAPTER FOUR

I

MY first emotion following the announcement of the turn in the wheel of the Heffernan fortune was one of pain and uneasiness. I could not analyse this emotion, or explain it. All I know is that a gloomy, ugly sensation came to me. Briscoe, I also noticed, looked dejected. She seemed to have lost some of the vigour of her movements, to have weakened at the hips. Perhaps it was because our monopoly in the Deerpark tragi-comedy was ended, perhaps it was because our loyalty was after all such a poor thing that it could now be paid off by a just and material reward, perhaps it was because of something in our peculiar Celtic psychology too elusive for me to diagnose—but whatever it was, Briscoe and myself had it, suffered from it. A miracle had happened at the wayside shrine where we worshipped and we knew that it would become commercialized. Even if Miss Heffernan, Briscoe, and myself, had resolved to suppress all knowledge of the miracle, even if we had barricaded Deerpark and put a gun at every window, we knew that we could not keep back the human tide which had already, in the person of Miss Silver, dressmaker and precursor, been heralded.

Mr. O'Moore, solicitor, a wiry, sandy, keen-eyed gentleman, having his office in the near-by town of Ballyrea, arrived and the case was put before him. He was immensely interested. We had several interviews with him, altogether agreeable. His manner of coming to the point, of accepting the miracle as an everyday occurrence, of mapping out the procedure with Messrs. Henshaw and Davidson, of informing us as to the Administration proceedings, made life in Deerpark enter on a new phase. Under its influence Mrs. Briscoe and myself shed our despondency. Miss Heffernan knew no despondency at any time. She had always believed in the existence of a valuable property. She had merely wakened from a dream to find that the dream was very like the waking reality. Ghosts in whom she had always a belief walked out of the shadows, assumed flesh and blood, and one could not say for certain whether they had been merely playing at ghosts, or were now playing at reality.

Mr. O'Moore had a clear, ringing, plump voice. He read particularly well. And his voice, quite intuitively I am sure, was regulated strictly according to the impor-

tance of the document which he perused. An acknowledgment of a letter, or an appeal on behalf of some public charity, he raced over harshly, almost incoherently.
The items of a bill of costs sang up out of his throat in a
pure tenor of distinct, sweet, perfectly formed and flexible quality. Thus it was that when he came to Deerpark
one afternoon with a communication from Messrs. Henshaw and Davidson, and read a list of the securities and
shares in the matter of the estate of the late Mr. George
Heffernan, I had the illusion that a lark had risen out of
the lawn.

Mr. George Heffernan had quite obviously only a
lukewarm interest in Australia in the arrangement of
his investments; he had only staked something on a
wool exporting company, and a bank (of which he had
had the intention of becoming a director were it not for
the treachery of his kidneys). His estimate of New Zealand, as expressed in the shares of oil companies, was
more emphatic. He had what one might call the traditional admiration of wealthy men for British Consuls,
he put American railroads in a neck-to-neck race with
them; he expanded visibly when he came to think of English thread and cotton, Irish linen, and woollens. It
was not, however, until he turned his eyes upon breweries both in Ireland and Great Britain that he rose to
his full stature as a speculator; his enthusiasm for the genius of his kith and kin to run and maintain successful
breweries was nothing short of superb. He practically

staked his all on it. His daring almost stunned me. Messrs. Henshaw and Davidson had given the dividends paid on foot of the various investments for the past three years—as an inkling of their value—and as Mr. O'Moore rounded his chiselled lips and trilled out the percentages I had the profound feeling, the splendid, sudden, rapture, which lifts one's soul when the notes of a supreme singer strike the drums of the ears. The concluding bars on the amount of the brewery shares, and the dividends paid on these brewery shares, rose up, note after note, until Mr. O'Moore's voice, extraordinarily sensitive to the measure, soared into a falsetto of haunting quality; one's mind strained, tense and profoundly moved, on that sweet and delicate vein of sound, swooning away with the last exquisite touch—30 per cent. and a bonus! I was so moved by this lyrical effort that I could scarcely follow the concluding paragraphs of the letter, which Mr. O'Moore delivered in the recitative manner, dealing with the transfer of these shares from the late Mr. George Heffernan to the legatee, Miss Mary Heffernan, and to arrangements with regard to the moneys (apart from all the securities mentioned) lying to credit of the account of Mr. Heffernan in the Bank of Australia at the time of his death and since augmented by the proceeds of the sales of sheep stations in New South Wales.

Miss Heffernan, into whose lap Mr. O'Moore was pouring all these gifts, sat quite unmoved in her chair, her interest in the proceedings intelligent, but her eyes now and again wandering to the familiar grey patch of sky visible through the nearest window. That patch of grey sky was the scroll upon which Miss Heffernan had read many wonders; the splendid canticle of dividends which Mr. O'Moore had just sung was no greater than the canticles which Miss Heffernan had heard sung in the grey sky over the hills.

II

A rumble of voices came up from the lower passages of Deerpark one day; I saw a half-dozen rats scurry along a passage and disappear, terrified, under the staircase. Through the fog came a dark active figure, the hands waving with energy; this dark figure was followed by a group of people in white suits, a team of silent acolytes. I stood amazed, then realized the situation. . . . The contractor who was to restore Deerpark had arrived, followed by his men. While the house was in his hands Miss Heffernan was induced to take a holiday at a quiet seaside place. She took Briscoe with her as companion.

It may be that my eyes saw more than the others. But it was all as vivid to my mind as a tense moment in drama. Her descent down the broad ancestral staircase was the physical expression of an extraordinary emancipation. The murmur of voices in the hall died down instinctively the moment she was seen descending. We drew up along by the walls, leaving a clear passage to the

door. Her carriage was unconsciously stately, deliberate, almost majestic. I could feel that those about me
caught the thrill of the moment. As she crossed the hall
I noticed some tremor in the figure, a little hesitation in
the steps; the black costume she wore accentuated the
ashen green pallor of the face, a pallor more noticeable
in this light than in the semi-dark rooms to which Miss
Heffernan had condemned herself. He eyes looked into
the unknown world a little fearfully. I walked quietly to
her side; I was conscious that she was grateful, that her
nervousness was lessened.

She stood for some moments in the portico, her breast
heaving more rapidly, her breath quickening. My mind
flew back to the night of gloom when men struggled and
cursed at the same spot as she arrived to take up the Heffernan burden. Then as now a carriage was drawn up at
the doorsteps. But the carriage that night was a black
spectre that had rumbled mysteriously out of a night of
horror; the carriage to-day was black, too, but a thing
that shone all over in the bright morning light like the
silk hat of a bridegroom. The carriage pair were magnificent chestnuts fresh from the Kish Massy stables. The
harness was silver-mounted. The coachman, like one
who was carved out with the vehicle itself, was the son
of a coachman who had driven a former Heffernan to
their joint deaths over a river bridge, returning from a
race. The door of the carriage was held open by a footman of magnificent diminutiveness, the grandson of a
footman whom a Heffernan had thrown over a banister

in Deerpark after a night of cards, of drinking, and what not. Miss Heffernan's hand trembled, and I helped her into the carriage. Briscoe followed, and they seated themselves.

Barlow, the coachman, made some slight movement of the ribbons, the pair of chestnuts snorted, pawed, showed the whites of their eyes, swung round, and away down the drive went the carriage. The audience on the doorsteps—mostly the old servants newly organized—waved their hats, their handkerchiefs, their hands, and from below the belt of trees a great cheer went up. There was no mistaking that "Ya-hoo! ya-hoo! ya-hoo!" It was the terrible slogan of the Land League, primitive, defiant, mad—music that sprang from the very bowels of agrarianism. The tenants had collected about the entrance of Deerpark to give their new landlord a friendly send-off.

I was going up the steps of the house when that "yahoo" struck my ears. I stopped dead; a quiver went up my spine and down my spine; my nails clammed into the palms of my hands, into the toes of my boots; my nostrils quivered and I sniffed at the very air with an animal instinct. Don't ask me to account for this sensation, which was quite splendidly painful while it lasted. Remember that I came of the blood of land agents. It passed in a moment. I continued my way into Deerpark, my mind anxious but elated at all the responsibilities which now rested upon it.

CHAPTER FIVE

I

WHEN Miss Heffernan returned from the seaside, where she spent several months, the restoration of Deerpark was almost complete. Her holiday had done her an immensity of good. She had no longer the ashen green pallor of the attic dweller. She was still pale, but it was a natural pallor. She had done a good deal of bathing in the open sea. Her flesh had a look of firmness. She was no longer gaunt, but it would be too much to say that she had grown plump. Her stately carriage was now stately with the grace of a freer and swifter motion. She took an immense interest in all the affairs of the house, and was at pains to see that the furnishing was kept well to tradition. The treasures which had been so long stacked away in an angle of the mansion were restored to their proper places. The old ledgers, the rent rolls, the parchment documents, were put away. The great bottle of smelling salts was seen no more.

The revival of the estate was within my special province. New books and records accumulated. I turned into the library, where due thought might be given to the revival of old activities on the property and the inauguration of new ones. Miss Heffernan was anxious to see around her an active rural community—if any rural community can be called active.

II

When I look back upon it, it seems curious to me that I was not quicker to observe the change in Miss Heffernan—for although I was aware of the altered conditions, they did not become significant of anything more than what might have been expected. One day it struck me suddenly that Miss Heffernan had her hair dressed in some new fashion that was still an old fashion.

We were in the library at the time, discussing the possibilities of the re-opening of the green marble and the limestone quarries. I was so struck with the change in the manner of her hair-dressing that I paused for quite a long time in the conversation. I was, of course, always aware that she had the yellow hair peculiar to the Heffernan family. But it had always been brushed flat into the skull, tied into an uncompromising hard knot behind, terribly expressive of her own life. Now when it got more play I was interested to find that it had quite a gleam, that it was not only yellow, but a rich yellow. It seemed curiously in harmony with the other family characteristics of the Heffernan face: pallid skin, but the pallid skin which conceals healthy, strong blood; long features, the nose somewhat hooked, the chin decisive but not aggressive; an expression of mildness which belied a gritty and passionate temperament; a tranquil outlook expressed in large grey eyes. The eyes, in Miss Heffernan's case, were unusually tranquil, but so warm in colour that they could hardly be described as grey. They expressed more her own temperament than any mere family characteristic.

The rather prolonged period of mourning which she had entered after the death of her nephew went by. I noticed the flash of some jewellery which had survived the storms. I had the feeling that Miss Heffernan's own manner brightened with the advent of the jewellery. The rustle of silks and satins betrayed her movements about the house. In her costumes she affected fashions new to her but not according to the conventions of the women of her day. This was deliberate; it did not arise from any failure on the part of Miss Heffernan to appreciate the fashions of the hour; it was simply that her tastes and her desires, spontaneously and almost unconsciously, went back to sacred and old and splendid things. She had always had the passion for robing her splendid body in rich colours. As the period of mourning lapsed this passion reasserted itself under conditions

of complete freedom. The touches of colour went on in-
creasing until she arrived at a point in her manner of
dress distinctly her own. The house had at this time
been completed, even to the restoration of the family
pictures on the walls, and Miss Heffernan had more
time to spend on her own personal adornment, and to
the direction of the revival of the gardens at the back of
the house.

One of the windows of the library looked down on a
corner of the flower gardens. Miss Heffernan spent a
great deal of her leisure hours in that garden, coming
into my view frequently. The flower beds were strictly
the product of the trained gardener; they were fashioned on a sweep of greensward around an ancient sun-
dial, shaped round, and oval, and diamond, with cute
little crescents between. They were geometrical to a
hair, displaying blooms as gloriously conventional as
their design. There was the fuchsia of the theatrical-
blossom variety drooping artistically in the centre,
round it flamed the scarlet geranium, round them shot
the blue lobelia, and like a thin line of froth the white
edging of alyssum. Amid these displays moved the form
of Miss Heffernan, arrayed in some print material of extraordinary colours, a filmy silk Eastern wrap across her
shoulders. And while she was the most brilliant thing
even among the creations of her gardeners, it seemed
the most natural thing in the world that she should be
so. Miss Heffernan had not alone the intuition but the

exceptional, racial, heroic lines to carry colours that were brilliantly harmonious. She seemed to me like a being out of a past which was greater than anything in our mean day.

Once I remember saying to her, as we looked down on this garden, "How geometrical the flower beds are! The mind of the gardener must be the least imaginative in the world." She considered the question for a moment in her deliberate way, crunching a leaf of southernwood between her fingers. "They never struck me that way," she said. "I only see the flowers."

"So the geometry does not count?" I asked.

"No," she said. "A scarlet geranium in my eye would dwarf all the geometry ever conceived." She turned and smiled a little at me saying, "Does it matter under what conditions beauty is created? If it is beauty, does anything else matter?"

"So I am never to mention geometry again?" I said.

"No," she replied. "Let all your eyes be for the great beauty of the flowers." I smiled, too, at the little lecture, and she moved across the room, leaving a suggestion of the perfume of the crushed leaf of southernwood behind her.

III

Families in the neighbourhood of Deerpark who had been oblivious to Miss Heffernan's existence now called upon her and were properly received. Miss Heffernan, on her part, returned the calls, and a mild social life developed. She gave an occasional dinner, an occasional tennis or croquet party assembled on the lawn, and we all enjoyed these little gatherings. Miss Heffernan liked to see her friends, but beyond her affection for Lady Newell she never had any enthusiasm for her neighbours. She seemed to understand them with wonderful quickness for one who had never had any intercourse with anybody beyond Mrs. Briscoe and myself. She was friendly with the rearguard of the land-owners who lingered in these parts, lonely comets cast off by a volcanic agrarian age, families who still clung to the feudal halls of their progenitors, most of them dowagers, ladies who sat all day at their windows speaking in mellow sadness of fallen fortunes, lapsed titles, dead romances, of things that had been and that had never been, prophesying evil for the generations to come, queer poor old grey owls moping in the holes of the immensely thick walls that were the keeps of other days, eternally droning out their family lamentations, unconscious plagiarists of Ezekiel and Jeremiah. I had a dread for a little time that since travel or town life made no appeal to Miss Heffernan, and that temperamentally she had no taste for society, she would fall into this sad life by the rural window. It was her habit in the evening to do some fancy work, to create in silk threads marigolds of a flat yellow immensity on white silk backgrounds, the stalks very brown and of wonderful thickness, the green leaves shaded with such powerful distinctness that they made one weep, the tendrils of the stalks fantastic looking as the tentacles of undersea monsters. These creations were destined for cushion covers.

When first I saw Miss Heffernan take her workbasket and her embroidery frame into a west window to create these wonders, I said, "Ah, she is settling down at the window! She will sit there until her hour has come! She will specialize in sunsets. It is the beginning of a traditional end." If she did not do fancy work, she read, and indeed it was better for her to read, for she read with intelligence and had a certain discrimination in her choice of books. But she never succumbed to the life by the window. She was outside the environment, beyond the reach of the influence of her neighbours. Her intercourse with them was perfect in its diplomacy. She would no more think of living like the ladies of Connacht than she would think of sharing with them a secret of consequence or picking with them a quarrel. "For," she once said, "quarrels and secrets are the two golden bridges to intimacy—and intimacy is always fatal."

She, therefore, never became one of the candles guttering out on the forsaken altars of feudalism. On the contrary, she developed an activity which seemed more and more to go back for its inspiration to other days.

Her voice changed. The tragic hoarseness which so well became her former condition disappeared. She even learned how to laugh again, and there was something extraordinary in that laugh—it was well bred and had some flavour of a rich newness that I cannot very well describe. Her step became light, and I once saw her at the top of the staircase gather up the folds of her dress—when she thought nobody was about—and with that extraordinary little ripple of laughter trip like a *debutante* down the carpeted stairs in slippers that looked eager to dance. Month after month I was a silent spectator of that wonderful transformation, noting with a silent pleasure—a pleasure that was a secret delight to my mind—the turns it took. And through it all Miss Heffernan retained her former self, all of her former self that was sweet and dignified.

I was always conscious that her outlook was instinctively for that which was good in the past rather than what might be good in the future. She had no craze for a gamble in futurity, and the present did not disturb her, for she rather ignored the conventions and agitations of her day. I don't know how the idea came to me first, but I oftentimes thought as I caught a glimpse of her— bending over her flowers in the garden, lifting up her arms, which were no longer thin, to fix up a strand of loose yellow hair, moving along one of the ancestral corridors in a trailing gown—at odd moments like these I was always reminded of certain miniatures of ladies in medallions and lockets which my mother greatly treasured and which had a fascination for me even as a boy.

They were, to my eyes at all events, delicately and beautifully painted miniatures of handsome women— relatives of our family—who lived long ago, dim pictures of women who gazed at one from a calm past, an age which they must have made sweet by their rare beauty and appealing charm. When I saw Miss Heffernan in certain lights and in odd poses I always remembered the dim pictures in the old medallions. Then she would pass me by quite closely, or stand beside me for a moment, and from the sound of her voice, a quick flash of the eye, a momentary heave of the bosom, perhaps even a swish of her garments, I would be keenly alive to the fact that a vital and very womanly personality was close at hand.

As one might have expected, Miss Heffernan took great joy in life out of doors. Quite frequently I accompanied her in her carriage, making little excursions to pleasant places, and it was most wonderful to observe the keen pleasure she took in everything that enfolded itself to the gaze.

The very air and the sun were, in a sense, new to her, for she had been a recluse practically since childhood. She was joyous in a subdued way, expressed her impressions in a quaint old-world manner and still with a frankness that held within it an element of the freshness of youth.

I could not, in thus accompanying her, in sharing her quiet enjoyments, help catching some of her spirit, her

tion was the most tender caress and at the same time an act of reverence.

"How beautiful the child is!" she said.

"Seven weeks old she is, your ladyship, and as quiet as a lamb," said the mother. "Born on the side of the road she was on me, a windy evening, too, but they sent the car from the workhouse and took us into the ward. The nuns were very good to me, your ladyship, and indeed they won't be without their reward in heaven. The holy Mother of God knows that."

I was becoming a little impatient and the beggar-woman was growing aggressive as she realized that she had come upon one who was not of the ordinary worldly mould. Miss Heffernan emptied her purse into the brown, sinewy, grasping hands of the woman, and the carriage moved on.

After this I noticed a certain pensiveness in the expression of my companion. Her eyes followed the sweep of the road, the arch of the trees, the patches of sunlight slanting through the leaves, the merry dancing of the light on the white dust of the road.

"All this is so fine," Miss Heffernan said, "but that little child—how exquisite it was above all earthly sights."

I said nothing, but an uneasy, almost disturbing feeling came to me which I could not at the time analyse. I knew that something significant, dominant, had come into the beautiful sensations of the new life of the lady of Deerpark.

CHAPTER SIX

I

I THINK I was a rather dull-minded man, lacking in perception, and in consequence regarded Miss Heffernan's altered life in too impersonal a way. I did not comprehend that if Miss Heffernan was changed in my eyes that so everybody else was readjusted to her new outlook. The old relations, the former standards of regard, had been put by. They were no more than the damp fogs which used to hang about the neglected passages of Deerpark. Gradually a perception of these things sank even through my thick sensibility. Miss Heffernan had such of that old-world way with her, combined with her new zest in life, that it was impossible for me to remain much longer in ignorance of what had come to pass.

The truth was, that a secret passion had sprung from old roots and burst into blossom in the general metamorphosis of Deerpark. It came to me as a great shock that I should be the object of this tender and peculiar passion. For it was peculiar, partaking of that startling openness which belonged to the love habits of the past. Miss Heffernan acquired a number of airs and graces, little sinuous movements of the body, restless passes of the hands, peculiar short laughs when there was really nothing to laugh at, swift sly glances, a habit of regarding me from remote angles of the room from under drooping lashes, pretences at bashfulness, tricks of retirement that were an incitement to investigation, coy attentions to my least behest, a significance attached to my most casual doing—all of which proceedings only slowly dawned on me as the wooing manners of ladies who practised that art in a departed age. The finest thing I can say for Miss Heffernan is that she carried these rather simpering airs without allowing a touch of modernity to vulgarize them. In all her gestures, in the tones of her voice, in her comings and goings, in the splendid parades about Deerpark in gloriously rich raiment, in the extraordinary manipulation of fans— which she gave a language of their own—in all these doings she was still in possession of that authoritative old-world charm which kept her as remote as the stars from a thing of burlesque. But for all that her overtures were the more patent, her seductions the more obvious. The women who took their funny little short runs about in crinolines, who were so devotedly conventional in their habits, so restricted in their freedom, so narrow in their environment, were, I am sure, the most wonderful and enterprising pursuers of the male which the world has ever known.

Take my word for it, the old-fashioned woman, the house mouse, is the woman who will always most eagerly go out after her man and stop at nothing to bring him to book.

Miss Heffernan did not wear crinolines, though I should have received no shock if some day she emerged from her room in hoops. She leaned more to the age of the flounces, long trains swept behind her when she dressed for dinner, and I don't think any peacock who ever strutted across her lawn was more proud of his tail than Miss Heffernan was of the trains which made the evenings in Deerpark so impressive. But although she affected flounces and trains she was nearer to the crinoline tradition in other respects, as I had very good reason to know.

I was greatly distressed. Since Miss Heffernan had come into her fortune I had been building up my own prospects, for my income had naturally increased with the revival of the estate and the resumption of other activities on the property, long lapsed. I had re-opened the fairly extensive green marble quarries, the limestone quarries, considerable sandpits; I had on hands the sale of some woods and a new plan of afforestation, and Miss Heffernan herself was very much interested in a scheme of cottage building and an experimental mixed farm. The management of these things was exclusively in my hands, and though naturally of an indolent disposition, the stimulus to make them a success and to get my own personal home in shape made me efficient in my supervision.

In the midst of all these interests, and in spite of the developments in the interior of Deerpark, I found opportunities for going up and down to Kilbeg, and these coming and goings were inspired by all the ardour which belongs to a certain condition. The truth is, of course, that the string of daisies which Betty Carolan had woven that day upon the little green mound had bound me as securely as if it had been forged of tempered steel. Perhaps if I had not heard her voice over the hedge that day, if her little dark passionate personality had not been so enchantingly fresh, if I had not seen under the fluttering lashes the heart's desire, perhaps—who knows!—I may not alone have responded to the tenderly daring overtures of Miss Heffernan, but gone out to meet them with proper old-time ardour. If anybody was entitled to share with her the fruits of the altered fortune of the family, if anybody had the right to assume the overlordship of the Deerpark estate and property, if anybody had the good luck to crown the happiness of a splendid woman, I was surely that man.

But it is idle to speculate upon such questions. I was in the hands of other gods: they held out to me that which is above all riches and all praise, that which is greater than any dower of wealth; they came to me, tripping to the tune of eternal music, bearing the goblet that can only be raised by the power of the hand of Youth; into my lips had flowed the nectar that is only exquisite in the noontide of life, and having drunk I could only look out with the eternal look which speaks of conquest and keeps the fire burning in the veins of the generations of men.

II

Whatever doubts lingered in my mind as to the condition of Miss Heffernan were finally dispelled by an interview which Mrs. Briscoe imposed upon me one day that I reached Deerpark. Mrs. Briscoe met me in the entrance-hall.

She said, "Mr. Jennings, I have a favour to ask you."

"Name it," I replied.

"I want you to help me in the education of a niece of mine, for I know you will soon be the master of Deerpark."

"Who told you that I will soon be master of Deerpark?" I asked, amazed.

Mrs. Briscoe clasped her hands in front of her and spoke with quiet courage. "Well," she said, "I have seen it coming a long time."

"Indeed?" I queried. Briscoe had evidently a keener intuition than I could lay claim to.

"Then," she added, "Miss Heffernan spoke to me herself last night."

"Spoke to you?" I was still more amazed.

"Yes, Mr. Jennings. She has been in the habit of speaking to me of her private affairs all her life." Briscoe at once assumed a new importance in my sight. She was the *confidante* of her mistress. I glanced around the hall, for I had an impression that a maid was hanging about, her ears cocked. I motioned Mrs. Briscoe into the breakfast-room, which was fortunately deserted, and there we sat down. I had an impression that Briscoe was enjoying the situation with an appalling feminine enjoyment.

"What did I understand you to say just now?" I asked, endeavouring to hide my anxiety.

Briscoe was quite sure of her ground. "Last night when I was preparing for bed," she related, "the mistress came to my room. She was in her pink dressing-gown, sir, and if you'll excuse me saying so, I was about taking the pins out of my hair. I knew she was kind of heightened in the mind. Well, pink don't suit Miss Mary and I'll always stick to that if I was to go on th gallows for it. The pink dressing-gown—"

"Cut it out, Mrs. Briscoe, cut it out," I cried, rocking one leg on the other.

Mrs. Briscoe's serenity was undisturbed. "It takes a complexion to live against a pink dressing-gown," she continued, "and Miss Heffernan didn't have no complexion last night, so she looked just woeful. After some

time, sir, your name was drawn down, if you'll excuse
me saying so. Myself I don't like drawing down names,
but we can't help other people nohow."

I groaned in spirit. Mrs. Briscoe used to speak like a
peasant in the old days, now she had fused into her
speech a garbled version of some of the special idioms of
an English footman.

I looked at my watch. "Any hope of us getting on between this and bed-time?" I asked.

"I don't think, Mr. Jennings," said Briscoe with a resentment that was grandly placid, "that there is occasion to check me over the hours I keep."

I hurriedly put the watch back in my pocket.

"I hope I am a respectable widow woman," added
Briscoe, "and that Briscoe has not found out anything
about me since he died that he did not know before the
horse kicked him in the stomach and inflammation did
the rest."

I bowed my head. Briscoe *was* enjoying herself, while
I——"

"With regard to Miss Heffernan," said Briscoe, "she
did not hide any of her feelings, and feelings is a thing I
always respect. 'Paul is very proud,' says she——"

"Paul?" I queried.

"That is what she called you, sir, if you'll excuse me
saying so. I won't wrong no person nohow. 'Paul is very
proud,' says she. 'For years,' she says, 'he stood by me in
great devotion, and thought I did not understand the

reasons of his steadfastness. But I knew all along,' she says, 'that he was sincerely attached to me.' Them were her words, for I would belie no person. You should see the way she looked, and I am sure her feelings were something dreadful."

My heart sank as I listened to Briscoe; I had not even the life in me to forbid any further disclosures. I sat at her mercy, my mind morbidly and fatally curious to hear more.

"She walked up and down," continued Briscoe, "her red slippers shooting out under the gown. 'Owing to the circumstances of the estate,' says she, 'Paul could not speak. He was,' she says, 'too chivalrous to take advantage of my impecuniosity. Now,' says she, 'he is too proud to speak because of my prosperity. He suffers in silence,' says she, 'like all noble souls.' Them were her sayings just the same as if you were to write them down in a book."

Briscoe looked at me with what I am sure was an abnormal satisfaction. I tried to look what I was farthest from feeling. When my mind cleared I intimated to Briscoe that I was thankful for her information and that our pleasant little interview was at an end. Briscoe did not stir.

"Miss Heffernan said something more," she added conscientiously. "She said, 'I cannot allow this false pride to stand between us longer. If Paul does not speak,' she says, 'I shall certainly speak myself.' That was what she said, and she in her pink dressing-gown and myself with the hairpins in my mouth. She tossed her head, Mr. Jennings, her steps high and her eyes on fire, just like one of them fine ladies in the old story books. So I thought you would like to know."

Briscoe at this time was fairly well on in life, God forgive her, and as sound as a bell. I intimated again that the interview was over. She rose and walked grandly to the door, where she turned round and remarked, "I think you're expected this afternoon, sir." The door closed and I was left sitting there alone, twelve stone of limp material.

I stood up suddenly, made an impatient gesture, walked up and down the room, a feeling of nervous anger seizing me. I was able to think again, and the position was all too clear and too humiliating to me. I realized that if Miss Heffernan wanted me and discovered that my affections were placed elsewhere my position would, indeed, be an embarrassing one. I saw that it might become so embarrassing that I should feel it incumbent to surrender my agency and management of the Deerpark estate. That meant a great deal to me. It meant a toppling down of my own personal ambitions, a cutting adrift from interests which were very near to me, a break in the traditional connexion of my family with the property, and it meant something very deep and not altogether selfish, for I had not spent so many days in that house and been through so much unusual

emotion with Miss Heffernan without feeling something that I could not analyse and that even now I cannot label. And yet the position of affairs seemed quite
hopeless—Mrs. Briscoe's crude disclosure revealed to
me how hopeless it was. As I dwelt upon the position,
and as I saw its impossibilities from so many stand-
points, a growing resentment against myself took possession of me. I blamed the whole proceedings of my
life, told myself I had allowed things to drift into the
present hopeless *impasse* by a criminal moral slackness,
cursed my luck and cursed myself. I was giving way to
a futile inward rage when suddenly I stopped dead. A
sound had vibrated through Deerpark.

III

I wondered if I had been mistaken? I listened intently,
distracted from my own heated and not very profitable
thoughts. Presently the same vibrating sound, but more
unmistakably, filled the house. The chords of a harp
had been struck. I went to the door, turned the handle
softly, opened it, and listened. The hands which
touched the strings were not casual hands; the notes
were perfectly controlled, and the player ventured on a
melody. It was played a little uncertainly, but to my ears
it sounded beautiful, something very personal in the
touch, the notes sounding as if they were wrapped up in
lavender. The music came from above, and then I remembered that the playing of the harp had been kept up

like other great traditions in the Heffernan family; they were, no doubt, descended from the line of Jubal, "father of all such as handle the harp." Back to my mind, too, jumped the picture of the weird room of the old days and the harp wrapped in the faded calico. Like so many other things in that room it had seemed to me to express something of the tragedy of Deerpark. Now it was responding to the touch of Miss Heffernan's hands, filling the house with melody, proclaiming the new life and—God help me!—conveying some message of a passion that was struggling for self-expression. I listened, fascinated, moved, almost quivering, until the melody had died faintly away, the house strangely silent after the effort. The last notes seemed to flutter down the corridors like little lost souls, to murmur as they passed through the rooms and to sigh as they escaped through the open windows, swooning in the foliage of the wistaria on the walls outside.

Turning back to the breakfast-room my eyes strayed to the portraits of numerous Heffernans hanging on the walls—haughty-looking people with the long features, the tranquil eyes, the slightly hooked nose of their kind, their yellow hair hanging in ringlets from their head, and they all appeared to have listened in approval to the performance of the child of Jubal. I sat down to consider the new situation, alone with all these silent spectators, and I had scarcely done so when the harp broke forth again, this time to the strains of an old-time polka. It

was not in the least like any of the hurried, inconsequent polkas that I had ever heard. It had a lilt that was
new to me and gave the polka a quality which any modern attempts I had heard lacked; it was danceable in an
ogling, quaintly humorous degree. So powerfully did I
feel the effects of the music that it seemed to me all the
Heffernans, men and women, stepped down from their
pictures on the walls and danced about the room. . . .
There they were, stout gentlemen in their powdered
wigs, their green or red silk coats, white silk knee-
breeches, shoes with silver buckles, going round and
round in the lilting polka, making little springs now and
again as if the spirit of levity was moving their staid
souls, all attention to the tall dames in the bright
dresses, their long earrings shaking about their ears,
beauty spots on their cheeks, diamonds flashing on their
necks, fans half hiding their coquetting faces. A young
pair dashed down the full length of the room, unconscious and uncaring for the couples they elbowed out of
their steps, and as they came along they showed their
white teeth, their brilliant eyes, their bodies swinging
together, kicking their heels in sheer delight, a pair of
lovers taking life at the noon-tide. A group of onlookers
stood at the end of the room, critical spectators of the
dance, helping themselves now and again to pinches of
snuff from silver boxes, dusting the snuff from their ruf-
fles with lace handkerchiefs which they carried in their
sleeves. The polka stopped suddenly, but was followed

immediately by a minuet, when another set of dancers, more stately than the last, took the floor, several old bucks putting out their legs, encased in silk hose, with a pride which plainly said, "There's a limb for you! Observe the sinewy thigh narrow down to the knee-cap, mark the breed of the knee itself, note the gradual beautiful line of the expanding calf, the slope to the ankle, the neat rise of the instep, the slenderness of the foot to the tapering toes. Just dwell on the symmetry of the whole creation as I take this step forward, my chest expanded, my head erect, my right arm horizontal, my lips firm, my lashes drooping on my eyes, the line of my waist well marked over the rigid hips. Have you, sirrah, ever seen a buck the equal of me before? Do you dance the minuet? Zounds, come along, then! My steps are as light as the kiss on a grandmother's cheek!" And the man who said most of this was stout, burdened with a paunch, and puffed as he went through the regulation movements of the minuet. And the ladies to whom the bucks paid deference, for whose benefit all the beauty of limb and leg was displayed, were themselves burdened with an antique style, their hair done up on the extreme crown of their heads, wearing bustles, making elaborate curtsies to their partners, going back on their haunches so gracefully but dangerously that to my eyes they appeared to sit down on their bustles on the floor. This seemed to me so droll that I laughed harshly, and immediately the room cleared. . . . There was nothing to be seen except the furniture and the thin streaks of the evening light falling about the place, the Heffernans in their frames on the walls looking as if they had never played a prank in their lives.

I shook myself together, my mind going back to the letters I had come to write. I regretted now I had not gone to the library at once and disposed of them while Miss Heffernan was wooing the harp in her boudoir. It was not yet too late, and as soon as the harp began again—this time it was an Irish war march played with unexpected spirit and with a surer touch than I had yet heard—I left the breakfast-room, crossed the hall, entered the interior of the house and ascended the staircase, resolving to get through my correspondence and clear out of the place before Miss Heffernan could be aware of my presence. As I mounted the stairs softly and swiftly Mrs. Briscoe's words, "I think you're expected this evening, sir," drummed in my ears. I felt like a criminal, a burglar, stealing through the house, my mind intent on getting through a little business and then clearing out before anybody could know anything about it. At the landing on the second flight of steps was a corridor with doors right and left leading into different apartments. The second door to the right was the library; the second last door on the left was Miss Heffernan's boudoir and I had fixed upon this place as the certain one for her evening's performance. The harp was much richer in tone now that I was nearer it and as

I stole down the corridor, straight in the centre of the carpet, I had a most uncomfortable feeling that the war march was timing and mocking my movements.

I breathed a little more freely as I reached the library door, turned the handle, and almost sprang into the room, closing the door sharply behind me. I had scarcely done so when I was aware that the volume of the sound filled the room. I stood stork still.

The library was dim in the evening light. Some of the blinds on the large west window were drawn. But a straight shaft of light fell on the harp and on the long fig-ure which bent over it, a little jewellery flashing on the fingers which caressed strings burnished like gold in the straight shaft of light.

The lady of Deerpark had chosen the library for her musical recital.

CHAPTER SEVEN

I

THE shock of finding Miss Heffernan performing on the harp in the library was so great that it steadied my nerves, gave me some degree of self-possession. She quieted the strings and rose as I stood immediately inside the door. I bowed, apologized for my intrusion. She smiled, dismissing the apology with a little shrug of the shoulders, moved away from the shaft of light, a long train trailing after her, a filmy wrap on her shoulders fluttering as she moved. I could see at a glance that there were changes in the library. One or two seats had been added to the furniture, and in an alcove beside the west window was a lounge almost hidden behind some evergreens. Tall palms and enormous aspidistras stood about like sombre sentinels; by the window there was an elaborate flower-stand banked with hot-house plants in gorgeous bloom. The perfume of azaleas was in the air.

"The feast is spread for the sacrifice," I thought a little grimly. I took a bundle of keys from my pocket and walked down to the desk which was not very far from the west window and the embankment of flowers. I sought that desk as my sheet-anchor in this hour of danger. I rattled my keys and, unlocking the desk, shot up the cover. I sat down at once and began to arrange my papers, my air one of decided business. I took the correspondence which had to be disposed of first and laid it to one side. I frowned over these letters; I selected a pen with deliberate care; I squared my shoulders. I felt, rather than saw, that Miss Heffernan had moved along by the book-shelves on the other side of the room. I could hear her take some volumes from the shelves, open them, close them, put them back again. I was conscious that she was very observant and interested in my movements at the desk. I put on the manner of a man in something of a temper. I stood up and shot up one of the blinds on the window, returning to the desk with a preoccupied air. I began a letter to a firm of agricultural fertilizing manufacturers.

"All business this afternoon," Miss Heffernan said across the room. I knew she was regarding me from out of half-drooped lids. There was a faintly bantering note in her voice.

"Yes, indeed," I replied, dipping the pen in the ink-bottle. I wrote some formal words. She crossed the room slowly: I heard the swish of her train; her shadow fell across the desk; I got the scent of roses; I could feel that she hovered over me; my hand shook on the paper, and this weakness annoyed me. I spelt guano with two "n's."

After some hesitation Miss Heffernan sat down on a chair beside the desk. There was nothing unusual in this, for we had often had talks in much the same position. But her presence under the new dispositions seemed an invasion of the business corner of the room which I was preserving against the more romantic atmosphere which she had been creating in the library. I began to complain, in a testy tone, of certain affairs on the property, declaring with some truth that things were not going to my liking. All my words were hard on the bone of business.

Miss Heffernan sat very still, regarded me quietly. As I lodged my complaints I had a swift survey of her. She was in evening dress, splendidly and carefully attired, in colours quieter than usual but bright brown and gold. A cluster of deep yellow roses lay on her bosom. Her hands clasped a little lambskin-bound volume on her lap. She sat straight but restfully in her chair; she had dropped the coquetting air for a calm, straight, direct method. She had her hair smoothed down over her temples, it made a loop on her ears, the loose knot behind low down on the nape of the neck. The pallor of her face was relieved by a faint touch of colour, the only touch of colour I had ever seen there. She wore large long earrings of unbeaten gold. The filmy transparent wrap on her shoulders was very characteristic, brighter than the gown in colour, but very much in harmony with it.

Whatever vague undeveloped idea I had at the back of my head of anticipating Miss Heffernan, by making an announcement of my relations with Betty Carolan, died without a struggle as I gazed on her.

It may be that I have some moral defect in my nature, but I would do anything, suffer mental torture, involve myself in all kinds of hopeless misunderstandings, go from one blunder to another, utter lie after lie with a sinking heart, sooner than make a blunt statement of fact when I know that that statement of blunt fact would be as a dagger aimed at a sensitive nature like that of Miss Mary Heffernan's. No use in my reasoning that a frank avowal would be the manly, the proper, the imperative course. You might as well ask me to flourish a shillelagh over Miss Heffernan's head. I had just moral stamina enough to go on talking about affairs on the estate in the hope that I might stave off the romance which threatened. And as I went on talking crude business I could not help thinking how more than ever Miss Heffernan reminded me of the portraits in the medallions. There was an extraordinary calmness in her demeanour, a calmness that could only come out of an environment which certainly did not belong to our day. The charm and the grace of this personality was disturbing, almost overpowering.

To this day I do not know how I raked up all the complaints about the enterprises on the property. I was inspired with a glibness which astonished even myself. I gathered some hope, as I paced along, that the cumulative effect of all the wrong-doing would temporarily frighten more tender thoughts away from her. What a child of life I was! I noticed that Miss Heffernan's face took on a slow expression of kindly humour, a tolerant smile playing about the lips. Suddenly she broke in upon my glibly serious chatter.

"Dear boy," she said.

The words dammed up my flow of speech. I frowned.

"How angry you are!" she cried. I knew then that no matter what I did or what I said I would appear wonderful to the sight of Miss Heffernan. I was translated into a male glory, a god whose sanctuary this splendid female creature was privileged to approach.

"Yes, I am angry," I said, clinging to the prosaic world I felt slipping from me. I rocked myself a little on the revolving chair; I looked exceedingly grim and determined, an angry and a jealous deity. I emphasized the prophecy that the green marble quarries would be dragged down to an ignominious failure.

"Does it matter so much that Kavanagh is drinking?" she asked archly, the tolerant smile playing about her mouth.

"Yes, it does," I insisted. "He's foreman there and re-

sponsible for the whole backwardness of the works, not
to speak of the bad example he is giving. I won't have it
from Kavanagh."

"Dear boy," she murmured again. I was splendid in
my rage!

II

I went on more desperately than ever with my inter-
minable complaints. . . . A valuable mowing machine
had been wrecked only the evening before, spiked, I believed, in a meadow. Was that to be tolerated? I put the
question sternly to Miss Heffernan and waited for a reply. There was no reply; only the cluster of roses palpi-
tated on her white bosom. . . . Did she hear about the
brood mare and the foal? No! A fowling-piece was carelessly discharged near them by a workman. Result: the
foal bounded blindly across a field and tumbled into a
quarry, thirty-five feet of a drop. It was dead there now.
Was I to stand that? Miss Heffernan's eyes met my glare
with her mysterious smile. . . . I tapped significantly
the letters before me on the desk. What were they
about? Miss Heffernan shook her head in a slow negative; the earrings swung about her cheeks, looking like
great golden fuchsia drops. Well, these letters were all
bitter complaints, every one of them! I was on the verge
of a big law suit with the contractor who had restored
Deerpark, for his "extras" were a patent swindle. And
who could tell how an action of the kind would turn out?

Miss Heffernan sighed, but not in sorrow for the uncertainty of the law. . . . There was another letter, from a monumental sculptor who was sick waiting for his slabs of limestone, ordered God only knew how long ago. Was it fair to the man? Again I held Miss Heffernan in a stern demand. But her fingers only fondled the little volume of verse she held in her lap. . . .

"What does it all matter?" she asked quietly, then bent over the roses to scent their perfume.

I gave it up. No disaster upon the Deerpark property appeared to shake Miss Heffernan. I moved the correspondence about on my desk and said, "I suppose if one becomes really philosophical nothing that happens on this earth matters a pin."

Miss Heffernan shook her head. "I did not say that," she corrected.

"Then what matters?" I asked, but not without some misgiving.

She leaned a little forward, the cluster of roses drooping. "We matter," she said, her voice vibrant. "You and I—we two—we matter a great deal—nothing else on earth matters."

I could feel that a sudden hot rash burned redly across my forehead; I had no hope that Miss Heffernan would take it as a danger signal. She was entirely absorbed in her own emotion. And as I said nothing at all she went on, speaking rapidly, "What does it matter whether slabs of stone are blasted out of the earth or not? Who cares that a foolish animal has met with a stupid accident in the fields? What significance has Kavanagh's drunkenness to anybody except the girl who accepts his kisses? Is the loss of money to monumental sculptors anything to us? . . . What does anything in the world, in heaven or on earth, now or in eternity, matter to me except——"

Miss Heffernan was almost overcome by her emotion. I could not conceive that she could be so swept away by her own words. She rose, as if the outbreak was more than she could endure. I was again conscious of her shadow falling across the desk, of the nearness of her being, of the tumult that swept all her calmness away, and I was conscious too, that she waited. I made no move, spoke no word, only foolishly re-shuffled some envelopes on the desk. She moved away with an almost angry decision, striding to the fireplace, her long train swirling in a brilliant backwash over the grey carpet, the filmy wrap on her shoulders marking her course like a sunbeam. She stood at the mantelpiece, her hands toying idly with some ornament, the long gleam of white flesh between the shoulder-blades like a beacon to my pained and straining eyes.

III

My eyes still on the white beacon of her back, I arose slowly, pushed back my chair with a drive of the leg, dropped my pen on the letter to the fertilizing people, and presently found myself walking down the room in

Miss Heffernan's wake. If a sentry had challenged me on the road I could have given no account of my movements whatever. I could only tell him that I was going that road. When I actually arrived at the fireplace, I stood beside—or rather behind—Miss Heffernan and still said nothing. The truth was I had nothing to say, not a single word of any kind or description. My own silence made me morose. I was only conscious of the gleaming white shoulder so near to me; again I felt the influence of her personality, her nearness, her pulsating body. My eyes remained fixed, dully, stupidly, with a brooding fascination, upon the white shoulders. An overpowering temptation to bend over that white flesh and put my lips to it took possession of me. I bent forward, and that grim Signalman who leers in the Box overlooking all our roads pulled one of his mysterious levers and I was switched back to my destiny; for no sooner had I poised over Miss Heffernan's shoulder than the flimsy sheath of coloured silk fluttered lightly as a thought from her back. It shimmered down the shoulder-blade, along the side of the back, and got arrested on the outline of the hip. My eyes followed it foolishly, and when at length it got arrested I caught it in my hand. There was a moment of stupid indecision. And then I spoke.

"Your wrap has fallen, Miss Heffernan," I said. The tones of my voice were as level, my words as commonplace, as anything ever heard over a counter. I held the end of elusive silk quite reverently to her, but I must have looked exactly like a draper's assistant—some farmer's son with powerful agricultural hands—holding up a remnant of silk for the inspection of a very *chic* customer, her eyebrows elevated.

With a quick gesture she drew the wrap about her body. She moved away; my eyes followed her course across the room; her steps were scarcely audible on the carpet; in the deeper shadows of this part of the room she seemed some golden-brown argosy sailing to the dim harbour of the book-shelves. I saw the sparkle of a jewel on one of the fingers which moved about the book covers, seeking aimlessly for a space into which the small volume might be inserted. A waft of perfume from azaleas touched my senses. I heard a soft pad on the carpet and saw that Miss Heffernan had dropped the volume. There was a momentary hesitation, then she turned to stoop for the book, but I, with my mind less and less conscious of any directing thought, walked quickly across and picked up the book. There was a little murmur of thanks, and Miss Heffernan was not now turned away from me.

"I am afraid Briscoe is neglecting the books," I said.

"In what way?"

"They don't seem to have been very well dusted."

My words were banal again. Miss Heffernan made no reply, and before I had fully realized it she had moved away once more; she was standing more in the light and beside the evergreens; some movements of the body as her form became outlines against the foliage gave me a moment of uneasiness; she looked in some distress; she began to sway, her hand straying to her forehead with a gesture of pain; I remembered the malady from which she used to suffer in the old days, indeed I remembered suddenly that fainting was a common thing among women in former days, but less and less heard of as the earth cooled. Miss Heffernan swayed, her figure one of great distress; I sprang forward, and not a moment too soon. I was only in time to catch her tottering form. She swooned into my arms.

As I stood there, her form limp and passive in my arms, I had not the least idea what I should do. My mind was more a blank than ever. Whatever thinking I did was chaotic, like the jumbled-up things that parade before one in a disturbing dream. I was only aware of the silent room, the silent house, the fading light, the crunch of rose petals as I clutched Miss Heffernan in my arms. I had a fantastic idea, too, that in my arms I held Deerpark, its estate, its activities, its resources, its tenantry, its splendid old house, its grounds, its stables, its servants, its traditions, and with them British Government securities, American railroads, New Zealand oil wells, Australian Wool Companies, and breweries everywhere breweries paid a dividend. I looked at Miss

Heffernan. The light was very indistinct, but I could see that she was quite pale, the little touch of colour having got washed quite away.

A little happy sigh escaped her, and I was glad to think that already she was reviving. As I stood over her my eyes caught the red tassel of a bell-rope beside the window, and from sheer force of habit of the old days I leaned forward to pull that rope in order that Mrs. Briscoe might be summoned to the aid of her distressed mistress. But I had scarcely put out my hand when I felt Miss Heffernan make some move to prevent me; her hand groped for my hand and she detained me. I sat her down on the lounge, looking at her. She came to gradually, the eyes opening quite suddenly and widely, her fingers closing upon my wrist with a tight, wiry grasp, powerful and convulsive.

Miss Heffernan looked at me without speaking, and I looked at her without speaking. But slowly it broke upon me that she saw something in my face that I had no intention of expressing; it was as if I had suddenly become to her as an open book. A look of fear, of misery, of despair, crept over her face. She became ashen grey in colour. Slowly, imperceptibly, her grip on my wrist relaxed. It was as if some swift revelation had come to her, that something yawned between us which no power could bridge. It was the look of a woman who felt herself lost, and as I felt that grip relax the feeling I had was that I gazed upon a drowning woman. She lay back, now shrinking from me, on the end of the couch, her hair deranged, the cluster of roses crushed on her bosom, her eyes full of despair. I stooped forward, egged on by this fearful feeling that before my eyes a human soul, the soul of a woman, was sinking. A little cry broke from me as I put out my hands. But she only shrank back farther. What extraordinary intuition had come to her? I was blind with emotion, my thoughts whirled, and my whole soul urged me to approach her, to reach out my hands to her, to plunge into whatever abyss might yawn before me. . . . The door was thrown open. . . . The figure of a man strode into the room. Then a voice rang out, a rough, rousing voice which seemed to bring the whole outside world into the heated room.

"Say, Jennings, where the devil are you?" cried that voice.

It was Kish Massy who had come into the room.

CHAPTER EIGHT

I

IF by some contortion of history I had been the distressed daughter of the House of Brabant and Kish Massy had been Lohengrin, come to Deerpark in shining armour and on the back of a white swan, his advent could not have been more welcome or psychological. But the Deerpark Lohengrin had no sooner arrived than the necessity of getting him out again, and of transforming him into an unconscious rescuer, became part of the immediate ambition of my life.

The very bulk of Kish Massy's figure, the uncertainty of his surroundings in the dim light of a strange, large room, the clang of his heavy voice, his sharp reminder to me of a world still existing outside the confined space of the alcove of the Deerpark library, made me abnormally alert. Some movement at the end of the couch was like an urgent appeal from Miss Heffernan to prevent discovery. I moved behind the evergreens with the stealth of a man in a play, then strode casually, almost lazily, to the man blinking near the fireplace.

"Hello, Kish," I said. "When did you get back?"

He started, recovered himself, and put out his hand.

"Hello, Paul," he said. We shook hands, and I could not help importing fervour into my grasp. It encouraged the unconscious Lohengrin and he laid his hands on my shoulders, wheeling his own back to the window to see me more plainly. In this simple movement I accommodated him.

"You're looking grand, Paul," he said. "I never saw you so good. And I got home last night."

"We're all very glad to see you," I responded, speaking for an imaginary chorus.

"Thanks, Paul." He put his hands in his pockets. "Well, if I was not thunderstruck when I heard the news."

"What news?" I asked.

"The news of the great Deerpark recovery. It was like listening to a fairy-tale by the fire."

"Well, well," I commented—the comment of all mature philosophers.

"Sure, I thought——"

Now, I was nervous of what Kish Massy might have thought, so I put my hand affectionately through his arm. "We must have a big talk about it all," I said. "Come along with me." He had some idea that I was leading him to a more private den in Deerpark; we walked, arm-in-arm, out the door. As I turned to close it softly I caught a glimpse of the tall, sombre, flat leaves of a palm over the couch and beside it the bright outline of the now silent harp.

"I'm walking down your way," I said to Kish Massy when we reached the hall, "so we can have a talk on our way."

He was disappointed; but I was agreeable, and we walked down the drive and out on to the public road. My companion puffed a little as we went along, for I was making unintentional little bursts on the road.

Kish Massy asked me numerous questions. I answered disjointedly, wildly. I laughed like a fool. Kish Massy shot suspicious glances at me, but I did not mind. I was responsive to the freedom of the air, the flutter of leaves on the trees, the light-headed career of some dim clouds across the sky. We shook hands at the by-road leading to his stables, with the assurance that we were to meet soon again.

II

Having reached home I at once skirted the gable of the house, made for the stables at the back, saddled a cob, led him out, sprang upon his back and trotted down the road.

Everybody knows what a stimulating effect a sharp ride on a smart cob has at any time, and already I was

more than stimulated. For no sooner had I recovered
from the attack of foolish chatter with Kish Massy on
the road than my mind swooped back to Betty Carolan.
The affair of the evening suddenly presented itself to
my excited brain as a fearful wrong to the girl. A thousand sweet memories of her rose up in my mind, passing like a procession of accusers before me. I clutched
my knees more tightly in the saddle, the vital body of
the cob pulsating as we rattled along the road. The sentences joggled in my head to the stepping of the cob on
the hard road. . . . It was a wrong to Betty, it was a
wrong to Betty! I was a weakling and a scoundrel, a
scoundrel and a weakling! I did not deserve her good
grace, her good will. I had been a traitor to her, a traitor!
She would never look at me again; why should she look
at me again? What would I do if Betty turned from me?
I would, indeed, I would drink myself to death! I would
join Kavanagh, go to the devil with Kavanagh. . . . On
and on joggled the accusations, the harrowing reitera-
tions. And then suddenly my mind broke off in another
direction. . . . What had happened Betty this evening?
Something told me she was in danger. She had been
through some fearful ordeal. Maybe her father had
turned her out! Maybe she was gone away, abducted!
Would I ever see her again? Hadn't I better gallop the
rest of the way? . . . The cob stumbled at the sudden vicious dig of my heels in his ribs, recovered, and broke
into a gallop. Some calamity had surely happened to

Betty; the cob seemed to know that a calamity had happened to her. I was sick with fear when I pulled up near the house, glancing apprehensively over the hedge that bordered the road.

There was not a sound in the place. No light showed in the windows. I jumped down and led the cob to the gate, the little gate with its arch of Virginia creeper. Through this arch I saw a movement in an upper window. There was a crackling of leaves as somebody leaned out over the clustering rose trees. I could see the outline of a figure, a figure in a white blouse, the vague movement of an arm, and I stood quite motionless where I was. A faint sigh was wafted down from the window, a little flutter that caressed me as it went by, too subtle to carry the burden of any tangible existence, but powerful with all the magic of a spirit being. And that little fluttering thing had escaped from Betty's lips, even as Angus had commissioned his kisses into the air in the form of white birds!

"Betty," I said in a whisper which had as little body and as much magic as the maiden's own sigh. There was a movement among the rose leaves at the window.

I could see, as she leaned more forward, the outline of the girl's bust, the pose of a dark head above the glimmer of a slender neck.

"Paul," she whispered back.

I gazed up at her, still silently, too moved to speak,

but in my heart there was an evening hymn, a thanksgiving, and that evening hymn carried its own music, and if it had a voice to speak it would speak of a scented hour when a soft hand falls like dew on the rose leaves; of the white bust of a young girl in the frame of a dark window; of the light of young eyes in the agèd day; of a body vibrant in its dawning womanhood; of the confession in the rise and fall of little breasts; of the bright proclamation of a moon risen to a new epic among the stars. It would have cried, "O drunkenness of Youth, O insanity of Love, O splendid tragedy of Life!"

"Betty," I said, "come to me."

"Why, Paul?"

"Why? My God, ask the wind, the stars, the gravel on the path, the little leaves beside you—ask anything at all. Everything, everybody, knows."

"Then I must know, too?"

"And you know, too—only a great deal more."

Betty made some movement.

"Where is your father?" I asked.

"Gone up to the mill. I am all alone."

"May I not call on you, then?"

"Yes, anybody may call on me. I cannot abolish custom."

"Come down and let me in at once. I want a cup of tea."

She disappeared from the window; a moment later a

little vein of laughter sounded in the house. I secured the rein of the cob to one of the pillars of the wooden gate as Betty opened the door and came down the path.

She came in her trim, well-shaped figure, her air of decision, her deliberate movements. The hair made a dark cluster about her head; her face, as she drew near, was expectant, and the dark brows level over the eyes. I was responsive to all the fresh ardour of her being; my eyes were upon her with an emotion hungry in its exactions. For the thought swept me that only an hour or two ago something might have happened which would make it impossible for Betty and myself ever to meet like this. I swung open the gate and seized the girl with a violence that frightened her.

"What is the matter, Paul?" she asked when she could disentangle herself. She looked up at me in her serious way.

"Nothing at all matters now," I replied. "Everything is right, is good. The whole universe is pleased."

Betty smiled, her look at the same time critical. "You are——" she paused.

"What am I?" I insisted.

She put her hands between the bars of the gate and fondled the nose of the cob. "I won't tell you," she said. "I might tell the cob, though. Is he not a little bit silly, Phil? What made him gallop you down the road?" Phil only showed the whites of his eyes.

"How do you know I galloped down the road?"

"Oh, I have ears," said Betty. "I could hear that galloping ever so far off. I thought it was a priest or a doctor hurrying to somebody dying."

"Are you sure you did not know who it was that galloped and what it was the galloping was for?"

Betty wandered into the little lawn and I walked beside her.

"Well," she confessed, "I thought it might be some such person as yourself."

She looked up archly at me. I was feeling quite tranquil again, so pleased that I began to whistle. Betty hummed a little with me; our feet moved more quickly over the grass. I took one or two steps of a fantastic dance. Betty laughed. But I went on whistling. Some of my spirit caught her. She tried some of the steps, too. We went down the little lawn together, at first timidly, then more boldly, letting ourselves go, prancing and humming and laughing. The cob snorted at the gate, some small birds fluttered out of the hedge, alarmed at the sounds of revelry in this haven of quiet. We laughed together at the contempt of the cob, and I saw Betty's shining eyes, the flash of her teeth. I felt her warm pulsing body, the delicate sense of her youth; the scent of the evening air was about us, we swung round together in a slow rhythmical waltz, and I remembered the young pair who had pranced down the breakfast-room in Deerpark—how many years ago? With a common motion our bodies swayed together; for a long minute we might have been in mid-air, in the sky, and that patch of green grass was as the earth and all that it held beneath us. We whirled, and laughed, and kicking our heels danced into the house through the open door, a pair of lovers taking life at the noon-tide.

CHAPTER NINE

I

NEXT day I did not enter the Heffernan household, nor the day after. I found many things
to do about the farm, in the quarries, among
the tenantry, and even in the stables. I quarrelled with
Kavanagh in the quarries, disputed with tenants about
rents, let out at stable boys in the yard. "He's doing the
boss before his time," I overheard the coachman say to a
workman.

When, on the third day, I did enter the house and
made my way to the library, I found things had been restored to their old order. The palms and the flowers
were gone. So was the harp. I was relieved to note these
changes. I settled into my old position at the desk.

Just as I had concluded checking an account from a
firm of calf-cake manufacturers, a light knock sounded
on the door; when I looked up Miss Heffernan was in

the room. I rose at once, my tongue wandering aimlessly about the roof of my mouth.

"I wonder is this interview to terminate my connexion with Deerpark?" I thought as I put out my hand. Miss Heffernan moved down the room in her elegant carriage. We shook hands; as our eyes met, there was a swift and a mutual embarrassment. But this painful self-consciousness was mastered almost at once. It was as if Miss Heffernan had said, "No explanations, and therefore no recriminations. Let us ignore that episode if we cannot forget it." I was more than ever conscious of her inbred refinement, her self-possession. As to my dismissal: I knew now that it never suggested itself to Miss Heffernan. She had a belief in traditions; she would as soon think of removing me as she would of pulling down the demesne wall. The Jennings were an institution on the estate. As she seated herself I noticed that she was simply dressed, that she wore no flowers and only one piece of jewellery, a cameo brooch at the throat.

She had some letters in her hands and turned to them as soon as she had replied to my polite inquiries as to her health.

The letters were from her stockbrokers, concerning the transfer of certain shares which she was making on the advice of Captain Manning, and while she read them I had an opportunity of a long look at her. She was pallid, lines of suffering were about the mouth, the eyes were heavy and dark. In an inadequate way I realized that this woman had passed through an ordeal which it was a misery to think of. Remorse seized me, knocked at my heart, and never had a more acute sense of the old veneration for Miss Heffernan come to me. I call this feeling for Miss Heffernan "veneration" because I cannot think of any other word which comes nearer to express it, but it does not express it. Miss Heffernan was an unusually sensitive woman; that sensitiveness appeared part of the qualities which, in my sight, gave her a place in an age bigger than ours. This very sensitiveness was asserting itself now in her capacity to live down the disillusionment which she had sustained at my hands. If she had been a woman of the modern world, if she had been the "business" woman, she would have had her little weak complaints and she would have had the poor emotion of a temper; they would have expressed themselves in my dismissal. She was, however, the sensitive sort, and therefore the braver sort; for people of exceptional sensitiveness always stand up more spiritedly, more sanely, more uncomplainingly, to the ordeals of life. It is the thick of hide, the dolts, the braggarts, the cheap little egoists, who make up the whines of their generations. The weakling weaves out of life nothing but a chaplet of complaints. The sensitive ones spin fibre for their day, wire the *morale* of their generation. Miss Heffernan brought out from some storehouse of her nature a sensitiveness that was rare. Whatever may be my own shortcomings—and they are fairly obvious—I claim certain delicacies of feeling that may be called a sensitiveness. They were sufficient to now give me a sympathy and an understanding of Miss Heffernan which might have been beyond a cruder mortal. I was sensitive to the secret misery which Miss Heffernan had now to endure, and which she was schooling herself to endure without a murmur.

II

We sat quietly by the fire, discussing the transfer of the shares, all our words as colourless, our behaviour as neutral, as if we were the heads of some commercial concern in conference, and while we talked there was, in our casual words, in our very carelessness, our assumption of indifference, a tragedy more poignant, more human and more deadly than if that tragedy found expression in hoarse shouts of passion, in acts of crude violence.

We talked of the transfer of the shares, and then of the tillage scheme, the cottage building, and all the time there was the suffering and the pain, the sense that there was something between us which it was necessary to strangle. Now and again I had a racking feeling that there was a wounded bird struggling silently in the room, behind some piece of furniture, in some corner, and that I dared not move to its succour or even seem conscious that it writhed. And Miss Heffernan sat there and talked about her enterprises while she hid away her gnawing secret. I found it very difficult to recall the recent airiness of her ways, the gay moments of her moods, the vitality of her interests, the immense pride she took in clothing her fine body in bright raiment. She seemed to me now like a woman who sat mourning silently over the grave of her own womanhood. And nobody else would understand this except myself; I alone of all those around her would see that something intimate, something that was part of her own being, perhaps the best part of her being, had been shattered, that a secret sorrow was not alone sapping her vitality but eating the very flesh from her bones. And I, the one who understood, who was nearest to her, who was even still nearest to her by reason of that bond which I call veneration, I was the one—O irony of life!—to have struck the blow.

I do not honestly think that I could have gone on under such conditions, that I could have continued in my management of the Deerpark property and affairs; but the currents that wash us to our individual destinies were even then busy, preparing to shift us on to a new chain of events, events which led to something which to this day seems to brood over the very hills. I had risen from my chair in the course of the conversation, my eyes on a bronze figure on the chimney-piece, a study of a nigger boy with half-devilish lips. Miss Heffernan was seated directly before the fire, her feet on the fender. There was a knock at the door, and Mrs. Briscoe entered.

"A gentleman to see you downstairs, miss," she announced.

"Do you know him?"

"Yes; Mr. Kish Massy."

A pucker gathered on Miss Heffernan's brow. She hesitated.

"He possibly means to sell you a horse," I said.

"I suppose I had better see him."

"Shall I show him in?" Briscoe asked. Her tone was that of one who hoped she would have the honour of showing him out.

Miss Heffernan considered for a moment. A hard line gathered at the corners of her mouth. "No," she said, rising. "I shall see him in the hall."

She followed Briscoe from the room.

"Kish Massy is evidently not in favour," I thought. "I don't think he is likely to sell her a horse."

Some moments later Kish Massy's chest-deep laugh boomed downstairs. My eyes came with something of a snap from the figure of the nigger boy with the half-devilish lips.

And from that moment Kish Massy came stalking into our lives in all his vulgar humanity.

PART TWO

KISH MASSY

I

KISH MASSY turned the scales at something like sixteen stone. In his early days he made himself known as a skilful thrower of bowls on the roads, a game not yet quite abandoned in rural Ireland, possibly because it is illegal. His passion for climbing into trees, mounting telegraph poles, scaling high walls, was so real that it refused to die with his boyhood. Even the coming of the sixteen stone—gradual and insidious—did not quench the spirit of the squirrel in him. In the full tide of his manhood he won a championship as a thrower of the hammer and the fifty-six pounds weight. I have heard people describe him as a repulsive-looking man; this illusion arose from the heavy black look which passed like a cloud across his face when angry or suffering from the after-effects of drink. His face was large, the mouth unpleasant. His firm chin was handsomely dimpled, the habit of shaving indifferently leaving in the dip of the dimple a suggestion of scrub in a hollow. The head was long, had a back to it, was expressive of capacity, even power, the hair passing from a wiry pig black to a tough steel-grey. The eyes were hazel-brown, oblong, tilting somewhat at the ends, a little like and yet quite unlike the Japanese eye. They expressed slow, sly humour and intelligence. Above the eyebrows two lines twitched rapidly in moments of excitement or anger, disappearing altogether when the mood was tranquil. These tricky lines, obviously connected directly with the brain, were hitched upward at the ends in harmony with the make of the eyes. The nose was large, irregular, mottled, the nose of a campaigner, the lobes of the nostrils round and flexible, Kish Massy's habit of half squeezing and half stroking them during spells of reflection giving them a ruby complexion. Now and again he had a curious way of holding his hands palm upwards, the fingers twitching as if they had an instinct for possible gifts, grasping unseen things in the air.

All his movements expressed energy. He swung his thick legs as if they belonged to the golden age of his youth. Under the wide chest he carried with remarkable ease a considerable paunch. His arms were inclined to swing out in front of him when he walked, the elbows elevated and active, very like a man breasting the water when wading into the sea for a dip. This habit gave him a rather odd appearance. When people saw him for the first time they thought, "There goes a man who will trample upon anybody who stands in his way."

The Kish Massy stables were pitched almost midway

between my mother's house and Deerpark; they were extensive and famous. Kish Massy was, I believe, one of the best-known breeders of horses in Ireland. His fame and his name alike came to him through the exploits of one of his horses. While yet Peter Massy he was riding a colt down the road and chanced to meet an old man noted for his incurable pessimism.

"What do you say of this colt, Patch?" asked Massy, showing off the points of the animal. "Should he do well on the course?"

"Devil a fear of him doing well on the course," said Patch. "He's only fit to draw a kish of turf from the bog."

"Very well," said Massy, "I'll call him Kish."

And as Kish that horse subsequently won a series of sensational races all over Ireland and England. Now kish is a Gaelic word, meaning basket, and locally applied to the baskets straddled on the back of a donkey, a mode of transit still in favour in the hills. Therein lay the sarcasm of the old pessimist. There was so much loose writing in the papers about the exploits of Kish and the breeder of Kish that somebody, in a moment of confusion, made reference to Mr. Kish Massy. Not in the least offended Massy adopted the name; it found favour with everybody. "There's nothing," he said, "like handing out a name to the world that nobody else is likely to claim. I'm Kish Massy." Saying which he made a curiously active bow, his left arm what the pugilists call "jabbing."

I often heard conversations touching the astounding

sums of money Kish Massy made one way or another. There were stories of his speculations and the equally astonishing sum of money he lost upon them. He was spoken of in terms of a gambler, a "plunger," but as far as I am concerned I never had acquaintance with any man who had such a passion for making and holding money. He affected to me an impatience with the great profits on his stables and his stud, but I put this down to the weakness of men of his kind for incessant boasting.

Unsavoury stories floated about the country concerning him from time to time. He rather enjoyed a quarrel. I was present when the Master of the County Hounds attacked him openly at a meet, charging him with the doping of a horse. Kish Massy, his fists aloft, his oblong eyes aflame, his chest and stomach heaving in a passionate duet, raised himself in his saddle and met his accuser with great spirit. There was a volley of gingered words, some appalling threats, and both gentlemen charged their mounts at each other. Several members of the Hunt backed their hunters into the spot, to keep the combatants apart, a group of indignant horses clung together on the road, some awkward manoeuvring was carried out to the accompaniment of angry voices, the shuffling of hooves, a few unintelligent and undamaging cuts of the crops were exchanged, the horses detached themselves, and the Master's wife was heard to say, "Gerald, dear, this will never do; your stock's got quite crumpled. Come here until I fix you up."

What the papers called a *cause célèbre* ensued in the courts, out of which Kish Massy came worsted. But Massy did not in the least mind incidents like this. The human material which he valued clung to him: jockeys, trainers, grooms, stable-boys, all the gang of straddle-legged folk who breathe well when their lungs are charged with the robust air of the stables, whose tongues love to savour the direct speech of the stud, whose brain-cells are stocked with the wondrous mythology of the Turf, whose ear-cavities accommodate neglected hay-seeds, whose teeth find pleasure in chewing sweet straws, whose boots eternally crunch agreeably odorous horse-dung.

II

It was very like Kish Massy to enter Deerpark under circumstances already related immediately on returning from one of his trips abroad and learning of the miracle which had happened.

"So you are agent, manager, and I might say general boss of the whole place," he said to me on one of the few occasions he found me at home. We were smoking a pipe by the fire.

I shrugged my shoulders as if to say, "It is nothing."

"Just so," he agreed slowly, a suspicious light deepening in his eyes. I was very reticent, and Kish Massy was very inquisitive about Deerpark.

"Well," he said, "to tell you nothing only the truth, I

thought the young hare herself had roamed away long ago."

"Who is the young hare herself?" I demanded coldly.

He shrank at once; an indiscretion on his own part always annoyed him. He stooped forward, struck a match on a bar of the grate, and put the light to his pipe. "One thing," he said, "I was always a great admirer of the Heffernan family."

"They had a great many valuable admirers," I said, "once upon a time." I folded the newspaper lying on my lap and put it on the table.

"I don't believe I ever laid eyes on Miss Heffernan herself," he added, ignoring my ill humour. "Used she ever go out for a canter at all?"

"Never," I said, "she was too poor."

He took some slow puffs at his pipe, and said, "And now she's rich."

"And now she's rich," I agreed, "so everybody knows all about her."

"Especially yourself, Paul," he said slyly, at the same time anxious to draw me.

"I knew as much about her when she was poor as I do now that she's rich."

"That's greatly to your credit, especially a young fellow like yourself."

It was my turn to smoke without saying anything. Kish Massy leaned a little forward, the pipe in his left hand. His eyes were on the fire, but his body and his mind leaned towards me. I knew he was going to risk a question of importance.

"Tell me, Paul," he said, the tone low, confidential, "how much do you think she'd be worth?"

I shook my head. "No idea," I said.

"Roughly speaking?" he encouraged, the eyes coming to my face. Kish Massy was, like all men of character, something of a hypnotist, and I could feel that either consciously or unconsciously he was trying to subordinate my mind to his. And I was of the temperament which, almost unconsciously, too, sidetrack strong minds by a pretence at giving way to them.

"Between ourselves," I said, returning his gaze steadily, and then paused.

"Yes?" He was afraid I had repented of a valuable disclosure.

"Between ourselves," I repeated, and paused again. "I don't want this to go beyond ourselves," I added.

"Of course not. I understand that." Kish Massy was hopeful, eager, respectful to my mysterious manner.

"Between you and me and the wall," I added in a low voice, "Miss Heffernan is worth a tidy bit."

Kish was disappointed, but still had hope. "I guessed as much," he said, to flatter me, "and now you confirm it."

"I do confirm it," I said, the emphasis generous.

"In round numbers—just roughly—I wonder what would she be likely to be worth?" There was almost pain in his face.

I looked cautiously round the room, then leaned forward from my chair like Kish himself, giving him the illusion that a secret was about to be disclosed. Our figures hung over the fire; our eyes were on the burning coals; there was that tense silence which draws men into companionship, disclosures, indiscretions; Kish Massy's long head stooped forward to mine, my head responded by a nearer movement to his; we were good friends, we trusted each other; the moment was heavy with mutual interest in a woman and her fortunes. I spoke in the proper minor key.

"Do you know what?" I asked.

"What, Paul?"

"They say——" A cinder fell in the grate.

"Yes?" I heard his teeth crunch on the shank of the pipe.

"They say she might be a millionaire."

No part of Kish Massy moved except his upturned hands; the fingers began some nervous movements, but movements that seemed to have meaning. I watched them as the red glow of the fire shone between them; they were like the legs of a spider spinning invisible threads. Slowly, almost imperceptibly, the busy movements slackened, as if the hidden mechanism which started them had concluded its revolutions. They stopped altogether, the finger-tips drooped into the palms and the palms themselves slowly turned downward, and the knuckles once more shone redly in the firelight.

"Dear God!" Kish Massy sighed at last—"a millionaire!"

I stood up, put my back to the fire, and looked down with a smile at the top of his long head. The pig-black and the grey hairs were about evens on the field. His eyes remained on the coals, the pipe went out, presently he put it in his pocket and got up to go. The subject of Miss Heffernan and her fortune was not further discussed.

"Look here, Paul," Kish Massy said, "I was almost forgetting—I want a nice piece of poetry."

"Poetry?" I stared bewildered at him.

"Aye, a piece of poetry about horses."

I sat down and wiped my brow.

"I don't expect *you* to write it," Kish Massy said, almost irritably. "What some other fellow composed, you know, some piece out of a book."

"I cannot say how much relieved I am, Kish."

"But," he warned me, "I don't want any kind of inferior stuff. No namby-pamby, Babes-in-the-wood business. Give me something with breeding to it—something with a kick in every line."

"What do you want it for?"

"That I'll acquaint you of at my discretion."

"I know; you want it as a striking quotation at the top or bottom of the posters advertising your famous stallions."

"Paul Jennings," said Kish Massy with sudden anger, "the stallions in my stud don't want any damn poetry to bolster up their pedigrees. They're not tramps or agricultural riff-raff." He strode to the door and turned back. "Can you give me the piece of poetry?"

"Let me see," I said—"about a horse?"

"Yes, about a horse. Had any of them the guts to write about a horse?"

"I think Shakespeare has done some little thing or other that way."

"Well—yes—Shakespeare. Maybe he would do."

"They say he was a middling good man at his trade."

"Was he high class? What about his pedigree?"

"I heard he used to hang about stables one time."

"That's done it. He's bound to have a snap in him. We'll give Shakespeare a trial. Write it on a piece of paper and send it up to me."

And Kish Massy strode out, having tapped my knowledge to his satisfaction—for nothing.

III

Miss Heffernan drove in her carriage to the hunt whenever the meet was within striking distance of Deerpark. She liked to chat with the people there, drive along the road and follow the chase as far as it was possible to follow it from the road. There was for her an excitement in seeing the men ride up in their scarlet coats, white breeches, and top hats, the women in their riding habits on fine hunters. She was interested in the casual chatter to be heard from horse-back, carriage, phaeton, trap. She enjoyed the coming of the pack; she marvelled at the genius of the whips in calling individual dogs by their names. They were to her eyes a number of identical white, black and tan patches; even the wagging of the curled tails appeared to her as regular and drilled as the movements of a stage ballet. There was a joy in watching the draw of some covert. The dogs with their snouts to the ground, twisting and whisking about the furze bushes, the curled tails incessantly quivering, the followers of the chase spread out like a fan, the weird cries of the whips, the shouting and noise of the beaters, the excitement of the ragged gang of volunteers who turn up at every meet, the sudden mournful bay—like an Irish keen—of the hounds when a trail is picked up, the career of a red fox over the grey landscape, the tension of the whole field as his dead, calculated gallop draws the assembly in his wake—all these things warmed something in the Heffernan blood, gave her the sensation that she was linked up with a tradition, part of a privilege, an upholder of a custom which gave rural life some quality of ancient fullbloodedness.

The leaves of the chestnuts and the elms were dropping like conscious things to the grass of the lawn, making the autumn vivid, one day that I arrived at Deerpark and met Miss Heffernan as she came out under the portico, awaiting the carriage to take her to the meet. We greeted each other quietly, and stood for some moments together, Miss Heffernan drawing on her gloves. She looked pinched and unhappy; I had the same uneasy, guilty feeling which had brought restless nights to me since the affair in the library.

"I wonder what keeps Barlow?" Miss Heffernan said, a little impatiently. She moved down some steps to the drive, then stood, a murmur of surprise escaping her. In another moment Barlow, the coachman, drew up the carriage in front of the house. To the carriage were harnessed two splendid bays which I had never seen before and which did not belong to the Deerpark stables.

"Why, what on earth has happened?" Miss Heffernan asked, walking down to the drive. I was so interested that I followed.

Barlow saluted smartly. "I was backing the chestnuts into the shafts, Miss," he said, "when Mr. Kish Massy galloped into the yard with these two bays. He insisted on them going in instead of the chestnuts. Said it was your orders."

"My orders?"

"Yes, miss."

"But I never gave such an order. I don't own these horses."

"Well, that's what he said, miss."

We were looking up at Barlow, and Barlow was looking down at us, the footman, arms folded, sphinx-like on the box, his unemotional eyes unswervingly on unseen things beyond the shrubberies. In another moment round the gable from the direction of the stables came the figure of Kish Massy, his thick legs pushing hard, his arms out in front of him, his elbows making short backward drives, comical as a man doing a frog walk in the water.

"Good morning, Miss Heffernan," he panted; "good morning, Mr. Jennings. I was in dread of my very life I'd miss you, that you'd be gone on me." He stood before us, breathless but keen. One of the bays turned his head, swung the neck, pawed the ground.

"Barlow informs me——" Miss Heffernan began, but Kish Massy interrupted in the most affable way.

"Don't blame Barlow," he said. " 'Twas my doing. I had my heart set on them two bays stepping into the meet to-day, and hearing you were going I took the liberty of sending them up."

"Really, Mr. Massy, I'm afraid——"

"Now, don't disappoint me, Miss Heffernan."

"I should much prefer to drive my own horses." Miss Heffernan spoke with some asperity.

"The chestnuts are right enough, but they've got a bit fat and are drowsy in themselves on account of it."

"I'm not going in for driving competitions, Mr. Massy."

"Indeed, I know that. But there are the bays now, only too willing to show their points to the meet, harnessed and all, and what's the use of changing them for the chestnuts? It will only put Barlow to a lot of rounds, and he's cursed me already in the yard."

Miss Heffernan did not seem able to keep back the flicker of a smile.

"It will do them all good at the meet to see that pair of bays."

"I assure you," said Miss Heffernan, "I have no ambition whatever to parade at the meet in borrowed plumes—or borrowed bays, should I say?"

Kish Massy laughed in his hearty way, pushed back his hat on his head, and looked delighted.

"Massy is incorrigible," I said.

One of the bays snorted, raised his head, held it rigid, the ears forward, and he appeared to concentrate with the footman on unseen things beyond the shrubberies. The heads of horse and footman looked strikingly alike, almost mentally intimate in their concentration.

"I want you to drive them bays, Miss Heffernan," said Kish Massy, "and let me know what you think of their paces."

"Surely you could have found a better judge?"

"I'd never put the judgment of a horse beyond one of the Heffernan blood."

"Miss Heffernan looked as if she wished to say,

"What on earth can I do?" and the desire ended in a shrug of the shoulders. Kish Massy, starting a most curiously agreeable sound through his lips, walked to the horses, moved about them, giving the harness a rattle here, a chuck there, stroking the horses on the legs, fondling them on the necks, slapping them on the bellies, diving under them, making passes of the hands, buzzing about them like some great wizard. The bays were conscious of his attentions, nervous under his influence, like brutes who felt they were being judged. It was not possible to remain uninterested either in them or their master. They were splendid animals, matched to the faint crescents on their grey quarters. The snouts were soft black and moist, exactly like the back of a black snail, speaking of perfect condition and health. The eyes were clear, with a flash of daring, the skin pink and clean, the hair silky, the mouths sensitive, inclined to foam. Here and there nerves twitched, making the skin quiver; they whisked active mops over the shapely haunches, now and again champed the bits in their mouths.

Kish Massy stood before us, having worked up our interest, spread his legs a little, laid his hand on the muzzle of the nearest horse, and said: "Is there anything better than a horse? What does the poet say?" And to my amazement he recited the words of the quotation I had sent him a week previously—

"Look, when a painter would surpass the life
In limning out a well-proportioned steed,
His art with nature's workmanship at strife,
As if the dead the living should exceed;
  So did this horse excel a common one
  In shape, in courage, colour, pace, and bone.
Round-hoofed, short-jointed, fetlocks shag and long,
Broad breast, full eye, small head, and nostrils wide,
High crest, short ears, straight legs and passing strong,
Thin man, thick tail, broad buttock, tender hide;
  Look, what a horse should have he did not lack
  Save some proud lady seated at his back."

There was some stable quality in his voice which gave the words a sympathy, a sincerity. Miss Heffernan gazed at him like one who could tolerate a survey of his personality for the first time. Kish Massy pulled out his watch.

"Bless my soul, Miss Heffernan," he said, "it will give Barlow and the bays all they can do to get you to the meet in time. They'll be drawing the coverts up by Ardclough first, and there are foxes there, too. Don't let us be keeping you any longer."

Miss Heffernan looked embarrassed for a moment.

"If you wanted the bays to be taken out itself there's no time for it now. It's gone beyond discussion, as they say in Parliament. You'll have a grand view of the draw around Ardclough, and if the brush goes down by the lakes you'll see as nice a chase as ever was, and plenty of good stone walls for the Blazers."

Miss Heffernan could not, I knew, be "bluffed" into doing a thing she did not wish to do. But if she insisted on the bays coming out Kish Massy would have found other obstructive tactics: it would be the sort of situation his talent revelled in. Miss Heffernan hated scenes. A lesser woman might have found it necessary to make the scene. She stepped into the carriage. Kish Massy made a movement to help her in, but she was too quick for him. Some sense of self-preservation made her step in with surprising agility, and the footman, who had dropped like a hawk from the box, was snapping the handle of the carriage door before Kish Massy could do anything. A moment later the bays were going down the drive, throwing their paws as if half swimming through the air.

I was not surprised when making my way to the library to see the tall still figure of Mrs. Briscoe thrown against the background of heavy plush *portières* which cut off the passage to the kitchen and other mysterious regions of Deerpark. From this spot she had been a spectator of events on the drive.

"That was a good one," said Briscoe in a dry voice, "about as good as ever I saw." Then in a more animated tone, elevating her chin, "Well, I never!"

"Kish Massy is making progress," I remarked.

"Rather!" Briscoe declared. "When he called the other evening Miss Heffernan saw him on the doorstep. The interview lasted exactly twenty seconds by that hall clock." She glanced up at the time-piece. It had a round honest face. The deliberate ticks seemed to say, "Briscoe is right, Briscoe is always right." A Persian cat, known to all as the Shah, parted the *portières*, came through, elevated his great tail, brushed the front of the housekeeper's skirt, and seemed to say, "Of course Briscoe is right. We all stand by Briscoe."

I could not strike a discordant note in the household. "Briscoe," I said, looking with admiration at her dramatic pose, "You're a marvel for exact information."

She made no acknowledgment, but the Shah looked up at me with a mild smile of thanks.

CHAPTER TWO

I

I FOUND Kish Massy on the doorsteps, a coil of rope under his arm, obviously waiting for somebody and passing the time by humming a little out-of-tune song. It nettled me to find him there; I pulled the Deerpark hall-door to with a bang.

"Has Miss Heffernan got back?" he asked at once.

"That I don't know," I replied. He was quick to note some impatience in my tone.

"I thought I might ask at all events," he said.

"No harm done," I replied airily.

With that the carriage came down the drive. Barlow, I could see, was handling the bays with delight. There was something of the pride of a swan breasting the water in the manner in which they throw out their chests.

Miss Heffernan was rather surprised to find us awaiting her—I doubt if she was pleased—for it looked as if we had not left the spot since morning, although I had, meanwhile, put in several hours' work in the library.

"The bays were much admired," she said to Kish Massy, but in a rather bored voice.

"There was no carriage pair to touch them at the meet, I go bail," said Kish Massy.

Miss Heffernan turned to Barlow. "See that the horses are properly attended to and returned to Mr. Massy's place," she said.

Barlow touched his hat; the footman maintained his ascetic aloofness; the carriage disappeared in the direction of the stables.

Miss Heffernan had mounted the steps to the house; Kish Massy moved to a corner of the flight; I was some yards out on the drive. We described the First Proposition of Euclid; we were the points of an equilateral triangle. Miss Heffernan stood when Kish Massy addressed her—

"If you'll excuse me, Miss Heffernan, there won't be any occasion to take the bays from Deerpark again."

If Kish Massy was about to force a sale his methods were crude; I think Miss Heffernan expected something of the kind. She looked less annoyed.

"I don't quite understand," she said, turning down the collar of her heavy coat. I thought she looked tired. The rather biting autumn wind—that subtle first nip which has the venom of winter in its young heart—had sharpened the dark lines under her eyes, made the lips pallid.

"I hope you'll excuse me, Miss Heffernan," said Kish Massy, looking at her deliberately, "but if you'll accept the pair of bays as a gift you'll be doing me a great honour." He spoke quickly, jerked the coil of rope expertly in his hand.

I think my underjaw dropped. Miss Heffernan moved a little along the step, mounted to another one, looking at Kish Massy with wide eyes.

"Really, Mr. Massy," she said, a nervousness that was also a hostility in her voice.

Kish Massy raised his hat and bowed. "A very great honour indeed," he said.

"But why—why on earth should you make *me* a present of the bays?" she asked. The question was reasonable though hardly flattering to the donor.

I saw some movement of Kish Massy's thick legs as if he were setting himself into an attitude. His oblong eyes, from his corner of the triangle, took Miss Heffernan and myself in with a quick sweep. I had the feeling that he was about to spring something upon us.

"I ask you to accept the horses, Miss Heffernan," he said quietly, "in return for a great favour once done me by a member of your family."

"I never knew—I never heard," said Miss Heffernan, looking bewildered. Her hand toyed with a button of her coat.

"You could not know," said Kish Massy, "because the kindness was bestowed upon me at the other end of the earth." He paused, ranging the triangle with his swift eyes, adding, "Out in the Bush of Australia."

Both our eyes were instantly upon Kish Massy. The silence which followed was heavy with interest. A flock of pigeons circled overhead, their wings sounding with a strong leathery beat. Miss Heffernan betrayed some agitation.

"Were you in Australia?" I asked directly, incredulity in my voice.

"My last trip was to Australia," said Kish Massy.

I had assumed that it had been, like a few previous trips, to America. I recalled rapidly that he had been away quite a long time, perhaps close on three years. We had begun to forget him. The stables during his absence were run by his brother Augustine, who was quite unlike Kish both in appearance and temperament, but had all his talent for handling horses.

"Do you mean you met my nephew there?" Miss Heffernan asked, not without some emotion in her voice. She opened some buttons of her coat nervously, absent-mindedly.

"Yes, I met Mr. George Heffernan in Australia," Kish Massy said in the same quiet voice. He jerked the coil of rope again.

"I had no idea you had. Why did you not let us know

at once?" Miss Heffernan's fingers buttoned the coat she had a moment before unbuttoned.

"I had not much opportunity, Miss Heffernan." Kish Massy looked up at her with a certain frankness. He raised his left foot on a step, resting it there. He was unexpectedly dignified. I remembered the short shrift he had got when he called on Miss Heffernan some evenings ago—twenty seconds by the hall clock. There was almost a painful pause. The flock of pigeons drove down in a wild slant over the roof of the house to the lofts of the stables at the back.

"Won't you come in and tell us all about it?" Miss Heffernan said, a timid note in her voice.

"Delighted, Miss Heffernan." Kish Massy tossed the coil of rope on to his elbow.

I turned to go.

"Perhaps you would join us, Mr. Jennings?" Miss Heffernan said. There was a certain appeal in her voice. I knew instinctively that she did not wish to entertain Kish Massy alone. I was conscious, too, that Kish Massy, from his angle of the First Proposition, was keen as a razor to get an understanding of the relations between us.

"You might join Mr. Massy in a glass of wine," Miss Heffernan suggested.

"With pleasure," I said.

The triangle dissolved. Miss Heffernan led the way

into the house, Kish Massy came next, I followed leisurely. In the hall Kish Massy coolly hung up his coil of
rope with his hat. I thought, as he followed Miss Heffernan into a reception-room, that he suppressed a swag-
ger of the thick limbs. I had a rapid glimpse of Mrs. Briscoe as she lurked somewhere in the neighbourhood of
the plush *portières*. Directly in front of her feet the Shah
was sitting on his haunches, his well-bred tail flat behind him on the ground, his mild-whiskered face elevated. He was saying, "Well, I never!"

II

The room was long and, like all the rooms in Deerpark,
furnished with judgment and, above all, restraint. Miss
Heffernan was not standing on any ceremony. She
moved to a tapestry couch under a window, indicating,
rather than inviting, Kish Massy and myself to select
our own seats. I got into my favourite place—a low, uncomfortable ottoman with twisted mahogany legs, near
the fire-place. In this spot I could observe whatever
drama was to follow and at the same time hug my knees
with my arms. Kish Massy hesitated, looking about
him. At last he deliberately walked to an antique chair,
or rather throne, with a step reaching to a little dais and
a long narrow high carved back. He rested his hands on
the arms of the throne and looked about him, pleased,
I could see, with his surroundings. Something like a
grunt of satisfaction broke from him. Miss Heffernan

removed her hat slowly and laid it beside her, something a little weary in her movements. The situation seemed unaccountably strained.

"When did you see George, Mr. Massy?" Miss Heffernan asked, some nervous quality in her voice.

"Something like two years ago," Kish Massy replied. He was almost directly facing Miss Heffernan, but nearer to me.

With some hesitation, some movements of the hands up and down the arm of the throne, some shifting of the legs, Kish Massy related to us the circumstances of his meeting with George Heffernan in a hotel in Sydney. That meeting was quite accidental. Kish Massy had seen letters in the rack of the hotel hall addressed to a Mr. George Heffernan, he made inquiries, discovered the identity of the visitor and they became friendly, having, of course, a great deal of interest in each other owing to their antecedents at home.

I have no clear recollection of the full story which Kish Massy went on to relate. Much more vividly do I remember the bulky figure on the throne, the carved woodwork reaching over the long head. A vague doubt as to the truth of what he related obsessed me. Some whispering which had gone the rounds at the time of his departure came back to my mind. It had been said he had gone away to avoid debts.

"Your nephew," said Kish Massy, "was at the time transacting very important business in Sydney with his stockbrokers." Kish Massy loved the sound of the word. The palms of his hands turned upward, the fingers twitching.

But the life that had attracted Kish Massy most was, he declared, the life of the Bush, the life spent on horseback, the pastoral life.

"It is easier for a man from Connacht to fall into that life than it is for most people," he declared. "We graze sheep mostly in Connacht, our countrysides are lonely, we do a great deal of our travelling on horseback. But there the resemblance ends. There is no real comparison when you get to the Bush."

He went on to speak of his delight at being invited by Mr. George Heffernan to visit one of his sheep stations in New South Wales. He dwelt on all the hospitality he had experienced while doing so. Miss Heffernan leaned forward, her elbows on her knees, her hands clasped, straining to hear every detail of the life of the man to whom she owed all her present possessions, the man who had redeemed the family name. Kish Massy inclined from his throne to her as he praised the family hero. As the story went on I could not help thinking, what an amazing contrast they made: Miss Heffernan tall, elegant, unhappy, something broken in her life, sensitive to an exceeding degree, old-world, refined, a charm in all her simple ways. Her profile was between me and the light of the window; I could see the partings of the moist lips as she listened to the words of Kish

Massy, her yellow hair disordered above her head. And Kish Massy: He had settled into the throne. The thick legs were well apart, a stout pair of pillars, the paunch reaching across them like a dome, a splendid piece of architecture the style of which dated back to the period of the Garden of Eden. His hands now rested on his knees, the palms turned upward, two red cups fashioned to receive gifts. The lips while he spoke seemed extraordinarily eloquent. Out of the oblong eyes there were glances hungry in their eagerness to observe and to impress. This strange god, almost bronze in colour, was alive in every nerve, vulgar, aggressive, unscrupulous, humorous, and at the moment extremely happy. As I beheld him on the throne I said to myself, "Suppose some artist or sculptor sought a model of Crom Cruach, the evil god who had twelve evil sub-gods, what a chance this would be!" While he talked from his throne he was putting forth all that personal hypnotic influence which was part of his aggressive character, the hypnotic influence which he used with such splendid effect upon animals, upon his followers at the stable, and upon most of those who came within his range. He looked pleased because the situation favoured him. He was undoubtedly making an impression as a voice from the Bush.

As I have said, I have no recollection of the more or less connected story which Kish Massy related. Only stray snatches of it remain with me. I remember a little description of himself and George Heffernan sitting on a veranda outside his house at a sheep station, smoking an evening pipe. Kish was disappointed with life in Australia and grew to dislike it: the management of horses was so different. The conditions were outside his scope. "Every man in that place," said Kish Massy, "was like a trick circus rider, and they used to remind me of this by telling me I had no place on their programme."

The long rides made no appeal to him, and as to loneliness and vast spaces, why Connacht was a thriving populated place beside it. He had learned some tricks of mounting and dismounting, methods of curbing the tempers of fiery steeds, and a band of lads from Argentina whom he struck had taught him the art of lassoing. There was some vividness in the short, jerky sentences in which he talked of long rides with border men whose main business it was to succour sheep who had tumbled over on their backs, unable to regain their legs again on account of the heavy fleeces. I was interested for a little in his account of one of the few birds which refused to move back with the receding wilderness of the real Bush and which found a living on the maggots of the sheep: in its hunt for the maggots it had discovered the kidneys of the animal, took greatly to them as a luxury, and consequently became a very great pest. It was inevitable that he should speak about the rabbits and the hares, the wonder of their numbers. While he was talking Broderick, the butler, brought a bottle of wine and some glasses. Kish Massy held his glass in one of the red cups of his hands after the manner of a god. Miss Heffernan, during the interruption, moved from the sofa to a chair nearer the corner of the window. She had listened quietly to Kish Massy's story.

It was, he said, an attack of dysentery which had laid him low in Australia and brought about his final dislike of the country. His life was in danger. At mention of this fact he sipped some wine. He waxed a little sentimental about his ailment and looked in such very fine fettle that it was difficult to restrain a smile at his past distress. He was convinced that he would have died in the Bush were it not for the kindness and the good heart of one man. That man was Mr. George Heffernan. He inclined to Miss Heffernan as he made the declaration; she clasped her hands in her lap as she listened. . . . In the cool of the evening and during the night Mr. George Heffernan had driven Kish Massy across a desolate tract of country, arid, parched and hopeless in a fearful drought, to his sheep station, and there had him cared and nursed until he was by a miracle restored. That act he would never forget to Mr. George Heffernan, his memory or his kind. He spent weeks on a bed of pain after the night journey across the arid Bush, but was so carefully nursed that his strength came back to him, he returned to Sydney, went from thence to New Zealand, where he engaged for some time in the cutting down of timber, then returned to Ireland. Kish Massy stirred himself upon his throne and attempted to wind up his panegyric with a little peroration.

"A finer man, a kinder friend, a larger-hearted gentleman, never drew breath of life than Mr. George Heffernan. Thank God I have lived to speak these words of him in the house where all his race were bred and nurtured."

"By heavens," I said to myself, "Kish is doing splendidly."

Miss Heffernan was, I could see, greatly touched by the story. Kish Massy was so moved by his own emotion that I rose and replenished his glass.

"Did George look ill or delicate when you saw him?" Miss Heffernan asked.

"Not a bit," replied Kish Massy. "He was, like most of the men out there, thin, wiry, and fit as a fiddle."

Miss Heffernan returned to the sofa. Kish Massy sipped his wine, his oblong eyes following her movements over the edge of his glass.

"Did George never speak of those at home?" Miss Heffernan asked slowly, hesitantly, almost nervously. Her hand began to fondle the buttons of her coat.

Kish Massy lowered his glass and paused before he replied. I was standing by a side table. I held the bottle of wine over the tray. Something tense had come over the atmosphere of the room.

"I will answer you truly, Miss Heffernan," Kish Massy said. "I don't believe he ever worried much about

his old home or those at home. I don't think he understood the circumstances. But when we talked about the
old land and when I told him the way it was with the
Deerpark property he appeared to think more of it and
to be more concerned about its revival."

There was dead silence after this declaration. I put
down the bottle of wine noiselessly on the tray. There
could be no doubt of the significance of the announcement. It had linked up Kish Massy with the whole wonder of the resurrection of Deerpark, revealed him as the
instrument chosen by Providence to fire George Heffernan with inspiration which resulted in the fortune
which had come to Miss Heffernan.

"This," I told myself, "is a pretty stroke."

III

Miss Heffernan had built in her mind a shrine sacred to
the memory of her nephew, George Heffernan. There
was enthroned an idol at which no heretic dare point a
profane finger. In the most wonderfully intimate way
this idol was part of her belief in the greatness of the
family, her veneration for the estate, her worship of the
thing which had justified her long years of certainty in a
resurrection which happened. She could at best have
only a dim recollection of her nephew as a small boy; the
memory of a man whom she never saw but who had
been a torture to her mind because of his potency to ruin
or redeem the estate must have a sharper place in her

recollection. But all these things had now been woven into harmony in the romance of the property. George Heffernan was assuming in her mind the attributes of all mythical heroes. He was a wonder-man, wearing his halo as befitted a Heffernan.

I do not know how far Kish Massy could have grasped Miss Heffernan's mental attitude with regard to her nephew, but certain it is that the revelation of a friendship which had led to the resurrection of Deerpark was giving Kish Massy a place in Miss Heffernan's thoughts which she herself could not deny him. Her early prejudices against him were obvious; she did not make any attempt to conceal them. How could these prejudices stand up to the appeal of the story which had come from the throne? Already Miss Heffernan must be upbraiding herself for the manner in which Kish Massy had been treated. The very appearance which he carried about with him of Bush life in Australia, not so very far removed from the primitive environment of his home occupation, was surely now a thing that would stand to his credit in the eyes of Miss Heffernan? Kish Massy was a holy pilgrim who had been to the Mecca of Miss Heffernan's dreams. He was the only one she could ever hope to know who had beheld the glory of the Heffernan manhood.

I do not wish to deny Kish Massy's capacities. He had not that long head of his for nothing. He had a rough-and-ready understanding of humanity and no scruple about playing upon its weaknesses. This rough-and-ready capacity, coloured with some cunning, makes for more success in the ordinary affairs of life than the finer and more subtle intelligences. The fool who rushes in where angels fear to tread has more laughs at the expense of the angels than we suspect.

"I am so pleased you have told me all this," Miss Heffernan said after a long pause. Her hands were on either side of her as she sat back on the tapestry couch.

"Not a bit more pleased than I am myself," said Kish Massy.

I walked from the side table to the fire-place.

"Extremely interesting," I said. It may be that some harsh note sounded in my voice, but both of them looked at me at once.

Miss Heffernan took up her hat ready for departure. I made some movement to the door. Kish Massy clung firmly to his throne.

"I suppose, Miss Heffernan," he said, "that I will now have the pleasure of hearing that you will accept the pair of bays."

We had both forgotten the bays! For a second the old look of annoyance, almost pain, swept across Miss Heffernan's face. It vanished at once.

"I am sure George would be very displeased if I were to refuse," she said. "I am very grateful to you, Mr. Massy, and the horses are a magnificent gift."

"Well spoken," declared Kish Massy, rising from his

throne. Turning to me he said, "Here, Jennings, let us drink to Miss Heffernan, to her health, prosperity and long life."

I had rather expected his ingrained vulgarity would break out in some banality of the kind. Miss Heffernan's eyes drooped while he drained his glass, and I, feeling red and embarrassed, raised mine, although there was nothing in it.

In the hall Kish Massy said, as he took down his hat and coil of rope, "If you don't mind, I'll go round by the stables myself and acquaint Barlow as to the bays."

Without waiting to hear the reply I bowed and walked down the drive, swinging my stick as I went. I had not gone very far, however, when suddenly I heard a swish about my ears, and the next moment I felt my arms pinned to my side. I looked down to see, with amazement, that a rope was coiled round my body. A little jerk tightened it most uncomfortably across my chest. For a second I was bewildered; a perspiration of indignation broke out on my body as the truth dawned upon me. I had been lassoed by Kish Massy! He had given an exhibition of one of his Australian accomplishments!

I turned round, anger in every nerve of my body. Miss Heffernan was standing at the top of the steps, her expression one of dismay struggling with uncontrollable laughter. Some way down the steps was Kish

Massy, the other end of the rope in his hands, his fat active figure stooped forward like an athlete about to start in a race, his face one shining ray of malicious delight.

"Ha-ha!" he cried, "I've got you, Paul!"

I staggered a little as the rope got a powerful chuck.

CHAPTER THREE

I

MRS. HUGH QUIRKE'S accent rose over the faint babble, dominant as the gobble of a turkey in a poultry yard. A voice hailed me from behind.

"Ah, Jennings!"

It was Dr. O'Sullivan, the local practitioner. We entered together. Miss Heffernan moved across the room to greet us. She had been speaking to his lordship, Dr. Noel Mitchel, the bishop of the diocese, turning to him again when she had greeted us.

"The chrysanthemums would be most welcome for the *quarant ore*," I heard the bishop say.

Dr. O'Sullivan and myself moved down the room, joining the first group we met. Here was Colonel Algernon Burke, a very likeable man whose figure was somewhat misshapen; he spoke with a lisp, and had at one time made an essay into politics but received such a rough handling that he was now solely interested in poor law reform, his whole passion in life centred on an amalgamation of workhouses. He was expounding his scheme to Captain Manning. The captain grunted now and again in agreement with the colonel, the captain's figure sturdy and a little aloof. He had bought his title in the Militia in his youth and had devoted all his days since to the grazing of sheep and cattle, making a great success of it. It was said of the captain that he knew how to sell wool better than any man who had ever seen a shears.

"Mr. Kish Massy," announced the footman. I wheeled around sharply, scarcely believing my ears.

Could it be possible Kish Massy had been invited to a dinner party at Deerpark, that he was to be incorporated in this select little society in the hills, about to be taken up by Miss Heffernan? Could it be possible he had arrived? By Heaven, there he was at the door, looking enormous, and in evening dress, too! His white shirt front looked like some swelling white sail bearing a dark barge down the bright room. I could have snorted in sheer repugnance.

"Wethers went better and I got the top price for the hoggets," said Captain Manning to somebody farther down the room.

I wondered if Miss Heffernan had invited Kish Massy as a sequel to his story of the Bush, a sort of compensation for the snubs which had been offered him? He looked very cheerful as he sailed down the room, anchoring somewhere near the hearth with Mrs. Hugh Quirke, a lady keenly interested in horses. That lady, whose origin was obscure, was very anxious to get on in local society, and her idea of doing so was to stare very hard and to speak in a loud chopping voice which always reminded me of the turkeys in the poultry yard. She was now gobbling with great spirit at Kish Massy.

"The whole system is w'ong," declared Colonel Burke. "Amalgamate them and——"

I moved away, some annoyance coming to me at the presence of Kish Massy. As I moved away Lady Agatha Newell was announced. This was Miss Heffernan's great friend, and I was glad to hear she had come.

Lady Newell was understood to have spent all her life between Paris, London, Vienna, and the Riviera. The spaces between she dismissed with a shrug of the shoulders. "Where they grow the vegetables," she said. Suddenly two branches of the Newell family, long hostile, launched into a fearful legal contest, involving both their fortunes. A storm raged in the courts, Lady Newell's end of the beam eventually gave, so that, the storm abated, she discovered she had been washed into a dower-house—a long barrack-like damp building— over the hills and far away! Here she had languished ever since, a distinguished but broken-hearted deposit. Her sanity she had preserved by taking to the breeding of prize Pomeranian dogs, her spirits she had spasmodically maintained on Miss Heffernan's cellars, and her tongue she whetted on all of us, perversely holding her local neighbours responsible for the *débâcle* of the Newell family. That tongue was a source of amusement and alarm to her friends, albeit that she affected difficulties with the English language. She came into the room now leaning on an ebony stick with a gold knob, her walk a reminiscence of the Alexandra limp, her gown remarkable mostly for the number of laces that fluttered about her. On her golden head she wore a diminutive creation in black lace which had a far-out cousinship to a cap. Her face, although made up, was made up with unusual skill and almost pallid, the features and the eyes giving a strong hint of the beauty which, it had been said, had once, combined with her wit, made Paris talk.

"Marie," she cried making straight down the room for the fire, "what an evening to bring one out! Winds the most terrible, the most bitter, the most hateful! My poor bones, how they ache! I am so cold I no longer care to live. Ah, I am glad of the logs so bright."

There was no seat convenient to the hearth, and Kish Massy at once wheeled an armchair to the spot. He looked, as he did so, as if he were backing a horse into the shafts. My eyes followed his movements with scorn. Lady Newell sank into the chair without as much as looking at him. Miss Heffernan moved quietly to her guest and they exchanged a light kiss on the cheeks.

"*Ma chère*, it was good of you to think of the logs, for I famish."

"The weather has certainly been very bad," Miss Heffernan admitted. Her tall, distinguished figure towered over Lady Newell's chair, and again it annoyed me to see Kish Massy very anxious to join them in conversation.

"It's the east wind that caught you on the bog road, Lady Newell," he said.

At the sound of the voice Lady Newell raised her lorgnette and through it surveyed Kish Massy. It did not require any artificial aid to see him, but Lady Newell ranged about his figure with a scrutiny which would have appalled most people. She leaned backward and forward, swayed from side to side as if endeavouring in vain to estimate his girth.

"Why, who have we here by the *cheminée?*" she asked at length.

Miss Heffernan presented Kish Massy. She did so quietly. Kish Massy made a stiff quick bow, his shirt front jumping out smartly at the chest.

"Who did you say we have here, Marie?" Lady Newell persisted, making braver efforts to see round his figure.

"Mr. Kish Massy," Miss Heffernan repeated. I strained my ears because I thought I caught an unconscious note of apology in the voice.

"Ah, now I know! He is of the horses so famous! And

as for the stoutness, it is immense. How can you look so well in this climate, monsieur? Behold me. I am on the bone."

"You are really too hard on our climate, Lady Newell," said Dr. Mitchel, strolling over to the hearth.

"Ah, my good bishop, you are here and already you preach to me." She gave him the tip of her elegant fingers.

"Not preaching, remonstrating very mildly," said the bishop.

"It is the same. And it is of no use. There is no hell; there is only this *pays sauvage*, this Connacht most dreadful."

"It is merely your own——"

"Do not speak to me of my sins. They were many, but I am punished." She swerved away from the bishop. "Marie," she said, "you know Jacques, the toy chocolate, the father of so many families?"

"Yes, a beauty."

"What do you think? This morning he got a forepaw in a rat-trap. And the howls!" She put her fingers over her ears.

"One of the little Pomeranians, is it?" asked Kish Massy. Lady Newell looked beyond him as if he no longer existed, as if he were a transparency.

"Ah, Algernon," she called out, "there you are, talking about your tiresome workhouses! Come to me and shake hands."

Colonel Burke, an old friend, came up to the hearth and patted her on the cheeks.

"Well, Agwatha," lisped Colonel Burke, "how-do-you-do?"

"How do I do? How *could* I do? I am cold and into the bones."

"Did you get the wain yeste'day coming from the twain?"

"Rain? It was the Deluge! If I had not escaped, the good bishop would now be chanting the *De profundis*."

The dinner gong sounded.

II

Over the white table, the sparkle of cut-glass and silver and plate, the delicate tints of the chrysanthemums in the epergnes, the frail sprays of asparagus fern, above the comedy of the conversation, loomed that enormous figure in black and white, the light from the chandeliers overhead falling on the pig black and the steel-grey streaks of hair. It rose like a vague menace, a threat. The oblong eyes shifted from my face. I looked down at the wine Broderick was pouring into my glass.

"What right has he to come here?" I asked myself. "He should not be of the company." The clatter of cutlery on the plate, the occasional tinkle of the neck of a bottle on a glass sounded like an ironic comment on my thoughts. Somebody laughed and there was a lull in the general conversation.

"*Mon Dieu!*" Lady Newell exclaimed, leaning a little

to Miss Heffernan. "How can one eat like that and expect to rise from the table when the time comes?" Lady Newell's words had reference to Kish Massy, the figure looming over the table. A footman was fluttering about his chair with anxiety. He had been putting away great quantities of food.

"At the worst the butler can carry one out," said Miss Heffernan. As she spoke there was no smile on her face, but now and again there was that cloud of unhappiness. She seemed a little remote, like one removed from it all.

"Agwatha, my deah," chided Colonel Burke, "you do not mellow with the yeaws."

"No, Algernon," she replied, "I am not a bottle of old port in the cellar."

Kish Massy threw back his head. I gazed at him with some reproof. He returned the look with defiance. There was a gleam of triumph in his gaze. I looked away.

In the hall, as we came away, I overheard Miss Heffernan say to Kish Massy, "So very pleased you came and that you did not allow Lady Newell to terrorize you."

"Miss Heffernan," said Kish Massy, "I have not travelled round the world and remained a child."

I walked home alone. There were heavy black clouds resting like ugly gorged beasts on the grey sky. The wind came from the east. There were sharp cries from snipe who winged overhead.

"I don't know that I am so pleased to have gone to

Deerpark," I reflected. "I think it would have been more pleasant if I had gone to Betty Carolan. But how was I to know that Kish Massy would be there? I wonder was it given in his honour? I wonder why he gave Miss Heffernan the present of the pair of bays? I wonder——"

The snipe cried overhead.

CHAPTER FOUR

I

THE stable bell in the stone arch of the court-
yard of Deerpark clanged impatiently. It was
one o'clock. The raucous tone went out over the
fields, living long enough to touch the ears of the time-
keeper standing at the brow of the marble quarries. He
looked at his watch, waited some seconds, then blew his
whistle.

The harsh stroke of the sledge hammers on the drill-
bars, the "ya-ya" of the men who swung them, ceased in
the depths below. The men who turned the handles of
the cranes stopped, wiped their brows, drew on their
coats; the chains hanging from the jibs, swinging blocks
of stone from the bowels of the earth, no longer
groaned. The men leading the horses and carts turned
their heads about and jogged down to the road. Up the
rude passages men scrambled, calling to each other as

they came over the brows of the pits. They went away in little groups, their heavy boots scrunching on the heaps of grey splinters or sinking in the pyramids of yellow soft earth, making a zigzag down the landscape. Here and there stray souls who did their own cooking collected about the glowing braziers where the tar was kept boiling, ready for use in the making of the narrow line of rail which we were cutting down the hills, upon which a lorry service was to be soon inaugurated.

"It will be a great saving in haulage right enough," said Augustine Massy as his unemotional eyes followed the wake of the line of rail, littered with sleepers and workmen's tools, as yet only a fresh gap in the virgin soil.

I made no reply; Augustine Massy's conversation always sounded so remote that one's instinct was to ignore it. His languid hand stroked his black beard. He was not alone a negative of Kish, but almost a negative of everything, one of those subnormal mortals who live to tremendous ages, who keep up a sort of curiosity as to what is happening in the world about them but who remain apart from it all, super-nonentities. I forgot his presence completely as my eyes wandered away from the yawning gaps of the quarries to a road which wound through the hills some hundreds of yards lower down.

Along that road was moving a little cavalcade in the bright winter sun. It made me drop the stick I held in my hand, caused an exclamation of amazement to escape from my lips. My eyes fastened upon the cavalcade with a morbid fascination. First was a venerable phaeton drawn by a single and dejected horse. On the back seat of the phaeton lolled a bundle of brown furs. Inside the bundle of furs was the Lady Agatha Newell, one solitary eye peeping through the furs, keeping track of the outside world. Some little way behind the phaeton came Kish Massy mounted on a hunter. There was an ease in his pose, a consciousness that he looked at home and well on horseback. But I wasted hardly the fraction of a second on him. Some few yards behind him came the figure which I gazed upon in stupefaction. It was Miss Heffernan mounted on a big hunter!

"By God!" I said under my breath, but Augustine Massy heard.

"Oh, Miss Heffernan," he said casually.

This casual manner shocked me, even though I knew Augustine Massy to be casual in all things. Had he not seen this wonder? The manner in which the hunter whisked his tail, trotting with the light movement of an animal of blood who rates his going lightly—this, too, seemed frightfully casual for the burden he held on his back.

"By God!" I said softly again. It was the only expression which could voice my amazement.

"She's riding out a week or more now," said Augustine Massy, "tutored by Kish."

I had been losing track of developments in Deerpark.

I had been spending too much time at the marble quarries; I was too anxious about the cutting of the line of rail down through the hills. The grand manner of Kish Massy in leading the little cavalcade along the road made my lips tighten over my teeth.

"But," said Augustine Massy in his hollow lifeless voice, "the sorra much tutoring she wanted: 'tis in the blood."

Miss Heffernan rode easily. Her figure in the riding habit was about right. I imagined I had seen her in that garb, on that very hunter, big and easy, whisking his tail, quite often. The very knot of the yellow hair at the back of the hard hat appeared trite and as I had always known it. Bringing up the rear of the cavalcade was Barlow, the coachman, something deprecating and humorous in his appearance as he trotted along. The phaeton jolted round a turn in the road; the bundle of furs rocked; Kish Massy, leaning his hand on the haunch of his hunter for a moment, turned back to say something to Miss Heffernan, his face smiling pleasantly; Miss Heffernan urged her mount to a smarter pace, her long body pressing a little forward as she "humoured" the saddled; Barlow quickened his pace, too, and they all disappeared round a bend in the road.

"I suppose you saw the new trotter?" Augustine Massy asked.

"What trotter?"

"Miss Heffernan's American trotter."

"N—no."

"That's curious. A great stepper altogether, and a lovely trap for him, too. Bought from Kish the trotter was."

I walked away from Augustine Massy, making up by the brow of the quarries to a wooden structure, not unlike a bungalow, right at the head of the pits, which we called the office and which was now deserted, the time-keeper and the clerks having gone away to their dinner.

II

I sank into a chair, put my legs up on the safe, and looked out the office window, composing myself for a consideration of the new situation. Having seen what I had just seen, it seemed to me absurd that Miss Heffernan had not gone on horseback long ago; she could not help thinking the same thing herself. She had been a victim of environment. Those about her had assumed she would not want to ride because her early education in that way had been neglected. She had been considered in her proper place in a fine carriage and she had accepted that view. It was only when somebody keen enough to make good an early neglect had come along that she had found herself on horseback. Next season she would be riding to the hounds!

"Another score for Kish Massy!" I thought grimly.

There was a knock at the office door, and I turned my head in some annoyance. At the door stood a young lad, a messenger who carried certain dispatches between Betty Carolan and myself, a very discreet boy. His discretion arose solely from the fact that he was both deaf and dumb. He made some passages of the hands, smiled, came forward, handed me a letter and went away again.

The letter read—

KILBEG MILLS,

Friday.

DEAR PAUL,—You know the story of the pitcher which goes once too often to the well? I am afraid the same story holds good about our dear University: we have gone there once too often. You may remember that when we were coming out of the avenue on Monday evening a horseman went by on the road. I am sure he saw us, and that horseman was Augustine Massy. So our secret is out at last. I am quite sure father has heard about it. He has since been frightfully cantankerous, in one of his "touchy" moods. In the evenings he sits before the fire, black as a cloud, smoking and behaving very badly. He scowls into the fire, pushes out his lips, sucks them in, grunts, shifts on his chair, making faces at the coals. Now and then he mutters, "Ha!" or "Ho!" or "He!" Sometimes he says, "Indeed!" or "Well, to be sure," or "Why not, bedad?" or "We'll see about that." I know what he is thinking; I can read him like a book. And what a surly old book it is! Why need people be so very cross about other people? I sometimes wonder if he has ever been young himself, and if so if he ever went out to meet anybody of an evening. To-day he was worse. "Too much liberty you have, me lass," he said to me, "I had a right to keep you down." That's his whole gospel: keeping somebody down. I wonder he ever trusted himself to call me into the world at all. But I expect it was not myself he was expecting at all! To make matters worse, Barlow, the coachman, came here yesterday evening with a message from Miss Heffernan to say that Mr. Carolan would please not to supply any more grain or flour to Deerpark as orders were placed elsewhere. That added to father's lovely mood. He is like a dead weight in the home ever since. I wonder why the order for the grain was cancelled? Do you think we ought to abandon our studies at the University?

Yours,

BETTY

P.S.—Let them all go to hell.—B.

The University to which Betty referred was a little wayside schoolhouse. In an avenue at the back of that schoolhouse, after pupils and teachers had fled, we were in the habit of meeting. We had so far succeeded in keeping ourselves from becoming the subject of gossip, not alone because of the delicacy of the situation at Deerpark but because of Betty's father, a cantankerous old miller whose mind worked like some of the aged cogwheels on the machinery of his old mill. When I read this letter from Betty I knew that our secret was out, and I expected that Kish Massy would make an unscrupulous use of it at Deerpark. I connected the discovery directly with the other things that had happened. The figure of Kish Massy, vulgar and potent, rose up before my mind's eye like a monstrous threat.

I walked over to Deerpark that evening when I left the marble quarries. The old phaeton was turning out the entrance gate as I arrived; there was a movement in the bundle of furs, I heard Lady Newell's voice, and the phaeton pulled up. I stepped up to her. She put out a white hand, shapely, firm, expressive, and through a breach in the furs I got a glimpse of the face of the beauty and beside it the head of a diminutive sable Pomeranian pup. I was aware of a faint smell of decay exhaling from the old phaeton, and possibly from the old coachman and the old horse. All three looked and smelled as if they had been buried for some time and then dug up again.

We had some polite speech.

"I have seen the good Marie," Lady Newell said. "She has now taken to the saddle."

"So I have seen."

"And this Massy, this Kish, he is stout and nimble of the legs, a hunter great."

"No better tutor could be found," I said.

"And now he stalks the good doe in her park," said Lady Newell. She put her mouth to the black ear of the Pomeranian and said to him, '*La, la, ma petite*, he will bring the good doe down!' . . . *Au revoir*, Monsieur Paul."

She drove away. As I walked up the drive I felt my ears burning.

In Deerpark there was very little stir. Miss Heffernan did not make an appearance. I rang for Mrs. Briscoe after some time. The housekeeper looked worried.

"Miss Heffernan is not well this afternoon," she said.

"Nothing serious I hope?"

"I hope not." The Shah squealed at the door, Briscoe crossed the room to let him in. He came to the fire slowly with a slightly offended expression, then settled down on the hearthrug.

"Miss Heffernan," I said, "looked in perfect health today, riding a hunter."

"Perhaps that has something to do with her headache. She's got a very bad headache. But then I'm not surprised." Briscoe, seeing that I was anxious for information, liked to compel me to drag it out of her.

"Why are you not surprised?" I asked.

"Considering the way she cried her eyes out in her room last night. Something dreadful."

"What on earth made her cry?"

"I don't know, I'm sure, Mr. Jennings. She's had attacks of it on and off. I don't like it. And I am afraid there will be another attack to-night. I can see it coming on. I must steep some brown paper in vinegar."

She left the room quietly, the Shah following her. I did not tarry very long in the library and when leaving I

instinctively walked lightly. Silence reigned in the
house. There was no sign of the lamps being lighted although darkness was settling down. The sight of the
dim corridor, the vacant staircase, the heavy shadows
along by the walls, the stillness of the place, gave me a
strong impression of gloom, of sorrow, almost of tragedy. I stole quietly out of the house. And I left it with a
feeling that for the first time there was a definite breach
in the relations between Miss Heffernan and myself.

III

At home that night I sat before the fire thinking out the
whole position. Why, I asked myself again, had Miss
Heffernan cut me off in a matter of business? She had
made purchases of horses, of a dogcart, ended one of my
contracts for the supply of grain, without consulting
me. After all, had I not a right to be consulted? . . . But
had not Miss Heffernan a perfect right to order her own
life, her own affairs, as she thought proper? Had she
done anything more than assert a very ordinary personal independence? But was it an assertion of independence, or did it betray her first surrender to a new influence? Were these transactions by their very nature
unlike the Miss Heffernan I had known? And why was
Miss Heffernan given to these distresses in the secrecy
of her chamber at night? And why were my own
heartstrings touched at the thought of these distresses?
Had I the right to sympathize in so intimate a way? I

could not shut off my life in Deerpark, the things I had
lived through with Miss Heffernan. The bond was
there. And was all this a disloyalty to Betty? . . . I felt
racked between the conflict of all these thoughts. Why
had I not one supreme passion in my life, a passion
powerful enough to absorb within it all other emotions,
making for me a great content? Are the scratchings that
men leave on the disc of their generation only a record of
little frets, protests, discontents, strivings, disloyalties,
struggles, cries of pain?

As the coals glowed, died, falling to ashes in the
grate, so did my thoughts burn, fade, and pass away.
When I rose to go to bed I was merely in a more pensive
mood than when I had sat down. And as I mounted the
stairs the conviction came to me that something was
about to happen at Deerpark that would change everything and everybody. The discovery of my affair with
Betty Carolan could not have been made at a more delicate or fatal moment. I know that Kish Massy would
make a skilful use of it in furtherance of his own
ends. . . . How carefully, how splendidly as we
thought, had Betty and myself guarded our secret! I had
no idea that lovers could be so amazingly resourceful;
they are as cunning, as audacious, as tricky, as decep-
tive as criminals! How often had Betty and myself
laughed in gleeful derision at the world we hood-
winked, the friends we deceived? And there had always
been the possibility—to Betty the thrill of mysterious

delight, making danger a joyous part of her other emotions—of discovery. I read her letter again when I reached my bedroom. And when I had read it my mind went back to the wind-swept, lonely schoolhouse. It was there, as Betty used to say, we received our higher education. . . . I smiled as I remembered an evening of storm and rain, when Betty and myself had to cling to the narrow doorstep of the University because shelter was not to be had anywhere else. We clung, hand upon hand, to the doorknob, sparring at each other with the other hands like a pair of kittens, shouting things because the wind was too high for conversation. The maps of the world rattled on the walls inside, some slates were blown off the roof. Betty shouted, "They're conferring degrees!" But a terrific report behind the door—the blackboard was blown off its easel—suddenly made her spring clean from the step, and she made for the little gate, her young, sinuous body in a transparent bright blue oilcoat, so that her movement looked like the vivid flight of a kingfisher in the half-light. . . . Then I remembered Miss Heffernan and her hours of weeping, and the figure of Kish Massy rose to my mind's eye, and I groaned at the thought that some day—perhaps soon, if something was not done—he would be the master of all that estate, of that fine house, of all that wealth and the power which the mastership of Deerpark carried. I drew on my pyjamas with a feeling of great unhappiness and rolled painfully into bed.

I lay for a long time without sleeping, a mental movement of battledore and shuttlecock racking my poor brain, weaving a problem which offered no solution. But gradually a picture came more and more vividly to me, a picture of a young girl stooped over a table, writing a letter. Her shapely black head bent over the white paper; there was decision in the level, silky, gleaming brows; the hand moved with firmness; what she wrote was a reply to all my doubts and distractions, the words disposed of all fine distinctions, prudent anticipations, philosophic balancing. There was no weak evasion even in the spelling out of the word. Betty went straight and direct to all the problems of her life. There was no pretence, no sentimentality of a poor sort, no hypocrisy. She was a woman of her day, of her generation, a woman who would have counted no matter what sort of life she chose to live. While I lay tossing on the rack, a victim to conflicting emotions, groping for something definite and clear in the tangle of my life, Betty sat down and wrote the words, direct, indeed with something of the harshness and intolerance of youth, without equivocation or compromise, which now, as I lay in bed, came to me with all the force of an inspired direction. For across the ceiling of the dark room were the words, large as life, vivid as lightning, which she had written—

"P.S.—Let them all go to hell.—B."

CHAPTER FIVE

I

MISS HEFFERNAN was not able to continue her riding exercises that season. In fact she became quite ill and was altogether confined to her rooms, so that I did not again see her until we were quite near to the Christmas festival. She was anxious about a *fête* to the children on the Deerpark estate, and as I had, as usual, charge of the arrangements, Mrs. Briscoe informed me that Miss Heffernan would be glad if I joined her in a quiet cup of tea in her boudoir so that she might hear the details of the arrangements. She was still unable to move about the house.

I had only been in that room of Miss Heffernan's a few times during the years of my connexion with Deerpark. It was one of the rooms which she had preserved during the period of her poverty, and for that reason I think she cherished it. Briscoe showed me in, saying Miss Heffernan would be with me very soon. It was a longish, narrow room, tapestries on the wall, the quaint figures of which used to puzzle me very much in the years gone by. The room was lighted by a large standard lamp with a pink shade, and the quaint figures on the tapestries were in this light more elusive than ever. I looked around the room, which at once struck me as rather crowded, almost congested. It was a woman's room in every respect and expressed the temperament of its occupant. The personal note was obvious even in its lack of order. In the furniture, the draperies, the workbaskets, the flowers, the pictures, the few pieces of statuary, the odds and ends scattered about, there was, I said to myself, a homely carelessness. A little square table near one of the windows drew the eye irresistibly; it jumped out from the gay disorder of the room. For upon it was a pile of little stiff forms with cream and rosebud complexions and stout pink arms. They lay at all angles, startling in their effect. I crossed to the table to have a closer look. It was a pile of baby dolls, pink and white chubby images in long white clothes, some lying backwards, with their eyes closed, others upright, their glassy orbs staring vacantly across the room. The sight of these dolls gave me a most peculiar sensation, such a sensation that I glanced around the room to make sure that nobody had caught me gazing upon them. I wondered vaguely if the passion for dressing all these dumb pink staring creatures had any affinity to the change which had come over Miss Heffernan's life the day we had met the beggarwoman on the road? Was there anything peculiar, abnormal, in this craze for dressing baby dolls? On another table near by were other dolls, but not many, some gorgeous ladies in wedding and court dresses, one or two with vivid red petticoats, grey shawls wrapped about their shoulders, red speckled handkerchiefs on their heads, in imitation of the local peasant women. Several of these dolls were only half robed; in one or two cases the *négligée* of the gorgeous court ladies was quite scandalous. It was plain that Miss Heffernan had grown tired of them before their costumes had been completed. There was some pathos in their neglect, lying so stiffly there in the *débris* of material ends, skeins of thread, lengths of ribbon, gold braid, fluffy gay coloured pieces of chiffon, tinsels, bright beads. I walked uneasily away from the table piled up with the baby dolls, and as I went to the fireplace my foot crunched on something on the hearthrug. I stooped down and picked up a scissors which had fallen there. As I put it on the chimney-piece I noticed that here again were all kinds of odds and ends, remnants of bright materials. They looked like an attempt to do the chimney-piece out with bunting. And gradually, while I waited, I became aware that the disorder of the boudoir was not as I remembered it; there was something more than a normal carelessness in the room. My eyes wandered over the chairs, the stools, the couches, the numerous little tables and whatnots. A work-basket with pale blue silk lining had fallen behind a table and lay on the ground with its contents tumbled out. A bookcase between two windows looked as if it had been ransacked: volumes lay here, there, and everywhere; those on the shelves were at sixes and sevens. Miss Heffernan had evidently been glancing at a great many of them and as in the case of the half-dressed dolls they had failed to hold her interest; she had grown tired of them, dropping them whenever the feeling of boredom had attacked her. On her *secrétaire* a half-written letter lay on a blotting pad; a bottle of ink had rolled on to the carpet. Cushions trailed from one seat to another, looking as if they had been used for some short while and then impatiently tossed elsewhere. It all expressed the temperament of one who had not alone indulged in the luxury of carelessness in her own particular boudoir, but one who had become nervous, irritable, ill. I had an impression of Miss Heffernan moving about that room hour after hour, endeavouring to interest herself in things which were losing their appeal, in spasmodic efforts at distractions which were no longer a distraction but an agony. I could see the evidence of those bitter little struggles where the threads of her normal life were slipping from her fingers; I could quite realize now the moments of breakdown when those attacks of weeping overcame her, when the headaches Mrs. Briscoe had spoken of brought about physical prostration. Perhaps it was in this very chair at my elbow that Miss Heffernan had sunk in an hour of utter misery. The pathos of the room in its dim pink light was deepened almost to tragedy for me as my eye caught the outline of the harp beyond the disordered bookcase. An uncomfortable feeling burned at the back of my neck as I gazed upon it; I shifted my position, a little impatient at being left so long there, gazing upon the eloquent background of a pathos almost menacing to my sight.

The door opened at last, but it was Briscoe who entered, carrying a wax figure, quite two feet tall. The figure she deposited carefully on a table and retired at once.

"In a moment, Mr. Jennings," she said as she went out. I saw that the figure was most magnificently robed, the colour scheme purple, gold shining on the head, jewels sparkling on the robes. A moment later Miss Heffernan entered the room from an inward apartment. I was struck at once with the palpable fact that she had suffered a great deal. The thinness was accentuated. Her manner was somewhat nervous; she was, I thought, almost unsteady in some of her steps. Her voice had, if anything, grown more gentle; she had scarcely entered the room when I was conscious of that subtle womanly quality which had always made our intercourse so delicately precious. A wave of sympathy, intimate and poignant, seized me the moment I beheld the ugly physical effects of a profound distress.

"Dr. O'Sullivan says it was rather a bad attack of influenza," she said in reply to my inquiry, "but I am shaking it off." Her eyes looked around the room, uncertain, almost wandering. "I'm afraid this is rather a dangerous place for His Majesty," she said. "Somebody may tilt him over." She took up the wax figure Briscoe had laid on the table and conveyed it to a cabinet. "Won't you come and look at these figures, Mr. Jennings?" she said.

On the shelf of the cabinet were other figures much the same size, and I saw at once that they were a group, almost complete, to represent the Nativity, the scene in the stable at Bethlehem, the figures of a Christmas Crib. They were arresting and striking in the suggestion of strong, eternal, primitive drama. I looked on them with an eye that held something higher and better than a mere critical gaze. Miss Heffernan was very quick to interpret my impressions.

"I always like to see the Crib at Christmas, too," she said. "I often say to myself, 'There is the scene by which all Christianity must stand or fall.' And I like to see the scene set out with the greatest simplicity."

"You have certainly gone to pains in the robing of the figures," I said.

"Yes," she agreed, "I think the nuns in Ballyrea will like them very well."

"You are sending them there?"

"Yes; the suggestion was made to me by Mr. Massy that a gift of the kind would be appreciated."

As she gazed at the figures, re-grouping them more

carefully in the cabinet, I thought to myself that Kish Massy had come very much into her intimate life, her personal interests. There was no limit to his tastes, his talents. He had pleased and flattered Miss Heffernan by suggesting this gift; no doubt he would also levy a tax on the nuns in the shape of prayers and make a heavy entry on the credit side of the private ledger he kept with St. Peter. Knowing his peculiar spiritual outlook I said to myself, "God help the next man he sets out to do!"

"They look quite handsome," I said to Miss Heffernan.

"I was anxious to make the gift worth while," she said. "Do you admire the three Kings?" She turned them about so that I could the better view them.

"Yes," I replied, "the three Wise Men who followed the star are quite familiar and suggestive."

"You see the crowns better now in that light? They are of beaten gold and studded with sapphires and diamonds. The caskets in which they bear the gifts of frankincense and myrrh are also gold, made specially in Dublin from my own design. The cloak of the coloured King is hemmed with fine pearls; I worked them in very carefully myself. I think real simplicity lies in the contrast of these rich costumes with the plaids of the shepherds, the dull brown of St. Joseph, and the blue and white of the Virgin."

"The nuns must certainly be delighted," I said.

She closed the glass door of the cabinet, laughing

with pleasure, a short nervous laugh. But it was obvious that Kish Massy had given her the only interest that had appealed to her, the only little enthusiasm she had enjoyed for some time past. The pilgrim who had brought back great news from the holy Mecca of the Bush had also found good things to do at home. She drew a shawl which rested on her shoulders more closely about her as if a draught had touched her. I was aware of little twitches of the head now and again, the result of great nervousness, which she found difficulty in suppressing.

"So you have secured the schools for the *fête*?" she said, moving to the fire.

"Yes," I said. She moved by the table on which the baby dolls were piled, a strange medley, a nightmare of maternity, and her shawl almost touched them; for a moment she paused as if about to say something of them, then passed on in silence. I followed, paused for a moment at the same place, about to say something of them, then conscious of her hesitancy I, too, ignored them.

"I think everything will pass off all right at the *fête*," I said was we sat down by the fire.

II

As we discussed the Christmas *fête* I was all the time reminded of her nervous movements, the twitchings of her body, the pathos of her condition. More than once she shifted her armchair, extremely sensitive to the slightest draught. Indeed, I think she imagined the draughts as coming from all quarters of the room.

"Would you mind shifting that screen more to the door?" she asked.

I jumped up at once to obey. In shifting the draught screen I knocked a book from a little table; picking it up the volume opened at a page where there was a bookmark. It was a volume of Keats' poems, bound in red leather, and some of the words on the marked page were underlined. The poem was Keats' rendering of "Isabella" from the stories of Boccacio, and my eyes ran down the marked lines, which I read very rapidly, they were so familiar to me—

> "They could not in the selfsame mansion dwell
>   Without some stir of heart, some malady
> They could not sit at meals but feel how well
>   It soothed each to be the other by;
> They could not, sure, beneath the same roof sleep
>   But to each other dream, and nightly weep."

I put the book quietly away and resumed my seat at the fire. But now and again, as we continued a somewhat strained conversation, my mind wandered back to the underlined verse, to the double pencil lines under the last three lines "and nightly weep." . . . What had Mrs. Briscoe said about disturbing attacks of weeping? I looked at the wan eyes, the heavy marks under the lashes, on Miss Heffernan's face. What was the stir of heart, the malady, which had stricken her? Why was that room in its present condition? Why was I there alone with her, sitting by the fire, talking inconsequent small talk? An old sickening feeling of unhappiness came to me. The atmosphere of the room seemed to weigh like a heavy panting body about us.

"You will have a cup of tea, Mr. Jennings?" she asked.

"Yes, delighted," I said, my own manner catching some of her nervousness.

She rang the bell and a maid brought us a tray. As Miss Heffernan raised the silver teapot it quivered in her hand, as if the weight of it was too much for her, but I had to ignore this distress. She knocked the china cups together, all her movements now shaky. It seemed as if at odd moments she quaked at some hidden fear; she started once or twice, her eyes going to the door, as if she expected somebody to burst into the room and attack her. What was she afraid of? She used to be a singularly self-possessed woman, calm and fearless in her outlook. I could not help feeling that she had been brought under some influence which had dominated her will, taken from her the tranquillity which had been a personal heritage and part of her individuality, her charm. What was she afraid of? The sinister figure of Kish Massy rose up in my mind's eye. I remembered him as he had sat on the throne of the reception-room proclaiming his adventures in Australia, putting forward all that personal magnetism, the reserve battery of his vigorous character, while Miss Heffernan gazed at him with parted lips. He had, I told myself, gazing on the sugar-tongs she poised shakily over the tea-cup, since found opportunities for asserting his influence in this house, and the result was to be seen in the present condition of things. He had found a simple, an unwary, and to some extent a weak subject, and I knew he would have no scruple about taking advantage of the situation.

"How many lumps?" Miss Heffernan asked.

"Two, please."

She sat down, a little sigh escaping her, and as she sank back on the cushions I noted the frailness of her long body. I almost cried out as I thought of the vulgar, aggressive brute taking that sensitive, refined, almost broken creature to his embrace. And yet what could I do, what could I say, how could I raise any sort of honest protest? To do so would place me in a possession of the utmost embarrassment again. As the thoughts crowded like gloomy things about the fire-place a silence ensued and we sipped our tea.

In the midst of the gloomy silence something fell on the floor with a dull, ugly thud, striking the bare boards near the wall. I glanced around apprehensively, and Miss Heffernan glanced around, too. It was one of the baby dolls which had fallen from the table and now lay with its broken face against the wall, an arm, split to the shoulder, hanging from the draped body. I had an impulse to jump to the rescue of this broken figure, but suddenly checked it. Miss Heffernan pulled her shawl about her shoulders as if she felt a cold draught and we resumed the sipping of our tea without speaking.

"Another cake?"

She jerked up in her chair, rousing herself from a little reverie, as if it had suddenly occurred to her that she had been neglecting me.

"Yes, thanks—just this one."

"You have still the old taste for the cream puffs," she said, with the flicker of a smile.

"Yes," I said, "they are as delicious as ever on the tongue."

She sank back again, inert, moody, her eyes on the fire. There could be no doubt that she was ill and in an unaccountable way changed. I knew instinctively that she feared I would understand, sympathize, pity her. Her pride was ready to spring to the defence. To silence the impatience, the agony, of my own thoughts I told myself, "You are only a dog in the manger. You did not respond to this woman's advances, and now you storm inwardly and impotently because another offers to her his affections, such as they are."

"I hope we shall have frost and snow—an old-fashioned Christmas," she said.

"I hope so, too. It is always more pleasant."

While the platitudes dropped from our lips over the quiet cup of tea my mind stormed in silence. "Bah!" I said to myself. "He offers her no sort of affection. He simply schemes to get hold of her estate, her house, her property, her wealth; he has dreamt of all the power, influence and prestige the mastership of Deerpark carries. She herself, the woman, the personality, is the least thing in his thoughts. He regards her as fair game for his ambitions. Affection indeed!"

"I always think rain is so dreary, so unhealthy, about Christmas," said Miss Heffernan. "So many people get knocked up with colds."

"Yes, indeed, quite a great many. Dr. O'Sullivan always gets a brisk running about during a green Christmas."

And my thoughts cried within me, "Lady Newell has said the bitter but the true thing about this monstrous wooing. He simply stalks the good doe in her park. Once, long ago, in the first unguarded moments, he himself likened her to a wild hare. . . . That is the measure of his interest in her. It is because I had affection, and that I have still affection, nay veneration, for this woman that I shrink from entering into competition with Kish Massy in this unholy hunt."

"I am very glad Lady Newell has set herself to paint Christmas cards and fans for us," said Miss Heffernan. "She has quite a talent for that sort of thing."

"All our neighbours will give a helping hand," I said.

"Affections indeed!" my thoughts cried. "He never got so near to the woman as I did, or understood her, or appreciated her, and he never will."

"Another cup?"

I handed over the cup and she reached out to the little table. As she did so her eyes wandered to the door as if that hidden, secret fear came to her again. I was conscious myself of something lurking, something threatening, in the shadows of the room. The very stillness of the place, the vague pink light, the disorder of the room, the spectral babies staring with their glassy eyes into vacancy, brought to me an unhealthy sensation.

"Thanks," I said, taking the cup from Miss Heffernan.

She tarried over the tea-table, then said, "May I say something of a personal, rather delicate, nature to you, Mr. Jennings?" she asked.

"Certainly," I said at once, looking up at her.

"I hope you won't be angry with me," she said, then settled back in her seat. "While we sit here quietly is the best time to speak of it." There was a nervous quality in her voice, but she spoke with a certain clear decision. The tea seemed to have braced her.

"What I wanted to say," she ventured, her eyes on the fire, "was that in case there is any change here—in case I make any change in my life—that you will still continue as agent of the estate and manager of the property."

There was no mistaking the words. I knew Miss Heffernan long enough to gauge the delicacy of her mind, and I knew now that this was almost a formal announcement of the success of Kish Massy's campaign. She had already surrendered, or was on the point of surrendering to him. All the wealth and power that Deerpark held was already within the grasp of the red, twitching fingers. There could be no other change. There was significance in the very tone of her voice, in the expression of her face, in a sudden clutching of the ends of the shawl, in the quiver of the pale lashes on the dark skin under the eyes, the eyes which gazed upon the fire. I stirred the spoon about in my cup and as I did so I was not alone conscious of the significance of Miss Heffernan's words, but gradually I was conscious, too, that she awaited my reply, waited and, perhaps, hoped for words that would decide the whole future course of both our lives. And as I moved the spoon about in the cup, the thought challenged me: "Is this to give you a last chance? Does not everything hang upon this pregnant moment?"

CHAPTER SIX

I

"OF course," I said to Miss Heffernan, "my place in the Deerpark organization is a traditional one."

"Yes," Miss Heffernan agreed, her eyes rather lighting up, "it would be strange if one of your family did not follow the tradition."

I could feel that she waited my further words with a new hope. Something came to life in her face. She seemed to shake off that gloom, that hidden fear, which haunted her.

"On account of that tradition," I continued, "I should feel very much cutting my connexion with Deerpark. It would be like attacking something lying at the very roots of my own life."

She nodded in entire understanding, in complete sympathy. Both of us had that conservative worship of tradition which is of the very essence and spirit of the aristocrat and of the peasant. Customs, institutions, all things sanctified by time, founded on an unbroken lineage, had a powerful appeal to Miss Heffernan and to myself; they were a creed, a religion, to us.

"So long," I said, "as I have to follow the tradition and that my service is to you yourself as a Heffernan—as one in the apostolic succession, as I might say—I shall be very glad to serve."

"Yes, yes," she agreed quickly. "I can understand all that."

"But," I added deliberately, "if the Heffernan ownership of Deerpark is broken, then that moment I cut my connexion with the estate."

"All that I can understand," she said. "I did not mean that I was to cease as controller of the property."

"Then the change does not affect me," I said. "I shall have very great pleasure in continuing in the management of the property if you desire me to do so."

"Yes, I desire you to do so," she said, but I could see something die in her face. The hope vanished. My words were evidently not the words she expected. She had an idea, it was clear to me, that they would have led to something more intimate. She lay back in her chair like one exhausted. I put down my cup on the little table that stood between us.

"I hope, Miss Heffernan," I said, "that the change in your life which you contemplate will be a happy one."

She made no immediate answer. Her eyes were gazing into the fire, strained, tense, troubled, as if she would unearth mysteries from the heart of the flames. Slowly, very slowly, she detached herself from the fire and looked at me. It was such a look as one might bestow on a friend from whom one was parting for ever.

"I hope so," she said in a low voice.

I could not avoid the feeling that my expression of goodwill had brought to her unhappiness. Her nervousness was accentuated. She looked as if the hidden fear of something had come to her more powerfully than ever. It was so powerful that I had myself again that sense of something disturbing and threatening in the shadows of the room. By little impatient movements I knew that she was now anxious to conclude the interview, to get me out of the room. My heart was crying out weak, vain, impossible things, my spirit was heavy because the woman beside me suffered so intensely.

I rose to go. She rose slowly, too, her back to the fire. A feeling that the parting was the closing down of something in both our lives made the moments oppressive. I considered for a little, trying to think of words to speak which might lighten the poignancy of this parting. I could think of nothing to say, however, and moved away from the fire-place. My eyes caught the white shape of the baby doll lying shattered behind the table, its broken face to the wall, and I was aware that Miss Heffernan was slowly accompanying me to the door. But I stood abruptly, an impulse coming to me that I did not wish the servants to see us shake hands at the door.

"Good-bye," I said, and I could not control the emotion which sounded in my voice.

She gave me her hand slowly.

"Good-bye," she said in a lifeless tone.

I pressed her hand, and as I did so I could not refrain from bending down and kissing fervently the thin hand which burned in mine. I could feel the little tremor which shook her frame. She stooped forward in a sudden impulse and almost with motherly gentleness kissed me on the brow, one quick burning kiss.

"Dear boy," she murmured. It was the expression she

had used in the library—how long ago?—ages, generations, it seemed to me. The room, with its weird stack of
sleeping and staring baby dolls, with its kings and shepherds, its gorgeous ladies, its littered floors, seemed unreal and far off. A curious feeling of faintness swept me.
I was only dimly conscious that we had already parted,
that I had come there either for a parting or a complete
understanding—that some last desperate effort had
been made to stave something off—that once more I had
been a failure, a disappointment, that I had made more
miserable than ever the life of one cherished and vener-
ated—that in life it is those who are near to each other,
precious to each other, who alone stab each other, who
have it in their power to inflict the most bitter wounds.
As if she were very far off I saw Miss Heffernan's figure
silhouetted against the red light of the fire for a moment
and then sink into an armchair, and her figure sank as if
I, an assassin, had struck her a mortal blow. I turned
from the sight, groping my way for the door in the pink
light like a half-blind man, found the handle, hurried
out and down the corridor to the library, where I sank in
the chair before the desk. A sudden burst of laughter,
the response to some crude jest, sounded through the
open window from the garden down below where the
workmen were going by.

I sat in a mechanical attitude of work at the writing-
desk and rolled up the lid. I took some letters from the
pigeon-holes and looked at them, though not a written
word was intelligible to my sight. I leaned my elbows
down on the desk, staring blankly at the wall opposite.
Then I lay back in the chair, saying to myself, "I must
sit here for some time. I must recover some measure of

composure. Perhaps it is better that it is over, though it was very painful and I had no idea when I went there. . . . But I must forget all that. I must regain my composure. She possibly thinks I have left the house by this time, but I cannot go just yet. I might meet somebody on the way, and I am too agitated for that. They would possibly notice something."

I put the letters back into the pigeon-holes, shifted some ink-bottles and pens, tore an end off a blotting-sheet, and again sat back in my chair. Suddenly the chords of the harp in an amazingly strong, harsh stroke came crashing down the corridor outside. It seemed to tear through the silent house, something volcanic in its sudden escape. I had no idea that a harp could gather such strength in its penetrating strains. It seemed to leap at me like a living thing as I sat on the chair and it gripped me there. I could not move, I could scarcely breathe. I was intensely responsive to the emotion, for although I play no instrument I am unusually sensitive to the influence of music; this, again, gave me some nearness to Miss Heffernan, who was, I felt now more than ever, a daughter of Jubal, her soul instinctively seeking self-expression through the harp. The music that now held me so powerfully was not any conventional composition, and at first seemed not even a definite or connected composition. It was ugly, terrible, the notes sharp, the discords painful, but as it tore its way along I felt it aimed at something and expressed something. And above the harsh discords there struck out, thin and sharp, a *motif* that surely had its source in some folk tune, elemental and disturbing. And there was a certain crude rhythm in the tearing discords, the notes most powerful in their harshness, urged on as it were by some velocity that was vindictive, and above the brutal jargon of sound was that weird, very definite *motif*, shrilling up over it all, ironic and terrible. I felt moved, shaken, almost exhausted by this experience, and like a flash the thought went across my mind that all of emotion and hope and desire and despair that lay behind the platitudes Miss Heffernan had dropped in her boudoir was now speaking, clear and unmistakable, in this rush of mad sound. It did not come on any scale of harmony and yet with terribly flexible and unashamed meaning, the child of an inspiration that was itself too savage to obey a form, too crude to step to a technique.

I clutched the arms of my chair and said, "This is the music of something lost, this is a thing of hysteria and madness!" And as I listened I felt that in no way could this music be interpreted except, perhaps, by the dance of a woman who would have in her body and her limbs the hysteria and the madness, in her face and her gestures the horror of a lost soul. And instantly there came to my mind the memory of a scene witnessed on a little yellow road in Connemara, a scene that had brought me nightmares in the years gone by. A young tinker woman, comely and courageous in the daring beauty of her kind, wearing a gay petticoat of red and white stripes, a blue bodice, her rich brown hair tumbling about her shoulders, danced in her bare feet on the road, beating up the dust, something fantastic and insane in her movements. She danced in the bright sun of a summer day and she kept her face, ghastly pale, to the sun, her upper white teeth showing through the blue line of her lips. She had, I knew at once, danced up and down the road, her eyes half closed, for a longer time than a normal physical reserve would allow, and she would go on dancing, seeing nothing, paying attention to nothing, until she fell in a swoon in the yellow dust of the lonely mountain road. And as I went by that dancing mad woman, I saw under a heeled-up cart in the ditch the dead body of a young man, lying stark on his back, her husband or her lover, but one who had died of love. She was dancing up and down by the side of the cart under which he lay dead, and this music which now had broken forth in Deerpark was such music as the limbs of that young tinker woman might have interpreted, for the hysteria and the madness were in them. And it was such music as might have swept the seas and the nations and all time, and found its votaries. It was to music such as this that the limbs of Electra might have moved before the Eastern palace at the hour Arestes struck the blow which brought down the traitor mother queen, Clytemnestra. It was fit measure for the movements of Salome when she danced before the throne of Herod bearing on a dish the head of John the Baptist.

"God!" I cried, "this is the music of a soul writhing under the sense of damnation!" It stopped quite suddenly, as if from exhaustion, on a bar that sounded like a gash. I could visualize the trembling form of the broken woman rising from the harp, her bosom heaving, her hands now hanging inertly by her sides as she tottered down the disordered room, past the figures of the kings and shepherds, the baby dolls, the ladies in wedding dresses, between the tapestries with the quaint Biblical figures, panting in the heavy pink atmosphere, and, having expressed in music what she had hidden behind the platitudes of our tea-talk, throw herself, exhausted, broken, in an agony of despair, into an armchair by the fire.

II

I closed the desk quietly, locked it, and slipped out of the room. There was no movement in the house that I could hear, and I stood looking apprehensively down the wide vacant corridor. The shadows were heavy by the walls. A streak of the lingering evening light fell across the red carpet where the staircase opened into the landing. Everything—the floors, the walls, the ceilings —seemed to vibrate with the weird music which had just ceased, and I imagined they would hold the agony of the notes for ever. It was a house of gloom, of tragedy, and in this hour of agony I had a feeling that the ghost of every Heffernan who had ever known sorrow was crowding up the broad staircase and down from the rooms overhead. I listened very intently, for I could certainly hear whispering from the staircase. Was it the servants who had grouped themselves there, alarmed by the sudden harsh outburst of music? What was the light sound of brushing along the walls? Could it be the spirits of the race crowding down the corridor to group themselves around the door of one who had cried out in mortal pain? What was that curious shuffling and brushing by the walls in the dim light? Why had not the servants lit up the house?

I shuffled nervously down the stairs, and in the hall my hand shook as I reached for my hat and stick. A little wind was blowing, making a moan among the shrubberies, and there was the sharp scent of frost when I got

outside. I drew in some breaths of that sharp air grate-
fully. The bare branches of the elms were delicate and
distinct, graceful tracery work against the pale sky, and
the atmosphere was that half-luminous orange clearness which sometimes transforms the hills.

I had gone only some way down the drive when I
could hear the sound of footsteps approaching the house
from the entrance gate. Some oddness touched me, a
feeling that I was in no mood to meet a possible acquaintance, and I turned in through the trees and the grass of
the lawn, making for a side gate in the demesne wall
used by the workmen. When some way in through the
trees I stopped, for the visitor was now moving along by
the shrubberies. I could see the black bowler hat move
along quite distinctly over the laurels and the rhododen-
drons. An inquisitiveness, instinctive and quick, came
to me. I watched that hat until the figure stepped out
into the open space of the house. I could see quite distinctly in the luminous winter evening light.

It was Kish Massy who approached Deerpark. Instantly his appearance became potent and vivid to my
mind; I watched his figure as one might watch some
movement in a drama which is rarely intense. Was there
not something eager and at the same time stealthy in his
approach? The great legs swung him along in characteristic strides; he was as intent upon his approach as I was
alive to his movements. The house was still in darkness,
although it must by this time be quite dim in the interior. Only a light, faint and pink, shone in the window
of Miss Heffernan's boudoir. I thought there was something significant in the dark bulk of the old house, solid,
grim, almost threatening. I had strongly the impression

that Briscoe had charge of it and that the darkness and silence were expressive of her supervision. What was taking Kish Massy to Deerpark at this hour, in this romantic light? I watched his active but stealthy stride to the flight of steps. He paused for an imperceptible time there, glanced up at the windows, then the active limbs pushed up the steps. Was he making a call? Was he expected? Would he be admitted? He seemed to wipe his brow with his handkerchief as he moved under the portico. He looked like a man bracing himself for something; again he seemed to search the windows of the silent stark house. I saw him move under one of the pillars, hesitate, then put his arms about the pillar and mount it like a sailor climbing up a mast. Why had he behaved in this extraordinary way? Was it the old boyish love of climbing breaking out in him through pure high animal spirits? He ascended the granite pillar steadily, the active arms and limbs expert at the business. When he could go no higher he seemed again to gaze at the blank windows of the house. I beheld the performance with amazement. Presently he slid down the pillar like a streak, and again approached the hall-door. I saw his action as he pulled at the bell. In the silence I could hear the distant clang in the remote kitchen. There was a short silence. Would they let him in? Had he merely come to make a polite inquiry as to Miss Heffernan's health? A light moved in a lower window. Still the door was not open. He moved uneasily, then suddenly clanged the bell again. It was the ring of a man who was not going to stand any nonsense. Another light moved across some other windows, then the two narrow panes on either side of the hall-door were illuminated. The door itself swung back. The figure of a maid stood outlined for a moment, then she drew to one side and the figure of Kish Massy filled the space. He was stepping in, removing his hat, evidently speaking to the maid. He moved in the hall. The door swung to and closed with such a dull clang of awful finality that my heart sank. Suddenly the pink light in Miss Heffernan's room went out. It was immediately replaced by a more powerful white light. Lights also jumped in other windows both above and below. The house was stirred into sudden and active movement. Once the hurried figure of Briscoe showed at a window as she drew down a blind. There was the sense of hurry in the interior, the presence of a powerful personality had wakened Deerpark into life. "The conqueror," I told myself, "has arrived."

I turned away from the light dancing from window to window and made my way through the quivering trees to the side entrance in the demesne wall.

The following March a group of people was assembled outside the little parish church in the hills. They raised a moody cheer as the bride and bridegroom drove away after the marriage ceremony.

Kish Massy and Mary Heffernan had been joined in wedlock. When the carriage bearing the newly wedded couple drove up to Deerpark the daffodils in their golden bonnets were dancing in the lawn.

PART THREE

AFTER THE MARRIAGE

I

I WAS not among those who extended to Kish and Mrs. Massy a welcome when a month later they returned from the honeymoon. That same morning I had made a call at the house of Hugh Carolan, the miller, who was away at the Ballyrea market. In his unregretted absence his hospitable daughter Betty had entertained me. It was a morning for both of us of splendour of spirits; I left with the elation which one might carry from the house of a poet.

In the afternoon I repaired to Deerpark, offering my respects to the bridegroom and the bride. There was quite a flutter in the house. Servants were swift on the foot, the butler was authoritative as he superintended the lugging of trunks, dressing cases, hat boxes, rugs and umbrellas across the hall. The air was heavy with the scent of cooking.

"They are roasting an ox for Kish," I thought as I mounted the stairs.

"What? Is that Paul Jennings?" a familiar voice called down as I passed on my way to the library.

I was embarrassed but acknowledged my identity. "Good! I'll be with you in a whiff."

I had a vision of Kish Massy in his shirt sleeves, his bare arms and hairy chest steaming and soapy, hanging over the banister while he buttoned on a collar. He was after a wash-up. It was a picture straight from a tenement house. "A very discreet bridegroom indeed," I thought as I entered the library. A little later he burst in, pulsing, animated, beaming, joyous, sixteen stone. He ran to me with an "Ah-h-h," took my hand in both of his, wrung it, slapped me on the back, and looked into my face with eyes humid with emotion.

"I'm delighted, delighted," he cried, and I had the feeling that I was the bridegroom and that Kish Massy was congratulating me on my immensely good fortune. He was so demonstrative that I had nothing whatever to say.

"Draw down to the fire, Paul," he said hospitably. We sat down by the fire. "May is not feeling very well," he added cheerfully as he leaned out to poke up the fire. "She's fatigued after that long journey from Dublin."

May? It did not break upon me for quite twenty seconds that he referred to Mrs. Massy, his wife. Somehow the springtime pet name, never called her by mortal before, sounded incongruous and in all the circumstances ridiculous.

"Well," he said happily, "it's good to have it all over and to be at home."

The boisterous note of his first greeting quickly died

out. He sank back in his armchair. He struck out the two great limbs; his arms drooped inertly over the sides of the chair; he gave himself up to a great content. His eyes ranged about the room, following the ornaments on the chimney-piece, the great cheval mirror overhead, the pictures and old prints on the wall, the great shelves of books up to the cornice of the ceiling, then down to the solid, comfortable furniture, the grey pile of the carpet on the floor. "All this is mine—*mine*," he seemed to say. The oblong eyes revolved in their sockets; I could see the whites of those eyes terrible and nigger-like for a moment; they might, again, be the eye-movement seen in a horse-box in a dim stable. The stout limbs spread out from each other slowly, the chest expanded, the stomach heaved, the lips made some movements, and in the most fascinating way the feet began to rise from the ground, ascending with a sloth-like movement, uncanny as the suspension in mid-air of a body by some stage illusionist. The feet reached the marble chimney-piece and there they rested, still well apart. I felt inclined to applaud when the movement had been completed, but he was quite oblivious of my existence. The long head nestled into the soft back of the chair and his nose heaved up, rugged and mottled, the nose of a campaigner, the breaths coming from the wide flaps of the nostrils in audible puffs of satisfaction. Some obscure sound rumbled somewhere in the very depths of his being, it twitched across the stomach, caused the chest to heave, distinctly moved the apple in the loose flesh of the throat, the red fingers began to weave invisible threads about the upturned palms, rapid muscles worked over the eyebrows, the mouth quivered and from between the great wet lips there emerged a sigh or a grunt, a whisper or a soft whistle, a murmur or a squeak, or something of them all—but at all events an individual orchestral note that was purely of his own creation and his own soul.

"This," I told myself, "is an Ode to Deerpark by Kish Massy." I waited patiently while the ecstasy of his inspiration lasted. When his eyes became conscious of mundane things they rested on the bronze bell-knob beside the fire-place. It suggested to him a use. He stooped forward and pulled it. Presently the butler appeared.

"Broderick."

"Yessir."

"Cigars."

"Yessir."

"And I say, Broderick."

"Yessir."

"Decanter of brandy and a siphon of soda."

"Yessir."

II

The cigars were good, the brandy was good. Kish Massy rolled about in his chair as we enjoyed them and, growing sentimental, he talked of the estate. He began to patronize me a little. It was the great squire addressing his faithful steward. I did not like this, yawned, rose, and went to my desk, saying I had come for some letters. Kish put his back to the fire, elevating himself now on his heels, now on his toes, his words full of windy importance. I was so absent-minded that I failed to answer questions; when I did make an answer it was irrelevant. He strolled over to the desk and stood behind me. I bustled through my work. He was about to take a thoughtful stride away, his movement that of one with tremendous responsibilities, when he suddenly wheeled about, his nostrils sniffing.

"What's that?" he asked. The demand was so sharp that I looked up. His expression had undergone a complete change. His features expressed suspicion, alarm. All the pretence had vanished. It was the aboriginal Kish Massy I beheld, the twitching over the brows more rapid than I had ever seen them before. He sniffed again, his flat nostrils giving the impression of an animal sensitiveness to smell. It occurred to me that there was a most peculiar faint odor around the desk, an elusive perfume which I had noticed the previous day when opening the post-bag. On investigation I had discovered that it exhaled from a pale blue envelope addressed to Kish Massy and bearing the New York postmark. I had put it into a wicker letter basket with other letters addressed personally to Mrs. Massy. The basket now lay on the desk.

"Do you find that curious perfume, too?" I asked.

"Yes, yes," he replied sharply, his manner quite perturbed.

"I think it emanates from a letter addressed to yourself," I said. "I put it in the basket with Mrs. Massy's letters."

"Where is it?" He was quite nervous, pounced upon the basket, picked out the pale-blue envelope with an eagerness and a directness which I thought curious, then, as if feeling that he was giving something away, slipped it in a casual way into his pocket. He walked back to the fire-place to conceal his excitement.

"Who takes the letters from the box in the hall downstairs?" he asked after a time.

"As a rule Mrs. Briscoe, the housekeeper."

"She keeps the key?"

"Invariably, yes. A second post is brought by our own messenger in a post-bag and this I usually open myself. Any letters addressed to me are left in the library; Mrs. Massy's letters are taken to her apartments."

"I see." He stood motionless at the fire-place, but the fingers twitched behind the back, a jewel flashing on one of the rings. There was a knock at the door and Mrs. Briscoe entered.

"The mistress is anxious to know if any letters await her, Mr. Jennings," she said.

"Yes, quite an accumulation," I said, handing her the basket of letters, and she moved to the door.

"I say, Mrs. Briscoe," Kish Massy called out to her. There was a little pause between the "Mrs." and the "Briscoe."

Mrs. Briscoe stood at once. "Yes, sir," she said. There was a pause between the "yes" and the "sir." I could feel something electrical in the air. Mrs. Briscoe was on her dignity with her new master.

"That key of the letter-box downstairs," said Kish Massy carelessly—"I should like to have it."

"Certainly, sir." She detached a small key from her ring and handed it him.

"I will relieve you of the responsibility of clearing the box in the morning," he said. "It's only waste of your valuable time." The note of sarcasm was slight.

Briscoe inclined her head in acknowledgment, and tilting her chin made a magnificent exit. There was scorn, contempt, in the straight stiff long line of the back as she took the door.

"That basket of letters Briscoe has taken is going to Mrs. Massy?" he asked.

"Yes, that is the usual custom," I replied.

He was evidently thinking that he had intercepted the scented communication only in the nick of time.

"Great Christ!" The words broke from him in a half-whisper and quite involuntarily. He sat down by the fire as if he had grown suddenly weak. I looked at him, puzzled, for some time, then closed my desk. The action seemed to rouse him. He looked up at me, his eyes smouldering. "I did not wish May to see that letter," he said, "because it concerns certain speculations in real estate business in which I am interested in New York.

When I was there some years ago I dabbled a little in business."

"Has it worked out all right?" I asked.

"No—not very well," he said.

I could see that he had been disturbed a great deal by what had occurred. As there was, however, nothing more to be said I prepared to leave the room.

"Good evening, Kish," I said.

"Good evening, Paul. And I say—don't mention about that letter to anybody. It's of no consequence, of course, but I'd rather you wouldn't."

"No, certainly not."

Crossing the room the insidious perfume again assailed my nostrils for a moment. As I closed the door behind me I heard the quick rent of paper, as if an envelope was being eagerly torn open.

III

"By the way," said Kish Massy, "May and myself go to Colonel Burke's place this evening. We dine there."

We were in the library again, some weeks later. Kish Massy had been walking about, uneasy, trying to hide a certain excitement; I myself was at the desk.

"The Colonel is a most agreeable soul," I said, "and his dinners are always like him."

"Very big house party there at present," said Kish Massy. "Lord Elmtree is among the guests. A gay dog is Elmtree."

He was so elated at the prospect of this dinner and this meeting with a Peer of the Realm that he could no longer contain himself. His old boyish instinct for climbing up something took possession of him. His eyes caught the step-ladder by the book-shelves and up this he ran, nimble as a squirrel, squatting down on the topmost rung. The step-ladder quivered under him. He looked a little grotesque in his great bulk on the perch. I could not help smiling. I was reminded of what an old peasant woman once said of him: "Kish is like the roosting hen, hot with high notions."

"Elmtree will be there all right," he said.

"I thought he was dead," I said, my tone as inconsequent as I could make it.

"Lord Elmtree? God God, no! What put that into your head?"

"I had some idea that his tenants had drowned him in a bog hole or that something or other of that sort had happened."

"Nonsense," said Kish Massy. "I'll be breaking bread with him this very night. He's as lively as a salmon at the wier."

"I don't like Lord Elmtree," I declared with decision.

Kish Massy was so annoyed that he came down the step-ladder.

"He's a Peer of the Realm," he said. "He votes in the House of Lords and we ought not to forget that."

"I don't see that it is of any particular importance that

he votes in the House of Lords," I said, very glad that I had annoyed him.

"Are you aware of the extent of Lord Elmtree's estates?" he demanded, looking at me with gravity.

"Two hundred thousand acres of the worst managed estates in Europe," I replied. "A Paradise for pheasants, a Purgatory for peasants."

"Paul," said Kish Massy, "I hope you're not going to turn into a politician or a Nationalist or a moonlighter or something of that sort."

I was fixing a new nib on a pen-handle.

"The only thing you have to fear of me, Kish," I said, "is that the devil may some day tempt me to dip this nib in the ink-bottle."

Kish Massy looked at me puzzled, his annoyance growing. In the end he strode out of the room, banging the door behind him.

But some hours later he was back again, unable to resist the temptation of showing himself off in his fine feathers. He was in a heavy ulster with deep fur collar and cuffs. It was thrown open, displaying the magnificent girth in evening suit. I caught the sparkle of diamonds in the studs of the shirt front. He wore an orchid in the button-hole. He had oiled his hair. He was smoking a cigar.

"Have you got the correct time, Jennings?"

He studied a watch for the purpose of dangling a

gold, jewel-studded trinket at the end of the fob. "I've had an argument with May about that hall clock."

We adjusted our time. "It won't do to keep the Colonel waiting; the party's been out for a shoot to-day and will come back ravenous as a wolf." He seemed to be practising the conversation appropriate to the occasion.

"By the way," I said, "there are a few cheques here I am anxious to have sent away to-night."

"Then why the devil don't you sent them?"

He made the demand over the glowing end of his cigar.

"They are not signed."

"Oh!" He fingered some of the ash of the cigar and walked up and down.

"Won't you sign them while you await Mrs. Massy?" I suggested. "It won't take a moment."

"I'm not doing any business this afternoon," he said. "Everything in its proper place and time. You understand me, Jennings?"

There was a knock at the door and Mrs. Massy opened it.

"I'm ready," she said. Then added, smiling, "Good afternoon, Mr. Jennings." I made a little obeisance.

Mrs. Massy wore her rich brown furs over her evening attire. There was that look of delicacy about her which she seemed unable to shake off. It was true that she had lost some of the extreme nervousness which had attacked her in the winter months, before the marriage. For the brief periods I had seen her since the return the impression remained with me of a woman who had developed a hardness, almost peevishness.

"I am afraid I am responsible for delaying Mr. Massy," I said.

She moved some way into the room, drawing on her gloves. The fair lashes lay pallid on the dark skin under the downcast eyes.

"What is it all about?" she asked.

"I kept him to sign a few cheques," I said.

The fair lashes at once shot up and she looked directly at me. Kish Massy made some movement, then walked to the window. I was conscious that something had disturbed, even annoyed, both of them.

"Cheques for what, Mr. Jennings?" she asked quietly, coming slowly down the room.

"For accounts now due some time," I said, moving to the desk.

"On the farm?" she asked.

"Some on the farm, others on the quarries," I replied.

"The usual sort of accounts?" she asked.

"Yes, certainly. Here they are." I lifted up a number of bills pinned together.

"Leave all this until to-morrow," Kish Massy said, turning from the window.

"It won't take very long," Mrs. Massy replied deliberately.

"Barlow is waiting."

"So is Mr. Jennings."

The words passed with a little sharpness. Kish Massy made a characteristic short jab with the left arm. Mrs. Massy drew off her gloves, moving over to the desk.

"I sign all cheques as heretofore," she said, her voice very distinct. The silence which followed was almost painful. I merely bowed in acknowledgment of the proclamation, and while I did so I could see the twitches working over Kish Massy's brows. "Forked lightning," I said to myself.

Mrs. Massy settled herself at the desk, selected a pen, and signed the cheques which I had filled in. Kish kept his great back steadily to the room while the pen scratched over the paper, dramatic in the silence of the place. The hand appending the magic signature which gave the blue sips of paper value was deliberate.

"Would you mind blotting them, Mr. Jennings?" she asked when she had finished. I bent forward to comply. She rose from the desk.

"Well, I suppose we may go now?" Kish Massy asked, turning from the window. "The Colonel is swearing by this time."

His wife made no reply. She was drawing on the gloves again. "You understand about the cheques then?" she said to me in the same quiet but decided tone."

"Yes, certainly." I felt a little embarrassed.

"And all lodgments are to be made in the banks as formerly," Mrs. Massy continued. "The farm and household moneys are to be lodged to the No. 1 account, and the quarries and estate to No. 2."

I bowed again. Kish Massy moved away from the window, went to the book-shelves and stared blankly up at them. It was a painful moment. It was as if Mrs. Massy had said, "It is I, not my husband, who has got to sign the cheques, and it is to my credit all income must be lodged in the banks. I control the treasury of this household and property and I mean to continue in control of it. There has been no transfer of power over the purse as a result of the marriage. The banks will recognize my signature only. I am perfectly well protected."

"Now we may go," she said, moving to the door. Kish walked sullenly after her. The door stood open and they passed out, the woman tall, the carriage one of unmistakable distinction, the bulky figure of the man only vulgarized by his new equipment. I could not resist the thought that a more ill-matched pair were not likely to be on view at Colonel Burke's dinner party. I could hear them descending the stairs, and they passed through the house without conversation. Presently the carriage rumbled down the drive. I stood over the desk for a little while, indulged in a long soft whistle. I walked up and down the room, and at length said, "So she's got Kish chained up in his kennel."

CHAPTER TWO

I

THE tenants had been coming and going in little driblets all day, handing over the half year's
rent, or whatever rent they owed. To me, as I sat
behind a long mahogany table, they addressed their
opinions and their complaints. They passed through
the place with a low shuffle, to the accompaniment of incessant talk, leaving behind the memory of a procession
of tough spirits, of hard grey faces, of wiry hands finger-
ing money, of the production of long, faded calico satch-
els from some remote pocket in a garment hidden behind many waistcoats, of the reluctant tendering of
money wrapped in dirty wads of paper, of a long series
of arguments about crops and climate and diseases of
animals and everything on earth that was futile and eva-
sive. Women delved skinny yellow arms in half-exposed

bosoms, hunting for purses which appeared lost in unknown regions, and having miraculously discovered them handed over the rent with prayers for the souls of their dead. Now and then some angry man pushed into the room as if he had come to take my life; others slunk around the door, timorous and shaken, as if they expected me to whip them upon the back. A young woman or two came direct and close to me, their eyes full of challenge, adventure; others backed at the wall, making curtsies as if they found themselves in the sanctuary of some dread deity. A violent old man, who remembered the famine, with a mouth like a vacant potato-pit, attacked me with blazing eyes, shouting and cursing, disputing records of rents which had been disposed of twenty years ago, striking the table with quivering fists, driving home arguments which had been nursed by the fireside a dozen years, astonishing me by a quotation from Virgil, learned from a hedge schoolmaster; others entered without a word, did their business without a single comment, their thin lips drawn across their teeth tight as the skin of a drum, men from some famished hillside; a widow with a rich colour in her cheeks wept for fifteen minutes for a husband who had died of consumption sixteen years ago; now and then a preoccupied well-to-do person drove up on his side-car, came in with an air of business, wrote out a cheque, leaning hard on the pen and breathing heavily, talked of the County Council for a minute, and went out

with the whip in his hand; a woman who held her head
erect, the skin bright on her high cheek bones, her eyes
calculating and clear, said with an American accent, "I
guess I pay you good money for the pinch of dust between the rocks on Knockbwee"; a hand emaciated with
toil in the little hungry fields would reach for the rent re-
ceipt as if he were about to receive the Ark of the Cove-
nant; other hands shrank from the papers as if they were
death warrants.

And while this ceremony proceeded I wondered how
it was that Kish Massy did not come. The collection
took place in my mother's house, as had been the custom
on the Deerpark estate for generations. The Heffernans
never met the tenants on such an occasion; but Kish
Massy was not a Heffernan. It was such a proceeding as
would give him an opportunity of playing the rôle of
agrarian demi-god. I could imagine him behind the long
mahogany table: his hands spread out, his eyes com-
manding, his voice full of a terrible authority, his mind
eager for battle. The joy of lording it over these people
would be ecstasy to him. He would enter into all their
arguments, understand all the by-play of their obscure
but subtle minds, know how to play upon their emotions. He would shout back at the angry old man, throw
him curse for curse; he would weep with the widow the
fountain of whose woe was potent after sixteen years of
desolation; he would meet the curtsy of the abashed
with a faint acknowledgment; he would kindle to the

spark of the eye which held adventure. His great skin would swell until it creaked to feel the homage paid him by the hill-folk. . . . And yet he did not come! The last frieze coat, the last white bauneen, the last shawl and the last cloak, had made its individual entrance and exit and still the new landlord resisted the temptation to preside over this wayside levee. All that remained of the ceremony was the scent of the turf smoke from the clothes of the tenants, the little heaps of yellow clay from their boots and their bare feet on the floor, and on the table the agreeable piles of the gold, the silver, the notes, the copper, their dues on the estate, their reluctant offering on the feudal altar, the tribute that was the testimony of their bondage.

Doyle, the clerk, who sat at another table, checked and totted his accounts, made his reckoning, and for half an hour worried over a crown which could not be accounted for. Eventually he gave it up. "I'm afraid it must go into the Micawber account," he said.

I nodded and yawned. "Thank God another gale day has been concluded," I said. "They have all been here— all except the stragglers, the backsliders, the perverse ones whom as usual we shall have to legally beat out of their coverts."

II

Doyle went away, and I made a final count and reckoning of the rents. I was putting the coins into the cashbox in their respective little brown paper cartridges, when suddenly I had the feeling that I was under observation. I heard no sound whatever, but I had strongly that instinctive feeling that somebody was close to me and interested in my occupation. The window looking directly into the public road was right behind my back and I felt that the presence lay in that direction. I swerved sharply about, and had an idea that something moved away from the window; it was so swift a movement, however, that I was not quite clear. I waited, and a few seconds later Kish Massy came into the room. His eyes were directly on the cash-box. And there was an ill-concealed hunger in the gaze. "Ah, Paul," he said, "so your gale day is over."

"Just concluded," I said. I proceeded to methodically transfer the cartridges to the cash-box. He walked uneasily up and down the room between the mahogany tables. "It was a great sight to see the people gathering about the place—from the bogs, the mountains, across the hills."

"All bearing their honey to the one hive," I said, putting in the last packet.

Kish Massy laughed, but there was no mirth in the laugh. I closed the lid of the cash-box with a bang.

"What sort of a time had you at Colonel Burke's last night?" I asked.

He sat down and looked at me with his intelligent eyes, some eager calculation in them.

"A splendid time," he said. "Lord Elmtree and myself cottoned to each other wonderfully."

"Common interests, I suppose?"

"I expect so. He's coming over to Deerpark this evening to look at some blood stock of mine in the stables."

"So you combined business with pleasure last night."

His eyes were on the cash-box. I turned the key in the lock, and as I did so I could see a movement of his great shoulders. He gave me the impression of a man sick for money and baulked about it.

I was uneasy at the look in his eyes, wondering vaguely how it would fare with his wife if she continued to stand in his way in the complete overlordship of Deerpark. He rose and resumed his nervous walk up and down the room.

"How do you manage about this rent money?" he asked at length.

"Lock it up in the safe for the present," I replied.

"Here?"

"Yes."

"When is it taken to Deerpark?"

"It is never taken to Deerpark."

He stopped dead, his great feet crunching on the bare boards. His eyes had a dull ugliness as he swerved round to me.

"What do you mean by that?" he demanded.

"The money is taken direct from here to the bank in Ballyrea and there lodged to the credit of the estate."

"I see." He stood thinking for a moment, his face full of disappointment. I lifted the cash-box, bore it to the safe and locked it away. When I had finished he was sitting down, his gaze wandering thoughtfully out of the window. I wondered if his obvious hunger for money had anything to do with the arrival of the scented envelope from New York.

"I'm not at all in good humour," he said suddenly.

"No?" I asked, sitting down. It was at least a token of companionship with him in this his black hour.

"No," he said. "Something has happened." I waited and he added, "At Deerpark."

"Oh!"

"You know as well as I do, Paul, that women don't understand some things."

"Men, for instance?" I suggested.

"Exactly," he agreed. "And their requirements."

"All history rather contradicts you, does it not?" I said. "Think of the Garden of Eden, Kish, and all the little incidents that have parodied it ever since."

He made an impatient jab of the left arm. He was in no mood for trivial conversation of the kind. The Garden of Eden was too remote; the Chase in Deerpark was for him a more intimate business.

"We've had a tiff," he said sullenly.

"We?" I pretended a vacuous mind.

"May and myself."

I raised my eyebrows, trying to convey the unspoken word, "Impossible!"

"Oh, yes, we had. I got into a temper and just took a walk down here to cool myself off."

"An excellent exercise on all such occasions," I said.

"For one thing, we differed about Lord Elmtree," said Kish Massy. "As I say, I expect him to look at some of the young ones in the stables and there may be a very decent purchase. Naturally, I wanted to have a nice little dinner party in his honour. But May objected. Says she does not like Lord Elmtree or care to have him in the house. She could give no reasons, just like a woman! Women are like dogs, Paul—they just smell a man and come to some conclusion about him in the one whiff. After that they put their teeth in the calves of his legs or else follow him about for ever, wagging their tails and taking even kicks as compliments." He snorted contemptuously.

"Marriage has already made a cynic of him," I thought. Aloud I said, "Many women have very logical minds and powerful reasoning capacity." He made his pugilistic jab of the left arm and said, "I saw a woman with a sieve in her hands once, outside a barn door, winnowing oats, the wind blowing the red petticoat about her skinny yellow legs and I thought she looked nearly as right as a woman with a baby in her arms. She looked right because she was at the work of a slave."

"He must feel hurt to the soul about that banking account," I thought.

"In any case," he said, rising, "I intend to have Lord Elmtree to dinner. I would like you to join us."

"I'm afraid I can't bask under the shade of the Elmtree this evening," I said at once.

He turned a scowling face upon me. If he had been paying me to eat dinners at Deerpark he could not look much blacker.

"I'm off to a concert rehearsal in Kilbeg this evening," I said, "and nothing would induce me to miss it."

He walked up and down, his great limbs giving the illusion that he was trampling on the forms of fallen victims, a very Juggernaut in desire.

"I think," he said at last, "that we had better make a new arrangement about that rent money. Better have it sent over to Deerpark this evening and then we can see about its transfer to Ballyrea."

I felt the skin tighten over my mouth. He had struck me in the right spot. It was about time that we understood each other. I rose at once, determined to put things to the test. "I think," I said, "that the old arrangement must stand."

He stood at once; his broad back was level against me for a moment. He swung around slowly and looked at me. I walked a pace or two to the window, where he could have a good look at me in the full light. I awaited with interest to hear him proclaim himself master of Deerpark and give me definite orders as to how I was to dispose of the money. He hesitated too long. The "yellow streak" asserted itself somewhere in him.

"It would be a more reasonable arrangement than the present one," he said weakly.

"Up to this," I said deliberately, "I have been agent of

the estate and I don't purpose making any changes in the system of business followed—at least not without definite instructions from Mrs. Heffernan Massy whom I serve."

I could see the twitches coming and going over the eyebrows like angry thoughts. He hesitated, controlled himself, shrugged his shoulders, and walked up and down the room. In doing so he kicked the safe, stumbling a little as he did so. It was a solid article. He consulted his watch. "Elmtree may drive up to Deerpark at any moment," he said. "I must be off. Good evening, Jennings."

"Good evening."

CHAPTER THREE

I

NEXT day I accompanied my mother and Betty Carolan to the annual Hunt Club afternoon concert in Ballyrea. In the trap I fetched with me, at the same time, the cash-box containing the rents and duly lodged them in the local bank to the credit of the estate. I did so with the feeling that I was adding to the little annoyances of Kish Massy's new life.

When we arrived at the Town Hall an irregular queue of vehicles was drawn up about the door. As we ascended the staircase we got mixed up with Colonel Burke's house party, just arrived. The Colonel himself, pleasant and garrulous, limped up with Lady Newell, their aristocratic haunches working in harmonious distress as they mastered one step after the other. My eyes wandered over the party for Mrs. Heffernan Massy, who had, I knew, arranged to accompany Lady Newell, but she was nowhere in sight. The hall was almost crowded when we entered. There appeared a good deal of confusion; we wandered up and down looking for our seats.

"They go on for ever, these Irish concerts," said Lady Newell. "I have seen the programme—it is as long as a parish priest's funeral."

"I could forgive it all," drawled Colonel Burke, "if a young man from London, who has followed a niece of mine to Connacht, had not volunteered to tweat us to a mandolin solo."

"A mandolin solo, Algernon!" exclaimed Lady Newell. "Why did they not persuade him to tickle us with a quill behind the ears instead? Now I know I shall hate everybody who comes out from behind the palms. They shall all sing to me in vain."

"Not all of them, Lady Newell," I said. "You must make an exception. Miss Betty Carolan is on the programme."

"Ah, so that is why you are here, Monsieur Paul? You have come to hear the little song-bird. Betty Carolan, the old miller's daughter! How romantic the name! Is there a rustic bridge anywhere around the mill stream? And old ivy-clad walls? And does Betty not confess to freckles and sing at the dawn like a milkmaid? *Mon Dieu!* she is an old ballade!"

"Come this way, Colonel," said a young man in scarlet. "We must squeeze you in somewhere." As we made another journey up the hall Lady Newell turned to me.

"Poor Marie!" she said. "I thought she would be here with us. Now—" She shrugged her shoulders.

"Why has she not come?"

"Surely you have heard?"

"Heard what?"

"Of her accident."

"No. Has she had an accident?"

"But yes. And the doctor. I could not see her this morning at Deerpark. And Briscoe was so mysterious. What it was that had happened to her I could not discover."

Before I could hear anything more we got separated; several vacant seats were suddenly discovered between the embankments of millinery and we were bundled into them. Presently the concert began. It was conventional and proper. As it went on I wondered what accident could have befallen Mrs. Heffernan Massy. Lady Newell had hinted at some mystery. What was wrong?

Not until Betty came out to sing did I feel any interest in the proceedings. Then I woke up to an extraordinary anxiety. I was afraid Betty might break down! She looked so pretty but so girlishly timid as she stood before the crowd of sceptics! She turned the music over in her hands somewhat nervously while her accompanist played the opening bars of the song. Once she lowered her head for an instant, the enormous hat she wore hiding her face from view. "She's as nervous as a kitten," I told myself. But she looked out over the uneasy audience when the time came, a faint smile changed her expression, and at once her voice rang out nervously fresh and compelling in that piece of splendid musical rhetoric, the Jewel Song from *Faust*. There was a hesitancy still about her delivery, but she grew confident, and presently sang with a certain abandon, giving herself up to the gorgeous phrasing of the Song. A silence settled down over the restless audience, that silence which alone can be commanded by one who is in all essentials an artist. The young voice rose in the half-rapture, half-sigh, of the ecstatic Marguerite, exquisite in its delicate flexibility. "Betty is a wonder," I told myself. "She's doing splendidly. And this is her first concert, too! She looks sweet as a rosebud opening to a morning sun-ray." For a moment her eyes caught mine, and I noted the rise of the young bosom, the sudden white gleam of her neck, the grand confident pose of the dark head, the rich soprano ringing out with something more of passion than she had yet ventured. Some glint distracted my attention and I was conscious that at the end of a bench a man with a monocle was staring at me and reading my thoughts quite easily. He was a bald-headed person, gaunt and sceptical, a frozen smile on his glacial face. He seemed to be chuckling to himself and saying of me, "What a silly young fool to be taken in by these flowery notes! Of course she's singing middling well. Any sort of young girl with a voice and training could not help singing that music middling well. I have heard battalions of young girls like her. She's all right for a little concert. If she was put up on a stage proper, in a theatre, and had an orchestra before her, what a tin whistle we should have! Don't be a silly about her, young hopeful!"

I glared at this one-eyed critic, then looked down at my programme, for I feared my face was giving too much away. Betty won her encore and responded with a little light whiff of an Italian aria. She was wreathed in smiles as she was helped down from the platform.

II

There was a long interval, people moved about, tea-cups rattled, a racket of conversation broke over the hall. Lady Newell discovered us with her lorgnette and made her ground good to us, dragging Colonel Burke with her.

"Agwatha, you are westless as a gwasshoppeh," he complained. "You do run me about."

"What would you have, Algernon? You do not want to settle down like a fat toad, growing drowsy until it is time to go back to dinner."

"I like a leisurely life, Agwatha. You know vewy well it is the only civilized life; nothing vewy gweat eveh came out of any otheh kind of life. All awt, all litewa-tuwe, comes out of a fine wepose. . . . What a noise they make about the stage!" He settled down beside the mater.

"Ah, Monsieur Paul," Lady Newell said to me, "here

you sit so quiet beside the good mater. One might think you such a young Adonis. And what a charming voice has Mademoiselle Betty! Like herself, little and round and silky and of the passionate darkness. But what Italian!"

"You did not like her Italian accent, then?" I asked, amused.

"Accent, but no! I almost wept."

There was a little diversion at the door of a side entrance and Lord Elmtree stood there, having just arrived, a tall narrow figure, his face fair, irregular, the eyes small, blinking curiously, his expression a mixture of cynical humour and cunning.

"Ah," said Lady Newell, "there is the Elmtree which grew up a beanstalk."

Lord Elmtree stepped in to speak with some friends, and the place he vacated at the door was taken by Kish Massy.

"And there is the great Kish, heavy and filled," said Lady Newell. Then in an undertone, she sighed, "Ah, poor Marie!"

"Won't you tell me what has happened at Deerpark?" I asked.

"But I have nothing to tell. There has been an accident. She is in her bed. The doctor is with her. Nobody may see her. Briscoe is mysterious. That is all one can find out."

"The accident must be a trifling one, otherwise her husband would not come to this concert," I reasoned.

"I would never diagnose the case of the wife by the capacity of the husband to enjoy himself," said Lady Newell, shrugging her shoulders. She turned to my mother with one of her swift movements and they were soon engrossed in a lively conversation about the millinery which surrounded them.

My gaze wandered with a morbid fascination back to Kish Massy. He had the appearance of a man who had made a night of it; the complexion was mottled, the eye-rims seared. He did not look at home, and Lord Elmtree was steadily edging away from him. If Kish Massy was looking for snubs he had found the right company for them. The shouted words of greeting, the hearty good humour, the nods and smiles, the hand-shakes, the little salutes which were flying about, all concealed snubs and slights and insolent cuts. Every smile meant that somebody was deliberately overlooked, every shout conveyed that somebody else was ignored. The social life of the locality was anæmic, morally run down. The aristocracy was bastard. The professional class was inconsequent and trying to shake off the shop-keeping element. The shop-keepers were endeavouring to rise above their ancestral peasantry. The clergymen hung like afterthoughts on the flanks of all classes. A little group of peasants near the door stood gloomily austere and apart. I watched Kish Massy as he moved through a passage of snubs in Lord Elmtree's wake. I wondered again what had happened to his wife, and if the little incidents of the past few weeks had anything to do with her unexpected indisposition. Had the dog which she had chained up broken loose and done some harm? The feeling that something of the kind had happened, or was bound sooner or later to happen, oppressed me. I watched the progress of that bulky sinister figure through the animated crowd and it seemed to me that Lord Elmtree drew him on like a magnet.

The concert was resumed and seemed appallingly flat. Dulness succeeded dulness. Lady Newell sighed and chafed. Colonel Burke went to sleep in his seat. "Sometimes one envies Algernon his capacity for an animal happiness," Lady Newell said, gazing at him, his enormous underlip falling over his chin.

But right at the end of the programme our hearts went up with a bound. One of those things happened which are only possible at such an entertainment, which could only ripen in such an atmosphere. A little farce was staged, utterly stupid, but it had been put on to give Mrs. Hugh Quirke, a notoriously dashing horse-woman, an opportunity of introducing to our notice a sensation then new to the Western world—a skirt dance. Somebody in the farce said, "And now comes forth the fairy dancer!" Without another word of warning Mrs. Hugh sprang from the wings, prancing about the stage, throwing her legs in mid-air, shocking and horrifying, stimulating and delighting, a hard-looking thin woman, her eyes half closed, her breath coming short from her nostrils, her figure one of aggressive angles, her arms muscular, her elbows raw, her hands shaking the folds of her skirt about, displaying ankles that had no merit, shanks that were too wiry, limbs that were mercifully smothered in swathes of white frills under the semi-chorus-girl skirt.

"My God, it's Mrs. Hugh!" said Colonel Burke, waking up. "And to think Hugh is dead these twenty yeaws!"

III

On and on danced Mrs. Hugh Quirke, tossing herself about the confined stage, striking attitudes, ducking and diving, backing and revolving, making sudden plunges, her legs striking out wildly for such clear patches of the stage as afforded a foothold, some vague notion at the back of her enterprising head that she expressed a poetic motion, attained some obtuse artistic effect; but she was too tough, too flat at the hips, too meagre of chest, too eloquent of an unemotional age, too obviously a campaigner who had had her day, to convey anything except a grotesque parody of a stage emotion. Her exploit was received with an uproar: shouting, cheering, hand-clapping, whistling, laughter, and cries of amazement. I noticed that the bench on which we sat was quivering most curiously; I discovered that both my mother and Lady Newell were leaning back, both their bodies set into a rhythmical motion by uncontrollable mirth, both unable to speak, in the throes of a mer-

ciless duet of silent laughter at the expense of Mrs.
Hugh Quirke—for nobody is more intolerant of the elderly than the elderly—while Colonel Burke at the end
of the quivering bench muttered to himself, saying,
"God wrest your soul, Hugh Quirke, to-day!" But the
young cubs of the Hunt Club would toast Mrs Hugh
Quirke's health that night, assure each other she was a
ripping woman, a pioneer, hip, hip hurrah! . . . Some
seasons later, while following the Blazers, she came a
fearful cropper at an ugly stone wall. I was one of a
crowd of laggards who came upon her later. She was
lying under a clump of furze, her tongue lolling out of
her mouth, her eyes appalling, her neck cracked, a wren
on a branch of the furze above her body perking and
shrilling his merry little roundelay.

I hurried Betty down the stairs after the concert, finding it difficult to get her away from the people who
would flatter her—and many who would flirt with
her—as a result of her success. We overtook my mother,
Lady Newell and Colonel Burke.

"But no," Lady Newell was saying as we caught them
up. "If she came to us *à la nature* it would be so much to
the good. But the baby linen, the frills, the old joints
creaking behind! One has to go to Balzac for a woman
like Mrs. Hugh."

"Pooh Hugh, he died young," said Colonel Burke.

As we made our way through a crowd of people to
our trap Lord Elmtree and Kish Massy came from the

Town Hall together. Kish looked quite cheerful, almost merry, and he made an effort to reach us. I smiled, too, for I felt that he would tell me about the accident to Mrs. Heffernan Massy, and that the news would be reassuring. At last he reached us, ignored my mother and Betty, stooping over a little confidentially to me. As he did so I got a disagreeable whiff of raw onions and stale whiskey.

"Are you coming up to the hotel, Paul?" he asked and winked meaningly.

"I'm afraid not."

"Come along, man. Elmtree and myself are going up there."

"So sorry."

He stooped more to my ear, all confidence. At last I was to hear the news I awaited!

"Sold him two of the youngsters, all right," he whispered.

"Good price I hope?"

"Can't complain about the price. Are you coming to the hotel? We might as well make a night of it. Elmtree is in tremendous form, out to punish all the champagne in the place."

"I've got to drive my people home."

A little crowd of people cut us off from each other and we started for home without further delay.

As we drove along I felt puzzled, annoyed, at the news from Deerpark. What on earth had happened?

Could Lady Newell be mistaken? And if not, how was it Kish Massy did not consider the accident to his wife worth mentioning? Could it be possible the sale of the blood stock and his cultivation of the Earl of Elmtree were more important to him than the health of his wife? "And they were only married in March!" I thought ironically.

"Cheer up, Paul!" the mater said to me. "One would fancy that Betty broke down at the concert, you look so glum."

I looked across at Betty, her neat little figure, her young face eager and thoughtful, her eyes bright with triumph, her brows level and silky, and everything about her seemed inexpressibly precious. She was rolling her music in its black rainproof wrapper about in her hands, her movement conveying some of the excitement which inwardly consumed her. She had not been conscious of my gloomy mood; she was still tingling with the sensation which applause had brought to her. She smiled across at me. Even the powder which she had put on her young cheeks seemed a convention that might be forgiven!

"Instead of which I won my encore," she said, showing her white teeth.

CHAPTER FOUR

I

DOCTOR O'SULLIVAN was coming down the stairs at Deerpark when I called there next day. We shook hands. I inquired for Mrs. Heffernan Massy.

"There has been an accident?" I suggested.

"Well," the doctor said, his manner at once pompously professional, "not so much an accident, perhaps, as shock, very considerable shock, one might almost say a nervous breakdown."

"I understood there was an accident," I persisted.

The doctor beamed upon me, tolerant of my curiosity. "And so there has," he said. "I have mentioned that there has been a little accident. She tells how she tripped over an unseen cushion on the floor, stumbled, lost her balance, fell, her face striking against the leg of a table, causing a rather severe and painful braisure on the left cheek."

"That was unfortunate," I said.

"Most unfortunate," Dr. O'Sullivan agreed cheerfully. "She's rather poorly to-day and must rest. Good morning, Mr. Jennings."

I found but a few letters awaiting me in the library. I dallied over them for some time. People passed up and down the corridor outside; there was that stealthy, restless movement in the house which denotes illness. A feeling of unhappiness oppressed me. Two maids spoke in undertones outside the door. "She fell and so did I," one of them said in a note of sarcasm. I crossed the room, opened the door, startling the maids, and requested that they might inform Mrs. Briscoe that I was anxious to see her. They fled to obey, and after some time Briscoe, followed by the inevitable Shah, made her appearance. She looked fatigued; her manner was constrained, she sat down with an air of weariness. The Shah rolled himself into a ball before the fire.

"I don't like how things are going in this house, Mr. Jennings."

"What has happened?" I asked.

"What happened exactly I don't know, and I won't wrong no person nohow." Briscoe took pleasure in stating this great guiding principle in her life under the most depressing of conditions.

"The trouble seemed to come with Lord Elmtree," she added. "He dined here evening before last and stayed that night. I don't think the mistress was pleased. And the master and his lordship sat up most of the night. Broderick says they got very tight."

"Broderick is a good butler and every good butler knows what he knows," I said.

"When Lord Elmtree and Mr. Massy got up late next morning," said Briscoe, "Mrs. Massy had already left Deerpark for Lady Newell's place and did not arrive back until his lordship had gone. It was after she got back that the scene took place."

"Then there was a scene?"

"Yes, between the mistress and Mr. Massy. I don't know what was said, or what happened, but I could hear his voice, very angry and terrible. I was all of a tremble. But it died down. Then he left the house. When I went to the mistress she was in her bedroom, sitting before the fire, a handkerchief to her face." Mrs. Briscoe paused.

"Well?" I queried.

"Under the handkerchief," she said in a low voice, "there was blood."

I sprang from my chair, every nerve of my body tingling.

"It is abominable!" I cried.

Briscoe looked pained, even distressed.

"It was an accident," she said. "The mistress had struck her face against the half-open door in the darkness. She told me so."

I sat down again, telling myself in a hopeless way that it was none of my affair.

"Did Mrs. Massy say anything about tripping over an unseen cushion on the floor, striking her face against a table?" I asked.

"Not a word," Mrs. Briscoe replied.

Something, I knew, was being hidden. The story of the accident was a myth.

I knew by Mrs. Briscoe's uneasiness that she, too, scented something more than an accident, and there was a mute understanding on both sides that the subject was not one to pursue any further. There was silence in the room for some time, the Shah turning over on his back in a sheer orgy of self-indulgence, the paws limp, the white line of the belly palpitating softly, two yellow teeth showing over the underlip, giving him the illusion of a sardonic grin. From this picture of pamperdom my eyes wandered to the desk.

"There have not been many letters to-day," I said.

"There are others locked up in the letter-box downstairs," Mrs. Briscoe replied. "Nobody to open it."

"Why, where is the master?"

"I'm sure I don't know. He left for a concert in Ballyrea yesterday and he's not yet got back."

Briscoe was called away to the sick chamber but was back again within a very few minutes.

"The mistress would like to speak with you, Mr. Jennings."

"I wonder if it is good for her to see people? Dr. O'-Sullivan said something about quiet."

"I think you had better come. She appears anxious about something."

II

I found Mrs. Heffernan Massy propped up in an armchair beside the fire. Her face was of green pallor, the poor body inert and frail as she lay back on the pillows. There was some dressing on the left cheek; her fingers plucked at the shawl; her eyes were too open and too bright; the breathing was irregular. She gave me her long hand with a smile.

"Confess to it at once," she said. "Confess that I look a beauty."

"So sorry to hear you've had an accident," I murmured.

"Yes, it was so stupid of me," she said. There was a pause. "I wanted to see you about a little personal affair," she said, "and I am so glad you've come."

"Do you think it quite wise to bother about your affairs just now? Would it not be better to leave it over until you are about again."

"There are some things that should never be allowed to hang fire," she said, "and this is one of them. I have neglected it quite long enough. One never knows——" Her eyes closed a little wearily. Briscoe, who had been looking after the fire, quietly left the room.

"Anything which makes a tax on one's strength ought to be put aside on occasions such as this," I said. "No personal affair ought to be allowed to usurp the place of one's health."

"It would be a mercy if people would refrain from inflicting useless homilies upon me," she said with a sigh.

"I don't mean to lecture," I said quietly.

She looked at me slowly, and smiled faintly.

"Did Briscoe not tell you?" she asked.

"Tell me what?"

"That I've got quite cross, quite testy?"

"We all have our moments of testiness," I said.

She hitched herself more up on her pillows, the movement appearing to distress her.

"I hope you won't take alarm at a question I wish to ask you," she said.

"I don't think I am easily alarmed."

She plucked at the shawl and moistened her lips.

"I wondered," she said slowly, "if you knew anything about the making of a will?"

"Making of a will?" I repeated in surprise.

"What I mean," she added anxiously, "is, how one might begin it, in the proper legal wording, the correct formula. That should be important. If one once got under way it should be easy to set down what one wanted done. It is a mere technical point, and that is all I wished to know about it. A mere technical point." She appeared painfully anxious to make it clear to me that there was nothing more than an inquiry in this matter.

"I'm afraid I am a very bad adviser," I said. "I really don't know the formula you speak of, or if there is any formula. I don't believe I ever read a will in my life."

She sank in the pillows, disappointed, almost exhausted. It was plain to me that she was greatly disturbed, that she wanted very badly to make a will and to make it as secretly as possible. I could not help connecting that desire with what had occurred in Deerpark within the past few days. Some resolve had taken hold of her and had become a passion in her condition of physical semi-prostration. Did she fear death? And if so to whom would she will all she held in her frail hands?

"Of course," I said, "a solicitor—your own solicitor—is the proper person to advise in a serious matter of the kind."

"Yes, I thought of that, too," she said, "but I don't want to make a fuss." She again hitched herself on the chair and I had the impression that she was angry with herself for having consulted me to no practical purpose. "I thought, perhaps, you might be able to enlighten me, but it is of no particular importance."

"I am afraid I must venture on a lecture again," I said.

"You make a very great mistake to worry about such questions until you are first able to get about."

"I have my medical adviser to consult in all these matters," she answered. "I am entirely surrounded by experts. I am a most enviable personage, and cannot possibly make a mistake."

This note of bitter irony on the part of the lady of Deerpark was quite new to her. But I could see that in the shaken body there was battle, a determination, characteristic of the family, to assert her own will as far as she could.

I rose to go.

"I would be thankful," she said, "if you write a note to Mr. O'Moore, asking him to come out to see me if possible this evening."

"Certainly," I said.

"You might send Barlow with it and have it delivered by hand. If the solicitor is not too busy perhaps he would avail of a seat with Barlow on the journey back. It would be the quickest way."

Before more could be said footsteps sounded outside, there was a brisk knock at the door, it was thrown open, and Kish Massy stood there. His expression was hateful.

"What's this?" he demanded, his voice ringing over the room with a command and a challenge. Mrs. Briscoe came in behind him, her tall figure spectral in its pessimism.

Mrs. Massy looked at her husband with a smile which was disagreeable. It reminded me a little of the sardonic expression of the Shah. His eyes wandered from her face to mine.

"So you are here, Jennings?" he asked.

"Yes, at Mrs. Massy's request," I replied.

He walked down the room and stood gazing at his wife.

"What's the matter with you, May?" he asked, and the voice was not unkind. I wondered for a moment if I had been wronging him in my thoughts. But the look which Mrs. Massy returned to him was unmistakable. There was hatred in the eyes, eyes pathetic in their sickly light.

"Nothing," she answered wearily. Her eyelids quivered over the eyes. Massy bent over her, his frame massive and towering; he laid his great red hand on her head, and looked into her face. I was conscious of a renewal of some struggle, some battle of wills, some contest that was sinister. The frail woman breathing so painfully as she reclined in the chair looked like a hunted bird quivering under the fascinating gaze of some great hungry vulture. And in her eyes was that frank look of hatred and resistance, coming and going, blanching and glowing, under the steady scrutiny of her husband. Mrs. Briscoe moved quietly behind the invalid's chair. The scene was one which I would like to have avoided and I could not refrain from making some movement of protest. Kish Massy at once responded. Without stirring from his position his eyes turned to me.

"What are you doing here?" he demanded.

"I have told you already I came at Mrs. Massy's request," I said.

"To tell her about the song-birds at the concert?" he leered.

"No," I said, "she was troubled about some legal point on which I could not enlighten her."

"Some legal point?" he queried, his manner more alert than ever.

Mrs. Massy's fingers rapidly but aimlessly toyed with the fringe of the shawl.

"Some technicality in the making of a will," I said, determined to leave nothing hidden.

"By God Almighty!" swore Kish Massy, jerking back from his wife's chair. His face was like a thundercloud, the forked lightning flashing over the brows.

"Mrs. Massy is anxious to see her solicitor," I said.

"See damnation!" He roared the words, raising his right hand, the fist clenched. Mrs. Massy raised two trembling hands as if she would ward off a blow, her body shrinking into the cushions.

"Ah," she said in a weak voice, "don't. Don't make another scene. I can't bear it."

Mrs. Briscoe bent over the patient, soothing her. "The mistress must be left alone," she said. "Dr. O'Sullivan said she must have quiet."

I bowed quickly to the poor inert figure in the chair and walked out of the room and the house.

CHAPTER FIVE

I

MRS. HEFFERNAN MASSY'S indisposition continued. Indeed it was announced immediately following the scene in the bedroom that she was quite ill. But her illness was altogether eclipsed by stories of the actsof devotion of her husband. He never left her bedside. He watched over her night and day. To this end he sacrificed his own comforts. He neglected himself. He did not even sleep. He brushed aside all remonstrances. The supreme duty to his suffering wife came before everything. Once or twice I timidly intruded the question of the patient. But nobody appeared to have any definite information as to how she fared. Dr. O'Sullivan said she was still poorly; he met all cross-examination with a grand blandness. Mrs. Briscoe was only very rarely on view and one could see by her colour that she, too, was putting in a vigil in the sick room which must be at least equal to that of her master.

Such visitors as Captain Manning and Colonel Burke were not permitted to see the patient. The doctor, it was proclaimed, had banned all visitors, and Kish Massy was there to personally see to it that the ban was upheld.

Lady Newell alone succeeded in gaining admittance to the sick chamber. It was said she talked her way into it in French. One of the footmen could not resist the temptation to make the inevitable joke. Lady Newell's French leave was the subject of titter over the washing of every plate in the pantry. Once on her way from a visit to the patient Lady Newell came to the library for something to read. I questioned her as to Mrs. Massy's condition.

"Marie!" she exclaimed with a shrug, "there is no longer any Marie left."

"I am afraid I don't quite follow that, Lady Newell," I said.

"Well, there is the room, there is the white bed, and there she lies on it, an outline, a pencil sketch." She made a sudden movement with her ebony walking stick and the strokes were so rapidly eloquent that I could see the outline of a human skeleton across the book-shelves.

I looked hard at her still splendid features. What manner of woman was this? I asked myself. Have women like her any place in their hearts for the primitive emotions, the fundamental humanities? Not a trace of sympathy for the sufferer ruffled her. How could she speak like this of one who had for her affection, at the very least one whose wine it had been good to drink? The eyes, like faded woodland violets, the mobile rouged cheeks, the expressive rather full lips, the finely wrinkled, intelligent brow, the rather small but wonderfully chiselled nose, the golden wig, gave nothing away. All the harvest of her beauty was as implacable as the parchment face of a Chinese god. The figure with its curious little limp, a limp that appeared to plead for a former grace, moved down by the book-shelves, the figure that all its gay days had insinuated itself to admiring male glances along the saloons and boulevards of Paris, that had lolled under the bright skies of the Riviera, that had whirled around the ballrooms of Vienna and London. My scrutiny of her failed to discover even the suggestion of the slightest disturbance, although she had come straight from the bedside of her distressed friend, the good Marie.

She turned to me, having followed up a line of books, saying, "As for the great Kish, what a watchdog he has become! He looks so very wicked! Somebody must have given him a great fright; threatened to take from him his bone. . . . But you know, you saw. Monsieur Paul knows everything in Deerpark."

"I did not see," I said quietly.

"But no? Then you must know he sits by the window in view of the bed, enormous against the light, like that——" She made an outlandish imaginary drawing of a figure with her stick. "The eyes like the eyes of a sphynx; dumb, watchful, huge, animated, a stained-glass Colossus."

She followed down a line of fiction, talking incessantly, her golden head slanted as she read the titles. "What have we here? *Adam Bede*. No, I do not read George Eliot again. One would require so much leisure. . . . Ah, yes, the Kish is like a sentinel on the mountain frontier. There can be no more surprises by the enemy. . . . *The Autocrat*. I know; it is upon all shelves. Wherever there is no breakfast there is Oliver Wendell Holmes. . . . Like Saint Peter guarding the Golden Gates: that is now the great Kish. He sleeps on the hearth as the hare sleeps in the heather. And this one with the red cover? *Virgin Soil*. Ah, barbarous, anonymous Russia! Why should we who live in Connacht read Ivan Turgenev, Monsieur Paul? Do we not all look out through our windows? Melancholy can do for us no more. . . . If they seek a gamekeeper in the Park of the Lord, let them send an angel to summon the great Kish. He is magnificent! . . . *Wuthering Heights*. Good, very good, but Brontë might ease it about the relatives in the opening chapters. One has to ask so often who's who. . . . Poor Marie, she will do what she is told now. The fires out of the great Kish eyes have burned her down to the pillow. She is always tired, always on the verge of sleep and always awake. . . . Ah, how came it here among the Puritans, the Ironsides? *La Confession d'un Enfant Du Siècle*. I shall take and read it again. I must see if I cry or laugh at Octave and Brigitte after all these years. Ah, we have all lived! . . . Is that my old phaeton rolling up to the door, Monsieur Paul! Yes, yes, I know the thud of the old hooves, the tired fetlock. Go and shake up my old coachman, *mon ami*, but gently, pray, or you may knock the whole—what do the peasants call it?—'contraption' to pieces! Then I should have to set out on foot and it would be my luck to sink in the bog so black."

I watched her drive away in the aged phaeton, her golden head lolling scornfully on the drab cushions, the coachman and the old mare full of a heartbreaking sorrow as they bore her down the lawn between the laurels.

Her visit and her conversation had left me miserable to the marrow of my bones. I could not settle down to do anything. Everywhere I saw the picture of the stained glass Colossus and the pencil sketch on the white bed. God, what a picture, what a vigil, what a struggle, what a house! I gazed up at the rows of books on the shelves. They held no magic for me. I walked away, for across them again had come the picture of the watcher by the window and the patient burned down to the pillows of her bed.

I went to the window and gazed upon the trees. The sap was oozing from the buds and soon the branches would be rolling in a drunken orgy of foliage, chestnut shouting to larch, beech calling to ash, the cherry trees in the orchard laughing up at the pears, and oziers singing up somewhere from a swamp! They had been doing that from the first tick of time and the sap would ooze on the branches when the last fire to consume the world would leap at the bark.

I looked beyond them to the hills, the Connacht hills which make the buckle of the belly-band of mountains which strap the body of Ireland. It is a good belly-band and there is no fear that we shall ever heave over into the Atlantic. "The hills often look gay and make men feel happy," I thought. But now they were ashen in a grey light and over them hung a grey sky with white foam scattered upon it from the angry mouth of God. A light rain was washing down the face of the hills and the music it made was an *ologone*, for it was trying to wipe from them the sorrows of seven centuries.

Why indeed, I asked myself, should we in Connacht read Ivan Turgenev? Do we not all look out through our windows?

II

When Mrs. Massy had been several weeks ill under the unwearying oblong eyes of her husband Mr. O'Moore, the solicitor, was fetched from Ballyrea. Broderick, the butler, acquainted me of this fact at the door of Deerpark, and as he did so his timid fat gaze seemed to say, "Ah, a crisis has come at last!"

As I crossed the hall the breakfast-room door was open and inside two men were seated by the wall. They sat on the edges of their chairs, dangling their hats between their legs, conscious that they were there because of some extraordinary circumstance. One was Augustine Massy, the other Doyle the clerk. As I made my way to the library I concluded that they were brought there as witnesses to a will which O'Moore had been fetched to execute. The struggle had ended. The woman who held so much in her frail hands had been well subdued by this time; she had been made to surrender to the stronger mind. She would do what she was told.

As I sat at the desk I heard Kish Massy hurry along the corridor. He went in a joyous buzz, his steps more rapid, eager, and at the same time more cautious than I had heard them before. He returned with two other people, bringing them in the direction of the sick chamber. They were the witnesses to the will. The document was about to be signed. The fate of all Deerpark, all the riches that had come to it, was about to be sealed by a drop of ink! Everything would be done in unimpeachable legal fashion; righteousness would shine upon the brow of Kish Massy. I hummed a little to myself as I sat at the desk, as men will hum during the seconds which are heavy with fate.

Twenty minutes or more passed in silence. Then a door opened and two people came along the passage; they went more quickly than they had come; they were glad to have it over; they did not speak to each other; they were the witnesses to whom no bequests could be made. In a little while another step went along the corridor. All these movements were now as significant to my tense mood as if I were a telegraph operator listening to the dots and dashes of the Morse code on a sounder. As I listened to the little patter along the carpet the dots and dashes said, "This is Mr. O'Moore, the solicitor, a Gladstone bag in his hand and a pleased look on his face. His is joined downstairs by Kish Massy. The carriage waits outside to drive him in state to Ballyrea. They come out together, looking very profound. Kish cannot resist an occasional sly admiring glance at the Gladstone bag. Inside it, tied with a red tape, lies the last will and testament of the lady of Deerpark. Kish grips Mr. O'-Moore's hands in a strong approving grip of friendship and the carriage drives off. Kish returns to the house with the air of a man of tremendous responsibilities and the gift to sustain them.

III

"But he does not return to the sick chamber. The vigil there is ended; it has ended in the manner in which it was intended it should end. May is quiet in her bed now. All nonsense had been driven out of her head! He turns into the breakfast-room. He drinks a glass of whiskey and soda, sits down by the fire, his head back, his nose in the air, his eyes half closed, his legs out to the heat. He says to himself: 'Well, it's over, everything passed off very well, there was no hitch and nothing was forgotten. No fuss and no excitement and no fear of a question being raised. O'Moore is in possession of a document precious beyond anything that has ever existed. So I can make my mind easy. . . . The priest can now come and anoint May as soon as he likes, and indeed it is about time she was anointed. She is very weak. I thought they'd never get her propped up on the pillows. I think she was putting it on a bit. My heart was in my mouth until she had the name scrawled; I never thought it could take anybody so long to scrawl out a name. I thought I felt myself turning grey while she fumbled with the pen—men often turn grey all of a sudden at a time like that. But she wrote her name all right. So I can make my mind easy. . . . The bishop himself may come to see her, for Dr. Mitchel always thought a lot about May and her azaleas. He will do anything he can for her, anything that is in his power, he will indeed. If it is in his power he will put up a special pontoon bridge from this world to the next, so that she will have no delay but to trip across into heaven. So I can make my mind easy. . . . I will do everything that a man can do for May. She has her doctor. She has her two nurses. She has her medicine. She can't expect to live for ever no more than any one else. Every one must move on sooner or later and make room for somebody else. She'll have to do the same. So I can make my mind easy. . . . I saw a woman dying one time, an aunt of mine, and she passed away without any bother. Just a kind of a shiver and all was over. May might go off like that. If she does everything will be done for her that can be done. I must remember to tell the nurses to cut the string tying her toes together before she's coffined, because I remember they forgot to do that for my aunt and she was spancelled when she was coffined. My mother said it was not becoming, and indeed it was not. They will put coins on May's eyes before they stiffen, and on her hands they will draw long white finest gloves. I'll take care they'll be silk gloves, the finest of silk. Flowers will be banked about her in the bed, lilies and tulips and carnations if they are to be had. There will be six tall silver candlesticks, three each side of her when she's laid out, with blessed wax candles burning in them. Every one that gazes upon her then will be sure to remark that she looks peaceful and happy and, sure, if she doesn't she can't say but that it was her own fault. So I can make my mind easy. . . . I'll wake her two nights running and I'll have the old-fashioned wake, but with no noise or singing. The people that come to the wake must be respectable. They'll get all they want in the line of eating and drinking. I'll have legs of mutton, hams, roast beef, fat ducks and game. I'll have a couple of barrels of porter tapped in the barn, and in the house there'll be whisky, brandy, wine, and tea. "Broderick," I'll say to the butler, "there must be no stint. 'Tisn't every day we bury our wife."

So I can make my mind easy. . . . All the prayers that can be said for anybody will be said for May. She'll have the benefit of them in three languages: English, Irish, and Latin. The tenants and every one else will be gathering about the house. I hope the *bean sidhe* will be heard the night before it happens, because the Heffernan family is as old as the next and I'd like the people at the wake to have it to say that they heard the keening. She's the last of the name, too, and that should make the *bean sidhe* put out a great crying in the dead hour of the night, giving us all the warning. They'll be praising her greatly at the wake, and there may be old people by the bed who can tell that they remember her grandmother. . . . I'll have her put in two coffins, one of lead and the other of best oak with plain brass mountings upon it. I don't know what age I'll put down for her on the breastplate, but I'll consult some one with knowledge of such things, for they hardly ever give the right age. So I can make my mind easy. . . . As to the funeral, I undertake that it will do every justice to May. I'll have men from the shops in Ballyrea giving out broad scarfs of white linen, one for the shoulders and one for the tall hat, of every priest who moves in the procession. Every layman will be given a crape for his hat. The number of vehicles, and of horsemen, and the tenants, and the crowds on foot will be beyond counting. I'll make them admit it was as fine a sight of a funeral as the eye could wish to behold, the old women raising a lament for the dead as we move down the hills to the churchyard of Gorrybeg. I'll be there myself, in a new black suit and a tall hat with a crape streaming respectably down behind. I'll walk three paces behind the coffin, and every one who stands by the road will say, "The Lord have mercy on the dead—and there he is himself, Kish Massy, the husband. God comfort him, 'tis a great cross." That day will be a remarkable and a notable day for me without any mistake. So I can make my mind easy. . . . Poor May, she's very weak, as limp as lard, with a little cold sweat on her upper lip and her nose, and the eyes looking scalded in her head. But what else could be expected. As to what happened between us, that's no concern of any one. It's all over and done. I'm willing to forget it and it is not worth May's while now but to keep her mouth shut. Even if she didn't what can be made about it? There was no one there at all but ourselves. There is no witness. And if it came to anything, my word is as good as hers. So I can make my mind easy. . . . I'm thinking it's nearly day with her. The life is hardly in her. A little shake and it would flutter out of her like a bee out of a buttercup. If it happens soon everything might be over and done in time for me, with the help of God, to attend the meeting at Leopardstown. So I can make my mind easy.'"

While Kish Massy stretched his legs before the fire, his pagan mind revelling in the Christian ritual of death, his vision morbidly intense as a Stringberg drama, I was sitting very still and miserably dull at the desk in the library. Nobody came near me. I was isolated in the midst of the great house. Around me was the heavy sense of tragedy. I was going down with the setting sun.

"You're about finished in Deerpark, Paul Jennings," I said to myself.

Suddenly the door opened and Kish Massy came in.

CHAPTER SIX

I

KISH MASSY had opened the door softly and come into the room. He had no sooner done so than the atmosphere of the place changed. I no longer experienced desertion. The feeling of isolation fled. I was keenly alive to quite another sensation. He hesitated as if feeling his way by a quick intuition. I looked up and waited, too.

"Good day, Paul," he said.

"Good day, Kish," I said.

The greeting on both sides was more a feeler than an exchange of good fellowship. It was an attempt by one to sense the mood of the other. Kish Massy stood with an air of indecision for a moment. I sat quite still at the desk. He wheeled a chair about to the fire, still, however, thoughtful. I rose from the desk, but did not move away from it. An abnormal sense of guardedness was manifested. One of Kish's hands ran along the back of the chair, as if he were feeling its smoothness. His eyes were on the chimney-piece.

"I came in to say that it occurred to me I may have dropped hasty words the other day," he said.

I nodded my head a little as he hesitated again. He found it difficult to choose his words and, through caution, I gave him no help. "If I said anything that may have sounded hasty or nasty I should regret it." A hard note in the voice proclaimed that he had no regrets whatever for anything he might have said. "I was, and I am, upset at May's illness." The words this time came out with a decision and a challenge. "It may be that I got into a bad temper." He straightened himself at the back of the chair and looked at me as if to say, "Now, it's your turn to say something, damn you!"

"It was nothing," I said—"at most a little misunderstanding." My words, even to my own ears, sounded contemptuous, and as I spoke I walked to the fire-place. Kish at the same moment left the back of the chair and stepped on to the hearthrug. We were standing quite close to each other.

II

There are moments in the lives of men that are as flash-lights, tense moments when innate things are revealed to us. Men look into each other's eyes and are astounded to behold something that puts out all former estimates as one may put out the life of a fly by the pressure of a finger. Kish Massy was never contemptuous of me and I was never contemptuous of Kish Massy by reason of the knowledge we had of each other. Our familiarity never bred in either of us a contempt. It was always salted by a toleration founded on good-humoured common sense. Now, in a moment, looking into each other's eyes, seeking, for the first time, something in the depths of each other's humanity, all the old values were gone, the traditional relationship destroyed. New personalities jumped into being and stood confronting each other, antagonists and enemies. It was a great strain to keep up the pretence that nothing had happened, that we were still the same two old mortals. The veils which had been suddenly torn from the tabernacle of our personalities had to be ignored.

We were standing so close together that we could hear each other breathe. The respiration was quickened immediately following the dramatic moment of revelation, the disclosures of a supreme eye-flash. It was as if the place had become suddenly laden with the atmosphere of another climate. A sense of oppression appeared to press in upon my temples. I could feel the heat that came from Kish Massy's body, I watched the perspiration that stood out in his brow in crowded little trembling capsules. I scented his laboured breath, and I was quite conscious that he scented my breath, our nostrils quivering with the emotion of the moment. A strange feeling of animalism swept me. I felt I could, at a moment's alarm, spring like a tiger and behave like a tiger.

My glance, keen and burning, ran down Kish Massy's body as if measuring and despising his existence. Kish Massy's glance measured my body with calculation and contempt. It was as if I had said to him, "I now see what you are. I know what you are capable of. Do not expect me to forget that attack on a tottering woman. I don't know what happened, I have no clear proof of it, but——" My eye conveyed the rest. And it was as if Kish Massy said to me, "You stand before me in all your little secret soul. Do not expect me to forget your intrigue with my wife over that will. I don't know what you did, I have no clear proof of it, but——" His eye conveyed the rest.

Whatever we might say to each other again, however we might be able to control our feelings, however much we might keep to the conventional toleration of man for man, these words and these thoughts would always lie somewhere about our hearts ready in a provocative hour to burst into the storm of a human passion. And all this had come into our lives in one appalling second!

Some instinct more powerful than our hatred kept us from emptying out our charged minds in a torrent of hot words. We held back from the first word, the first overt act, which would have led to a violent physical struggle. The sense that the woman who was in both our thoughts lay at the point of death only a few doors away kept us subdued, within the bounds of a deadening oppression. We had to cling to the conventions of existence to tide us over this hour of torment.

"How is Mrs. Massy to-day?" I heard my voice asking the question as if it were another being who spoke. And the voice sounded harsh and flat.

"No change whatever," Kish Massy replied, his tone just as harsh, his eye upon me for a moment again. And that eye said, "She will soon be dead, and when she is dead you go neck and crop from Deerpark."

I moved around to the fire and as I did so my coat touched lightly against his coat. Instinctively, and as if stung, we both pulled back a pace, then regarded each other with a still quickened breath. My eye in that moment said to Kish Massy, "One never knows! And at all events here I stay until the last moment, if for no other reason, then because it will rile you!"

His eyes fell to the grate and seemed to ponder upon the fender. My eyes went to the figure of the nigger boy on the chimney-piece. I became engrossed in the bony knee-caps, the art which had fashioned them, then the thought came to me that this new sensation with Kish Massy was impossible. The desire to gaze upon him for confirmation of it prompted me to look directly at him. At the same time his eyes were raised from the fender as if he, too, wanted corroboration of the situation. Our eyes met for a second. The desire to snort at each other was so powerful that Kish Massy raised one of his feet, pawing the hearthrug as a horse paws the ground. I locked my hands behind my back, and the seconds which followed were heavy with suppressed emotion.

Kish Massy walked up the room to the window, stood looking down at the garden. A silence followed. I sat on the edge of one of the arms of the armchair he had wheeled to the fire. Once he looked back at me, and I knew he was trying if this long-range view would make any difference to the new hostility, the ugly bitterness. And it did not. He again turned to the prospect of the garden outside.

"How the flowers have bloomed in May's garden!" he said half absently.

"Yes," I said, "the flowers have bloomed in her garden."

He moved uneasily. I rose and leaned against the chimney-piece. The stable bell clanged in the yard at the back. The men were quitting work. The faint sound of the timekeeper's whistle in the quarries came down the hills.

"Everything is bursting into life," he said.

"Everything is bursting into life, indeed!" I was unconscious, or partly unconscious, of the echoing of his word and of the mockery.

He made an angry gesture at the window, the familiar short jab of the left arm. He came back to the fire-place.

I could hear his breathing again. I could scent the hot sweat of his fat body, and we moved nervously about the hearthrug, like men sparring for openings. He wheeled about the armchair, just turning it on its castors, without shifting it from position. I pushed a low chair to the fire.

"Won't you pull down the blinds?" he asked.

"No," I replied.

He put out his hand suddenly and lifting a box of cigars from the chimney-piece he selected one, bit off the end of it viciously and spat it into the fire.

"Have a cigar?" he said, thrusting the box toward me without raising his eyes from the fire. He expected a curt refusal. And because I knew he did my hand went into the box, caught up a cigar, I bit the end of it and viciously spat it into the grate, too.

We lighted the cigars. Kish Massy puffed vigorously, then sat down on the armchair. I sat down on the other chair; we sat together by the fire, pulling at the cigars in short, quick, angry draughts. Not a word was spoken. Half-way through his cigar he suddenly fired it into the flames. I pulled more quietly at mine after that. I saw him lean back in his chair, his chin up, and his hand jerked down the collar from his neck. He was like a man who felt suffocating.

I blew out a long white luxurious whiff of smoke, it curled up in the air. He sprang to his feet and made for the door. At the door he hesitated, his back to me, as if

he were trying to think of something to say. But no
words came and he flung the door open, passed out, and
slammed it after him.

III

It seemed—at first—curious to me that the slackening
off in the vigils in the sick chamber by the master of
Deerpark should have led at once to a like slackening off
on the part of the housekeeper, Mrs. Briscoe. I noticed
that she, attended by the Shah, was more in evidence
about the house. Her face was quite pallid, but her
back, if anything, appeared to have improved its rigid
line.

She was so much restored to the normal that after a
week I was honoured with a call at the library. The Shah
expressed his approval by walking in first, the moment
the door opened. He licked his chumps as he smiled up
at me. The housekeeper was so friendly that she accepted a chair in front of the fire.

Mrs. Briscoe could babble as joyously as any old servant of an aristocratic family ever babbled. When she
liked she could be terse as a good playwright. Nay, fur-
thermore, Briscoe could be significant. Her habit of
pausing between the sentences, when she was in a certain mood, gave her an air of mystery. The listener felt
he had to conclude a great deal beyond the bare frame-
work of her spoken words. And it was part of her art
that when she talked most she said least; whereas when
she talked little she said most. I felt, as she sat down in

front of the fire, that she was in this peculiar mood. It warmed my curiosity.

"How do you think things are shaping out now?" I asked.

She considered the question carefully and said, "I like them better than they were."

"Has Mrs. Massy improved, then?" I asked eagerly. Briscoe checked my eagerness by her deliberation. She fingered the keys on her ring, looking down as if counting them.

"Doctor O'Sullivan says she's poorly," she replied, cocking one eye at the hollow of a small key.

"He's been saying that ever since he came to the house. He says it in every house. He says it of every patient. I don't remember ever hearing him say anything else. He has built up his reputation on the phrase. And it means nothing. He's the parrot of the medical profession."

Briscoe inclined her head in acknowledgment of my considered views.

"Doctor O'Sullivan says she's poorly," she repeated in her tranquil way. The repetition was a correction of my snappy manner and at the same time put the responsibility on the doctor's shoulders, leaving Mrs. Briscoe free to entertain her own views. The innuendo was characteristic of Briscoe in her present mood.

"What do you think yourself?" I asked quite humbly. Briscoe put her feet up on the fender.

"I've seen a great many Heffernans ill," she said, and

her eyes seemed to review a whole cycle of Heffernan history as she gazed into the coals. She maintained silence for a great while. She provoked me into an obvious question.

"Did you see any of them die?" I asked.

She looked at me at once and said, "You're very intelligent."

"Did you see any of them die?" I repeated, sticking to it.

"No," she said, "never!"

"And still they died," I ruminated—"every one of them except one, and she's——"

"They died, every one of them," she replied, "because they were killed, one way or another—mostly shot—some by accident, others by design, and when nobody else did it they did it themselves." Her hands fondled her knees and she looked up at the chimney-piece, saying at last in a lifeless voice, "Most of them were put out of the way; there was always somebody who wanted to put them out of the way."

The remark was so significant that I was unable to speak for some time. Out on the palms of my hands, on the hinge at the back of my neck, over the temples, a light perspiration broke. The long figure of the house-keeper, hooked on the chair, appeared to grow appallingly sinister. There was no mistaking not what she said but what she meant.

"How is Mrs. Massy at present?" I asked in a low voice.

"At present," she replied slowly and deliberately, "Mrs. Massy is weak. She's so weak that a fright, a shout, some threat, a little rough shake—something that was nothing and that nobody would notice—might very well finish her." The words seemed to me to come directly from the same train of thought that said "most of the Heffernans were put out of the way." And the words seemed, too, in close affinity to the thought which I had credited Kish Massy with as he sat before the breakfast-room fire, dreaming of her death: "The life is hardly in her. A little shake and it would flutter out of her like a bee out of a buttercup."

I wiped my brow with a handkerchief as Briscoe resumed her meditation by the fire. A feeling that the life of the house was sickening came to me.

"One good thing was done for the patient," said Mrs. Briscoe, stooping more over the fire. I waited for the inevitable pause. "She was put through it one day last week."

"Put through what?" I asked, although already I interpreted the words.

"Something that went against her grain," said Briscoe, and I knew she meant the making of the will. "To do something that went against the grain was always good for the Heffernans, no matter how weak they might happen to be."

"The desire to resist always braced them?" I suggested.

"It did. It was their best tonic. I always saw it and I always said it. Nobody about her seems to notice it—but since then she's come on."

I looked with a new eagerness at Briscoe. And as I gazed on her a sudden swift change came over her whole appearance. She jerked up, cocking her head. Her expression became one of extraordinary attention to something outside, her attitude that of a listener. Her old features hardened, something grim and dogged in their expression. Her body seemed as keen, as tense, as nervy, as a setter suddenly crouching for his bird. I could see that she had quite forgotten me in her sudden concentration on the movements outside. Her eyes went to the Shah, as if expecting something from him. That animal lay close to the fender, on his side, his paws over his face, in a heavenly sleep. Briscoe rose with a quiet, swift caution, crossed to the door with steps cat-like in their nervous buoyancy, and softly opened the door, her grip upon it at the same time expressive of an amazing power. She looked down the corridor, first one side then the other, closed the door quietly with the same powerful grip and came back to the fire, her eyes upon the cat. He still slept tranquilly. I was conscious, and it made me more uneasy still, of some indefinable likeness, some understanding or bond, between the cat and the woman. By the time Mrs. Briscoe had got back to the fire-place she had recovered herself. "It was only the butler," she said, seating herself.

"Why, who did you think it was?" I asked.

She evaded the question and it was a deliberate evasion. Instead she said, "Yes, we have to be very careful, very watchful, have we not, pet?" She touched the Shah with her shoe as she spoke, looking down at him. He removed the paw from over his eye and blinked up at her, going to sleep at once again.

"Why have we to be very watchful?" I asked, including myself in the company. This time Briscoe answered, but it was an answer to a question not put.

"Since Lady Newell spoke to me," she said. "Since she put it into my head."

"Put what into your head?" I demanded.

It was no use. Briscoe answered another question not put. "The nurse is not with the mistress now," she said. "She is alone by herself, in a sort of doze. And she is not to be left in the room by herself, Lady Newell says, especially if——" But Briscoe stopped.

The Shah had suddenly and noiselessly bounded right on to his feet, like a ball which had been hopped on the carpet. His face, the whiskers bristling, was towards the door, and his back humped up until it described a rigid half-circle. His thick tail, the guarantee of his pedigree, made a few angry quick swishes. In that attitude he remained.

Briscoe, at the first stir of the cat, rose from her chair, made the same noiseless movement to the door as before, her whole body tense. Footsteps came down the corridor. There was no mistaking them. They were the footsteps of the master of Deerpark, albeit that I thought he, too, walked with unusual softness along the carpet. Briscoe waited, still tense, behind the door until he had gone some way ahead, then she made one swift movement and was gone, the door closed. She was so swift that the Shah, who had also moved for the door, got cut off. He was left with me in the library. He stood there without a movement, his eyes fixed on the slit of the door at the jamb. I stood looking at him, the footsteps outside conveying to me that both Kish Massy and Mrs. Briscoe had gone in the direction of the chamber where the life struggle was so critical that "a fright, a shout, some threat, a little rough shake—something that was nothing and that nobody would notice—might finish her."

While I stood there I began to see the woodland violet eyes of Lady Newell in a new light. It was she who had "put it into" Mrs. Briscoe's head. . . . Kish Massy's footsteps passed back from the direction of the sick chamber. Shortly after Mrs. Briscoe entered the library.

"I'm so sorry," she said to the Shah. "And was the poor pet left all alone?"

The Shah brushed the front of her dress with his fur, a sign that she had been forgiven.

"That was Mr. Massy," Briscoe said, coming down the room a little. "He was in her chamber before I reached there." Then after a pause, "He was standing by the bed when I opened the door. I don't think he

heard me because he started—made a little spring—
when I drew near."

"Why should he make a little spring?" I asked.

"I'm sure I don't know. I won't wrong no person nohow. He said to me when he recovered himself, 'She's
sleeping easier than she used to,' and I said, 'She is indeed.' Then he went out."

"And *is* she sleeping easy?" I asked.

Briscoe's face brightened. "Very much easier," she
said. "Good evening, Mr. Jennings."

"Good evening, Mrs. Briscoe."

They went out together, the Shah looking back at me
from the door as if I had overlooked something.

"Good evening, old man," I added.

IV

The bulletins from the sick chamber improved. First,
Mrs. Massy continued to sleep well, she was taking her
medicine quite easily, her temperature went down.
Then her appetite revived. She was able to manage a
cup of weak tea and some toast. The limb of a chicken
tempted her. She was able to sit up in the bed. It did not
distress her to talk. She admitted some visitors, and
Lady Newell read to her daily. She was able to look over
the paper for herself. She began some inquiries about
affairs in the house, on the property. She was able to sit
by the fire. She signed some cheques. She walked about
the room. She found a glass of wine rather agreed with

her. She asked for a slice of ham and a potato with her chicken. Some early strawberries from Colonel Burke were greatly relished. She refused to take any more of Dr. O'Sullivan's medicine. She had a tiff with Lady Newell about the behaviour of Jaques, the toy chocolate Pomeranian. There was quite a flare-up, ending in Lady Newell kissing her on the cheek and in Mrs. Heffernan Massy ordering a new leash with gold mountings for Jaques. Finally, she sent to the village for Miss Silver, the dressmaker.

Broderick, the butler, reported that the master of Deerpark was run down. He refused his soup. He found fault with the dishes. He was liverish. He went for long lonely rides on the fieriest of the colts from his stables. He dismissed one of his best trainers. He was inclined to find fault with everybody. He said nobody wanted him. He struck his brother Augustine a vicious blow in the chin. He went to Leopardstown races with Lord Elmtree and stayed away a week; he returned alone, and with a cold in the head. He was given to wandering about the passages and rooms of Deerpark, in a sort of little trot, his head down, the heavy chumps hanging at the ends of his jowls, like a hound who had lost his quarry. By the time Mrs. Massy was able to take the air again, to go for a drive in her carriage, Mr. Massy looked as if he would take to the bed. When she joined a little afternoon party in the lawn, taking part in a gentle game of croquet, he sank before a fire in a back room, the servants telling each other with a leer that "master was studying form."

When the weather was warm enough Mrs. Massy, Lady Newell, Mrs. Briscoe and the Shah left Deerpark for Ballinacoorty, a bracing spot overlooking the Atlantic twenty miles away. There a nice house was placed at their disposal by Colonel Burke.

The same night Kish Massy was carried up to bed by the butler, two footmen and a pantry boy. He was noisy in his room. He was noisy next day. He wanted to climb up telegraph-poles on the public road. In the end he settled into it in the dining-room.

"He's drinking like a herring," said Broderick the butler. "There were sixty dozen in the cellar and now— I have not the heart to reckon them. They've got a fearful punishing."

His lugubrious brother Augustine and Doyle the clerk accompanied him the day he drove off to the railway station at Ballyrea *en route* for Mount St. Paul. If the bearded Guest Master of that famous Cistercian monastery saw Kish Massy arrive with quaking limbs and a passion for singing the same little out-of-tune song over and over again, he had the pleasure of packing him off, cured, a month later. He returned to the hills looking for recruits for the Anti-Treating League. Lally the footman, who never drank, became a member and wore the button.

A week later Kish Massy, accompanied by the Right

Hon. the Earl of Elmtree, left on a trip to the United States of America. The trip was, the butler told us, undertaken on the best medical advice.

"But what about the pale blue real estate business in New York City?" Betty asked naïvely when she heard the announcement.

'Not a word," I said. "Hold your——"

"Nostril?" Betty suggested.

CHAPTER SEVEN

I

THE ground of the Ballyrea fair green was sodden and smelt evilly. Men and women, cattle and sheep, ploughed bravely through it. They moved in a close confused medley. Men constantly made quick short journeys hither and thither. They moved with little sense of direction, half blindly, shouldering each other out of the way without compunction. The women, wrapped in warm bright shawls, their skirts tucked up over their petticoats, their beefy legs solid in the ground, stood mute and sceptical attendants on the passionate men. Wild-eyed bullocks, dribbling at the great mouths, made lunges about the crowd. Sheep took dispirited little trots whenever there was an opening, some rattling their fleeces, others, newly shorn, looking naked and wronged, for there was a cold sting in the autumn air. The constant whacking of sticks on the haunches of cattle sounded like a tattoo above the shout of the fair, the dull slopping in the wet ground. Herds moved about their flocks, whistling and crying, angry drill masters. Drovers hung on the verge of the fair, beaten looking mortals with swollen bare feet and swivel eyes, ready to take charge of the little lots of animals which now and again became detached from the main centre of the mart. Young country-men stood talking to each other, eyeing a girl whenever one was to be seen, their feet in puddles, sticks horizontal under their arms, indifferent as to the eyes of the passers-by they endangered. Raucous voices sounded from the inside of tents where refreshments were being served. Farmers and cattle buyers moved about among the beasts, their words brief and sharp and shouted when they spoke. An unreasonable resentment, and open distrust of everything said and done, a love of violent contradictions, an abandon to exaggeration, a belief that every man there had come to best some other man, a rush to get out of it first, alive, and, if possible, unbested, seized the fair community like a fever. The very mouths of the men, active and angry, seemed slit in their faces for the energetic business of the fair. The silence of the women, their patience, aloofness, was like a protest against it all. They stood about in a dumbness which seemed to cry, "We were made to bring forth men for better than this!"

In the streets of the town between the shops horses were being ridden up and down, crowded together;

men leaned from their saddles bargaining with buyers; others made short sprints of their nags whenever they found room, to show off their paces, whacking the brutes on the quarters as they rode, their coat-tails flying, a battle-light in their faces. Here the long mouth of a horse gaped, his eyes wild, as a man read his age by his teeth; there a mare was blowing after her wind-pipe had been gripped to test her wind. Men struck each other on the palms of the hand as they bargained. Little knots of eager people listened to the disputes. Small boys made sudden dives between the horses, risking their skins to cross the street, through pure love of the adventure. A blind man, tall, tranquil, his sightless face to the sun, came down the pathway shouting, "Halters! Halters!" The other side of the street a tinker woman in her bare head, a bright petticoat, a light grey shawl, cried "Halters! Halters!" and it was like an echo of the blind man's voice. In a side street a ballad singer and his wife were singing a song to a traditional air, a song about Robert Emmet, and selling song sheets. About them was a group of young men and young girls, attentive, silent, sympathetic, and behind them an old man with a white beard, who smiled, who had been a Fenian, and behind him a Peeler with a grim black muzzle.

I had left the ballad singers and was turning into the fair green when the figure of Captain Manning loomed ahead of me. He travelled sturdily, about him was a bodyguard of shepherds, their sheep crooks in the air.

He had the look of a man who was leading a foraging party. He wore a half tall hat, a loose black morning coat, dark tweed breeches, limp yellow buttoned gaiters somewhat crumpled on the legs, heavy square-toed boots. He gripped an umbrella in the centre. He was sprayed all over by the mud of the fair. He travelled over the sodden ground with the step of a man who was used to it and who found it agreeable. His heavy head was stooped as he listened to the words of a small farmer. He had reached the sheep pens before I overtook him.

II

Captain Manning was in good humour, almost talkative, for he was at home and happy in this atmosphere. A good fair, with a strong dash of anger and shouting and crowds, men and beasts thrown together higgledy-piggledy in a confined space, with buyers who knew how to pay for a good beast when they saw one, this was the Captain's idea of a purposeful life. He saw nothing in civilization beyond it. And he had again gotten the top price for all the animals it suited him to sell from his pastures.

We moved away together from the heart of the fair, walking up and down where it was less congested. I related my experience of the morning's business. The Captain advised and criticized. . . . I had no right to sell the ewes; *he* never parted with a ewe at that time of the year, except she was gone beyond the beyonds. Springers were very dear and scarce. He thought I did very well with the two long tails. £20 apiece was very good money as prices went.

"You're having a very quiet time at Deerpark these days," he said suddenly.

"Yes," I replied, "I'm all alone there in my glory."

"When is Massy coming back from America?"

The Captain spoke in the blunt dogmatic manner of the cattle dealer; sometimes he used the vivid phrases of peasant speech. A spot of black wet earth had splashed high on his cheek-bone and was drying out there a pale yellow, like a wart.

"I have no idea when he returns," I replied. "We do not correspond and his movements are altogether unknown to me."

"What was it brought him out there at all?"

"Nobody seems to know definitely. There was something about the best medical advice at the time of his sailing. But I really know nothing."

"Medical advice indeed!" cried the Captain. "A baggage like that to be talking about medical advice."

A small flock of sheep, recently shorn, looking nearer to the deer in their skin, went close by in front of us, bleating and confused.

"Ah!" said the Captain, drawing a deep breath, "that is the loveliest scent in the world! Do you find it,

Jennings? Clean and sweet! There is nothing like the smell of a sheep fresh from the dipping on an autumn morning."

The smells of the fair which I had been smelling all the morning had made no appeal to me whatever. They were, I thought, a trifle elementary! But I said nothing.

"Massy'll be home soon," said the Captain with sudden decision. "He can't stand that place, New York, on his allowance. The money goes there like chaff from the sieve—every little breeze taking some of it."

"I don't know that he has an allowance—outside of his own stables," I said. "I don't know that he has anything from Mrs. Massy."

"Oh, then, he has an allowance from Mrs. Massy. I know that. She made him an allowance from the day of the marriage and she made it to him on my advice."

The Captain ploughed through the mud, allowing his feet to slip gently at each step, his sturdy air that of a man who knew what he was about in this world. "If she didn't make that fellow an allowance he'd have got hold of everything that belonged to her and then it would be a case of 'O Fare-thee-well!' to Deerpark and all that it holds."

"I suppose an allowance was the best arrangement," I admitted. "But I daresay Kish considered he did not get enough."

"Of course he considered he did not get half enough.

Did you ever hear of a man who marries into a place or property who does not believe it was not half good enough for him? He becomes an old woman, always dissatisfied, grunting and grumbling like a little bloated fat pig. If there's one mortal I hate it's a man who has bought a place or a property or a position by selling his sex."

"I think Kish Massy looked on marriage a bit anxiously—but patronizingly," I said.

"And there he is in New York now, for what only the Lord knows, writing home making fresh demands of money upon her. What's more she's gone and sent him money."

"That I was not aware of either," I said.

Captain Manning stood to emphasize what he was about to say. He raised the hand which clutched the umbrella in the centre. He looked like the trunk of some strong oak with a solitary branch growing out of it.

"I was over in Ballinacoorty with Mrs. Massy yesterday," he said, "and I advised her to refuse point-blank the last demand he made and she has refused it."

"It will break poor Kish's heart," I said.

"Heart," scoffed the Captain. "When had any of them Massy's a heart that you could see on a white plate?"

To this question I could offer no answer.

"If he has any sense of decency at all," declared Captain Manning, "he'll come home, as he must know that the woman will soon be drawing near to the time of her lying-in. They're expecting it early in January."

III

Suddenly the whole scene took on a most faraway and fantastic look for me. Something seemed to revolve under my scalp. I found difficulty in pulling my legs along in the mud. I had to suppress a short harsh laugh. But shouts, primitive words, sentences in traditional arguments, resounded on all sides as the business of the fair proceeded and these shouted words in some irritating way became part of the struggle for lucidity in my brain. . . . "The two-year-olds will never leave me at the money. I'd see them roasting in hell first. . . . You broke your heart with your nine pound ten. Come here my decent man. Listen to me now. . . . I'll split no difference at all, not if I never stood over a beast again. . . . Put the raddle on her rump now, Johnny, and no more about it. . . . That I may be as dead as my father if I do. . . . I'll hold you a shilling she'll fatten like a fool. That I may never feel the weight of a luck-penny in me paw again if she doesn't. . . . Done! But you're the hardest man that ever walked behind a cow."

The babble of the mart went on as we turned back by the pens. Sticks flourished over the red shapes of the cattle; the crooks of herds shot at the white limbs of sheep. A scuffle took place inside a tent, the shapes of struggling men bulging out through the canvas. The tent-pole swayed like a mast in a storm. An old man, bent almost in two with age and infirmity, clung to the shaft of an upturned cart, coughing hideously, the sheep bleating around him. But the confusion which had gripped me made all this remote and unreal. So far was my capacity for lucid thought gone that I found myself dwelling upon something even more primitive than the Ballyrea fair. My thoughts jumped back to the period before the Flood! I remembered, in an insistent and curiously vivid way, the story in the Bible of Sarah, the wife of Abraham, who, in her tent one day "laughed within herself," because she overheard the promise at the tent door that she should bear a child.

"I suppose you heard that Mrs. Massy is expecting a baby?" asked Captain Manning.

"N-n-no," I said confused, and angry with myself for being confused. "I had no idea."

"Well, she is, then," he said. "I suppose it will go hard with her. . . . Did you sell, Stephen? Thirty two shillings a head for the hoggets? It's not bad at all considering. Springers are very slow. Are you holding back still, John? You have no courage. It's bad to be always behind the door."

He was already absorbed in the affairs of his neighbours, and turning his solid back walked away from me without more ado.

I walked from the fair green through the streets, in

the direction of the hotel where my car awaited me. I wanted to get away as quickly as possible. The streets were full of the noises of the fair. The voice of the blind man crying "Halters! Halters!" sounded over the uproar. A horse struck fire from its hoof on the road. Ash plants were everywhere rattling. Men swarmed around the counters of public-houses, the smell of porter came out the doors, a band of merry tinkers clattered up the road, driving a flock of unbridled donkeys before them, wild with joy at the heat of the fair. And as I went along the words kept knocking in my brain, "They're expecting it in January. . . . And Sarah said, God hath made me to laugh, so that all that hear will laugh with me."

CHAPTER EIGHT

I

AS not infrequently happens in Ireland the month of October turned out fine and warm, the summer persisting through short days and falling leaves. In consequence Mrs. Heffernan Massy and Lady Newell remained by the sea at Ballinacoorty. We were into the month of November when, accompanied by Colonel Burke, they returned to Deerpark.

Mrs. Massy looked astonishingly well. I beheld her as one beholds a wonder which periodically becomes more a wonder. The nervousness which appeared to have shattered her health early in the year was practically gone. She had got brown from wind and sea and sun. Her outlook was cheerful. As she ascended the steps I noticed for a moment that her movements were deliberate, that she wore rather loose-fitting garments.

She was almost gay as she acknowledged the smiles which greeted her on all sides.

Lady Newell had not permitted either the sun, the wind, or the sea to take liberties with her complexion. It was still the same even pallor under the golden wig. But her figure showed a disposition to plumpness. Colonel Burke was very pleased with the results of the sojourn, his liquid brown eyes merry in the large face, the flesh of the cheeks veined and mottled and bunching in light purple ridges whenever he smiled, the enormous lower lip hanging, a perpetual advertisement of his spacious aristocracy. The Colonel was always happy when attending on semi-distressed females. Lady Newell in one of her ironic moods had said of him, "Poor Algernon has a passion for women who are *passé*. I suppose he finds in their lavender charms something that stirs a memory of his purple youth. And what clover he is in here in Connacht!" But the Colonel did not really confine his sympathies to semi-distressed ladies. He was the sort of man whom shabby dogs or outcast cats approached with confidence, took his pats with gratitude, accompanied him some way on his road and left him with a wistful look on their tired faces. His passion for the amalgamation of workhouses arose from the same sense of fundamental sympathy, an instinct for the half abandoned.

They were all in very good spirits, hungry after the drive over the hills, and we had quite a joyous luncheon in honour of the return.

"I think, Agwatha," lisped Colonel Burke, "you must confess to the bishop afwesh."

"But why, Algernon?"

"You know you awe getting fat and that is to say you awe getting fond of Connacht. You've almost admitted as much you'self."

"It is too terrible to think of," said Lady Newell. "The humiliation would bring me to the door of death. Ah, Algernon, there may be a hell after all!"

"That is most splendid praise of Connacht," said Mrs. Massy.

"And my appetite, my gluttony for the food, what is it that I could not devour?" asked Lady Newell.

"You awe mowe the epicu'e in dwinks, ce'tainly," drawled the Colonel. All his "r's" seemed to slip fatally down the great underlip.

"And the mere fact that you talk so much about what you can eat and what you can drink looks as if you are being absorbed by the local environment," said Mrs. Massy. "You are nearly down to the level of all our animalism."

"Don't talk to me of it!" exclaimed Lady Newell. "Give me things to eat, food, meat, fats! The twenty miles of air over the hills has made me into a wild beast. . . . What have you on the sideboard, Broderick? What secrets lie under the cover dishes? The big one there—ah, mountain mutton! How lovely the carving knife looks in your pale white hand! Partridge did you say, and woodcock and a pheasant? Where had they the shoot? But it does not matter, nothing matters now except the carving knife! Broderick, the exquisite twirl of your wrist is full of hope. Broderick, I have confidence in you. Marie, Algernon, Monsieur Paul, do you not all hear that music? The rattle of dishes, the little shuffle of Broderick as he prances in his slippers before the sideboard. And now, *mon Dieu!* somebody is bringing mushrooms! I scent them afar; they make me swoon! I see nothing except the blade of a knife, the prong of a fork, the wing of something on a bright plate!"

II

I think we all had something of Lady Newell's relish for the luncheon, and Broderick was really very good to us. When we had eaten right heartily we dallied over the table.

"There is nothing now so good as a smoke," said Lady Newell. She selected an Egyptian cigarette, looking supremely happy as she lay back in her chair. Colonel Burke and myself declared for cigars.

"*Chacun à son goût*," said Lady Newell, striking a match. Although she never cultivated the smoking habit, Mrs. Massy liked the scent of tobacco and she liked little lapses when among her best friends.

Lady Newell looked at Colonel Burke through her half-closed woodland violet eyes and said, "After a liqueur—the splendid gift of the subtle alchemists of

Chartreuse—a whiff of the East. What do you say, Algernon?"

"I always thought you did you'self well, Agwatha."

"And only a little while ago I might have cried, 'My heart aches, and a drowsy numbness pains my sense as though of hemlock I had drunk.' "

"Yes, I remember the lines. But give us mowe of it, my deah. Is there not something about 'Dance and Provençal song and sunburnt mirth' and about 'beaded bubbles winking at the bwim'?"

"*Oui, oui*, Algernon, but do not expect me to say it. I can only think of it! Keats in that hour of his was divine." She closed her eyes.

Mrs. Massy fingered a Chinese ash-tray, but her eyes wandered through a window to the sky. I had already noticed these little detachments, these returns to the patch of sky over Deerpark, the reading of some new wonder in the grey scroll overhead. A curious, mysterious smile lit her face at odd moments, almost spiritualizing it, and now her lips moved for a second as if she were communing with herself, away from our company. Once or twice, too a quick little shudder seized her frame. We passed some minutes wholly in silence —some of those great companionable minutes of silence that come only to those who have the gift of fellowship.

"Has Mrs. Briscoe stayed on at Ballinacoorty?" I asked after a time, having, as they say, suddenly bethought myself of the housekeeper. The question roused all three. They looked at me in surprise.

"Could it be possible you have not heard?" asked Mrs. Massy.

I shook my head.

"Briscoe!" cried Lady Newell. "There is no longer Briscoe." She blew a white whiff of smoke from her lips into the air, as if Briscoe had some ethereal passing of the kind.

"Why, what on earth happened?" I asked.

"Bwiscoe has been twansfowmed into a cwab," said Colonel Burke. The flesh creased in comical puffs about the brown eyes as he chuckled. I knew by these manifestations that he had ventured a joke.

"Transformed into what?" I asked.

"Into a cwab."

"*Non, non*, Algernon, not a crab but a lobster."

"Yes, my deah, a lobsteh. It is much the same thing—a cweatu'e out of the sea with a gweat many legs. Bwiscoe is now a lobsteh, Jennings, a lobsteh, a blue-black lobsteh." Some of the puffs on the cheeks became vivid, shiny, through enjoyment of his own joke. He pulled a long pull at his cigar.

Mrs. Massy smiled, too, as if this new surprise were part of the hidden things which had been lighting her face.

"I heard of women who were turned into hares by fairies," I said. "It's quite a common practice of the

Good People when annoyed—but a lobster! I never heard of anybody being done into a lobster."

"Well, Briscoe has been done into a lobster and walked hindways into the sea," declared Lady Newell. "Never more shall we see poor Briscoe."

"And as for me," said Mrs. Massy, "I shall never ask to touch lobster again."

"It has been a season of lobster—let us call it Lobster Summer," said Lady Newell.

"Lobsteh soup and lobsteh salad!" drawled the Colonel.

"When she did not cook them," declared Lady Newell, "she talked of them or ate them or drilled them about the bottom of the baskets like Prussians. You should hear their shells crackling in the kitchen!"

"I'm afraid——" I began.

"When did you f'wst suspect Bwiscoe, Agwatha?" Colonel Burke asked.

"When I saw St. John the Baptist coming up the path to the door with his basket, saying, 'All alive! All alive!' "

"St. John the Baptist! Agwatha!" The Colonel's tone was one of admonishment. He did not like her irreverence.

"Ah well, that is my sin," said Lady Newell. "Look not as if you may have to go to the stake for me, Algernon! And I only speak of the picture as I saw it. A man, Monsieur Paul, with rich thick black beard combed only by the wind, with hair black as the raven hanging like thatch from the head, eyes burning black, and clothes so much abbreviated—almost *sans culottes*! A man who dwelt in a cave, who would eat of the wild honey and of the locusts if he could only get them. And he sold to all the lobster."

"But what has all this to do with Briscoe?" I asked.

"What has it to do? Everything!" Lady Newell made a sweep of the hand.

"Mrs. Briscoe has got married again," said Mrs. Massy quietly. She was gazing out through the window, the little smile playing about her mouth.

"Married! Surely——?" I was, as Lady Newell might say, blank of the face. They all enjoyed my amazement.

"Mawwied she is," confirmed Colonel Burke. "We wewe all at the ceremony a week agone."

"Who on earth has she married?" I asked.

"John the Baptist," Lady Newell replied. The Colonel raised his plump hands and turned the palms dead against her.

"Well, then, John the Lobster. That is what they call him in Ballinacoorty."

"Yes, that is what they call him in Ballinacoorty. In such pwimitive places they always call each other names. It is ill-bwed, the weapon of the ignowamus."

"Emerson does not agree with you in that, Colonel," I ventured. "In his essay on Plato he says no orator can measure in effect with him who can give good nick-names."

"Then I don't agwee with Emewson at all. He w'ote watheh well but dogmatized too much in epigwams—always a dangewous dissipation. Weak dogma and strong epigwam, and *vice versa*, come nimbly fwom some lop-sided minds. I hold stwongly that nicknaming is the weapon of the ignowamus. It is the handmaid of scuwwility."

The Colonel was in a combative mood after his glass of wine.

"I stand by Emerson and Ballinacoorty as against Algernon," said Lady Newell.

"Besides, John the Lobster does not mind being called John the Lobster in the least," said Mrs. Massy. She drew a vase of flowers to her and scented them.

"Am I to really understand," I asked, "that Mrs. Briscoe is now Mrs. John the Lobster?"

"She'd be very indignant if you were to understand anything else," Mrs. Massy replied.

"When I saw Briscoe one day taking the basket from him to carry it over the black rocks I knew she was lost to us. I saw her fall sprawling, a dozen times, over the wet weeds, but still she clung to it, John the Lobster following her in his bare feet, jumping like a goat from rock to rock. '*Mon Dieu!*' I said, 'Briscoe is going from us. She's off with John the Lobster to his cave. It is enchantment! She will become his beast of burden, John the Lobster's beast of burden!' Marie would not believe me when I spoke."

"I concluded you exaggerated," Mrs. Massy said. "But when I found Briscoe doing her hair into barrel curls and taking to wearing pink blouses with ribbons at the throat and the wrists—well, I knew then that the world was once more shaken to its foundations."

"Ah, it was so lovely, Monsieur Paul!" Lady Newell said. "Briscoe in her barrel curls and ribbons sitting at the open window upstairs overlooking the sea, watching John the Lobster in his boat putting down the lobster-pots. And then there was that magnificent evening when she was with him under the brown sail, the old boat racing over the waves to Galway where they went to buy the Claddagh ring."

"It was a most astonishing womance," agreed the Colonel.

"And Briscoe had a great stocking of money," exclaimed Lady Newell. "She had been hoarding it up ever since the horse kicked Briscoe in the stomach and inflammation did the rest. Would you believe it, she was in a shot-silk costume when she went down to the cave and poured all her money into John the Lobster's hands. He told me himself how she came like a bird of Paradise on the wing."

"I'm afwaid, Agwatha," chided Colonel Burke,

"John the Lobsteh was too confiding to you. Your 'fow-eign' manner made him unsuspecting and too confidential."

"Yes, he told me all," agreed Lady Newell. "'She come to me and I salting a few gurnets,' said he, 'and the next thing the coins, silver and gold, was pouring like a stream into me palms and I holding them together. So when I saw that now, says I, 'tis the man I'll be entirely for I'll have me own nobbie on the sea and a crew by hire, going out into the deep places for the mackerel and the herring. Me nets will be in every tide and it's tired counting the catch the women will be the time I do reef me sails be the quays of Galway, or maybe round be Kinsale to make bargain with the Scotchmen. And says I to Herself and she standing fornist me like an angel in bright colours, From this day out, says I, they'll always be white bread in the house and red meat the round of the year and you yourself, me heart, putting the shag tobaccy in me briar pipe the evening I do be coming home to you in the house.' He was so droll, with the big tears in the black eyes."

"You are acquiring the remote Connacht manner very fast, Lady Newell," I said.

"But why not, monsieur? Am I not intelligent and a foreigner?"

"And I'm afwaid she's given you a watheh highly coloured idea of Bwiscoe's man," said Colonel Burke. "He's quite a wespectable fishewman and his weal name is John Mulcahy. As to his cave—it's a cottage." The merry brown eyes twinkled.

"We were all there yesterday afternoon and had tea with the family," said Mrs. Massy. "And Briscoe is quite happy." The mysterious smile played about her face.

"I can scarcely credit it still," I said. "Shall we never see Briscoe in Deerpark again?"

"Oh, yes," said Mrs. Massy. "She's coming for her things one of these days."

"Have the papehs come yet, Jennings?" Colonel Burke asked. "I'm anxious to see them. Tomorrow I go to Dublin to move that wesolution at the Amalgamation confewence. They'll muddle the whole thing again if I don't insist on——"

By common impulse we all three rose from the table. The Colonel had touched a subject that had broken up many little gatherings. I took my leave of the ladies without any delay. Mrs. Massy crossed the room with me to the door. She inquired if any personal letters awaited her.

"I don't think so," I said.

"Nothing from America?"

"Not that I noticed."

There was a faint shrug of the shoulders as much as to say, "It is really of no importance." Then she smiled and her smile seemed to say, "I am immensely happy."

I bowed and passed down through the house.

III

I had forgotten even Briscoe's astonishing romance until I reached the hall. There on the table lay a cablegram which had evidently been delivered while we sat together. It was addressed to Mrs. Massy. Of course it should have been taken to her at once. Briscoe's absence was already expressing itself in little household slacknesses! I felt pretty sure the cablegram came from Kish Massy, and as I raised it I wondered what he had cabled about. Possibly an urgent whip for money. The letter refusing further supplies, of which Captain Manning had spoken, would about have reached him by this time. I smiled grimly as I thought of the expectant Kish in New York.

There was no servant about and I walked back with the message to the dining-room. The place was, however, already deserted. I went upstairs and found Mrs. Massy and Lady Newell in the drawing-room.

Mrs. Massy was standing with her back to the window, a little table in front of her covered with cut flowers from the greenhouses. She was humming in a happy undertone as she arranged these flowers in blue vases. At the fire Lady Newell was seated on a Chesterfield armchair, a discarded magazine on her lap, her golden head fallen to one side. She was taking her siesta. I crossed the room lightly and handed Mrs. Massy the cablegram.

"Found it in the hall," I said.

She leaned across the flowers to receive it, the scent of the blooms filling the air. As she did so she smiled, and, nodding in the direction of the sleeping beauty, I withdrew quietly.

"Deerpark has not been so happy for many a day," I thought as I left the house.

CHAPTER NINE

I

MOTHER and myself, at breakfast next morning, were somewhat surprised to see Doctor O'Sullivan drive up to the door in his trap.

"Nobody ill in the house, is there?" I asked.

"Not that I know of," said my mother.

Doctor O'Sullivan was shown in, all apologies, but we induced him to sit down and drink a cup of tea.

"You haven't been to Deerpark this morning," he said, turning to me.

"No, not yet. Miss Heffernan Massy returned from Ballinacoorty yesterday afternoon."

"And went within an ace of going off again last night," said the doctor, putting milk in his tea.

I looked my surprise. "Going off to Ballinacoorty again, do you mean?" I asked.

"No, much farther this time. On a voyage to the great Beyond." The doctor sipped his tea.

"Dear me, has she been knocked up again?" my mother asked.

The doctor nodded. "I spent the best part of the night in Deerpark," he said. "It was a case of touch-and-go."

"But she was not in the least ill yesterday afternoon," I broke in. "Quite the contrary."

"Oh, well, something happened after you had left," said Doctor O'Sullivan. "The blow fell suddenly. Lady Newell found her prostrated in her room—in fact lying unconscious in a chair."

"Good God!" I said.

"But she has pulled through all right?" asked my mother. The room became heavy with a poignant anxiety.

"She has pulled through so far," said Doctor O'Sullivan. "But it was a terrible struggle, the like of which one does not care to see more than once in a lifetime. Things did not improve as the night wore on, and early this morning a baby arrived." There was silence in the room for some seconds following this announcement. Vivid leaves from the Virginia creeper outside rattled crisply on the window-panes as they dropped.

"My goodness!" exclaimed my mother at last. Her face bore an expression of stunned amazement. In a vague way I thought she was making some rapid mental calculations and puzzling over them.

"Yes, indeed, Mrs. Jennings," said Doctor O'Sullivan, wiping his moustache with his handkerchief, "a baby girl was born, one of these mysterious little lives that are hurried into the world before their time for the Lord only knows what reason. A seven months' child."

Again there was silence. I crunched some bread-crumbs between my fingers.

My mother leaned a little across the table to the doctor.

"Did the baby live, doctor?" she asked, her voice full of a moving sympathy, the maternal chord in her own heart, the mystery that is the very essence of all womanhood, profoundly touched.

"The baby lived," said Doctor O'Sullivan, glancing up at the leaves fluttering on the window-panes. As he raised his eyes to the light I could see he was quite fagged after the night's ordeal.

My mother leaned back in her chair, murmuring, "What a strange world!"

"You know Lady Newell?" asked the doctor, turning to her.

"Yes, quite well."

"I'm afraid I must stand up for her in future." Doctor O'Sullivan was the type of man who could not stand Lady Newell. His world was in exact ratio to the territory over which he enjoyed a practice; he was, in the most literal sense, local and very popular. And all Lady Newell's instincts led her to battle against everything that was local, to challenge every one who was popular.

"I must admit she behaved splendidly last night,"

said Doctor O'Sullivan. "They all lost their heads when Mrs. Massy was discovered unconscious, but Lady Newell soon had them in order and under discipline. She took charge of the affairs of the house. As to her behaviour in the sick room until the nurse arrived—and indeed after the nurse had arrived—it was a revelation to me. I would not know her to be the same Lady Newell."

"She was extremely attached to Mrs. Massy and Mrs. Massy to her," said my mother.

"And I don't believe anybody else could have managed Mrs. Massy so well under the more than distressing circumstances. I never in all my experience saw a patient so hysterical. For two mortal hours, Mrs. Jennings——"

The doctor's eyes wandered to me. He pulled up. He had evidently been struck with the thought that the theme was one which should not be developed in my bachelor presence. I was inwardly relieved that he thought so.

"I'm so very glad you've got things right again, doctor," broke in my mother. Like so many women she was a diplomatist at these embarrassing moments, helping the doctor to break off his disclosures the while she paid his professional skill a compliment.

"The crisis is over for the present," said the doctor, "but things are far from being all right again. In cases of this kind, Mrs. Jennings, one never knows! It's rather soon to prophesy, and the mother is only very poorly. And as to the baby—well, what could one expect? It's a weakling."

"Isn't it dreadful to think that her husband is away while all this happening?" said my mother, suddenly remembering Kish Massy. Doctor O'Sullivan rose from the table and crossed to the window.

"I found myself under something of an obligation in that matter," he said, "and took the liberty of cabling him this morning. This is a copy of what I said."

I crossed to the window and read on the slip of paper—

"Mrs. Massy gave premature birth to daughter this morning. Mother critical condition.

"O'Sullivan."

"Don't you think I was right in acquainting him at once?" the doctor asked.

"Quite right, I said.

"Lady Newell, who refuses to leave Deerpark until all danger is past, is anxious to see you, Jennings. I wanted a little blow of fresh air and decided to drive down to you myself, killing two birds with the one stone. Perhaps we had better drive back to Deerpark together when you are ready to come."

"I'm anxious to go at once," I said.

"Good," declared Doctor O'Sullivan.

As we drove away together he informed me that Lady

Newell had dispatched a groom the night before to Ballinacoorty for Mrs. Briscoe. She had probably arrived by this time.

When Deerpark came in sight through the trees some memory of what had passed there appeared to come back to the doctor.

"My God," he murmured a little absently, "what that gentle soul went through last night!"

II

Arrived at Deerpark, the doctor at once hurried upstairs to the patient. I went to the box at the back of the hall door to attend to the letters. The house was curiously alive to little hushed noises, the drift of leaves on the steps outside an accompaniment to them. I had a feeling of nervousness, as I fumbled for my key. The voices of two maids in conversation behind the *portières* came to me quite clearly.

"What time were you up, Lizzie?"

"A little after five. The shrieks wakened me."

"So you heard them, too?"

"Heard them! Will I ever forget them?"

"Wasn't it awful! But you weren't in the room?"

"No, I wasn't in the room."

I closed the letter-box with a bang and the voices stopped. Slippered feet scudded down in the direction of the kitchen. I crossed the hall murmuring, "My God!" and thinking how half the terrors of life, even the knowledge of life, come to us through overheard snatches of idle conversation. Other servants appeared as I made my way through the house; they looked very much like people who had been up all night. My coming seemed to bring them some measure of relief, as if they were glad to see some male of authority in the house. Broderick the butler ambled up to me on the stairs.

"No change in the condition of the mistress, sir," he said. "Nurse has just been down for hot water, and says there is no change. And Mrs. Mulcahy—Mrs. Briscoe that was—has arrived."

Something like a wan smile passed over his flabby face and I could see in his eye that he was itching to say, "I was up all night, sir."

I hurried up the stairs and as I made for the library Lady Newell came along the corridor from the opposite direction.

There was no change whatever in her appearance. She did not look in the least as if she had been up all night, or that she had done any nursing. She had evidently made a careful toilette, secured her rouge pot, used it with accustomed skill, arranged her wig, and all was well. Her aristocratic limp along the corridor was neither quicker nor slower than ordinarily; the hand on the knob of the ebony stick was as easily firm as its wont. The woodland violet eyes were as warm, the lips as expressive, as the first day I beheld them.

"*Bon jour*, Monsieur Paul," she said.

"*Bon jour*, madame."

I bowed her into the library. She limped down the room, threw open the window looking down on the garden, and seated herself there, breathing hungrily the morning air. I went to the writing-desk.

"I've heard what has happened," I said.

"And you survived," she said, drawing her chair more to the ledge of the window.

"I was greatly shocked," I said.

"But why?" she asked.

"Need you ask, Lady Newell?"

"Did you not know that Marie was *enciente*?" she demanded, her face full in the light.

"Well, yes, Captain Manning said something to me, but——" I was confused, disconcerted by her direct question. I think she deliberately wanted to embarrass me.

"The way of the world, *mon ami*, that it is all that it is. There is a new soul in Deerpark, a soul, oh, so *petite*! When I saw the little morsel, I said, 'What brings you to us in such great haste? What have you come to tell us that we do not know? What can you do that we have not already done? What pain can you speak of to us that we have not spoken of to each other? Are we not all bad enough and good enough as it is?' And the morsel that came in so great a hurry said nothing, Monsieur Paul, nothing at all—only the little heart ticked, ticked, fluttering under the shell-white breast, saying, 'Ah, I may have my day, too; I may have my day, too!' It is the way of the world."

Her eyes wandered down to the garden.

"There, Monsieur Paul, listen to that," she said, raising a finger. I listened. The drift of dry fallen leaves shifting about the paths, blown by little spasmodic breezes, sounded up from the garden and above it, sharp and clear, the song of the robin-redbreast.

"What a piping, what a dolorous tune!" she exclaimed. "It is the birds' Gregorian chant, churchyard melody, the *Dies iræ*!"

III

I turned uneasily in my chair at the desk. Lady Newell looked at me.

"Won't you tell me what happened yesterday evening?" I said. "Everything seemed so peaceful when I left. Certainly nobody expected anything of the kind to happen."

"Marie and myself were together," she said. "She was arranging some flowers by the window; I took a magazine to the fire. But I had eaten too much and fell asleep. When I woke up I was alone. Marie had fled. I saw the table, the flowers, two vases overturned, water on the carpet, flowers on the floor. Ah, all is not well, I said. Then there was an envelope on the floor. I picked it up."

"The envelope of a cablegram?" I asked, suddenly remembering the message I had taken to Mrs. Massy the previous evening.

"A cablegram, yes. I went to her room. There she was on the chair, her head back, rigid, white, the open cablegram under her hand on the lap. She was like one dead. I gave the alarm and they came. We put her to bed, the doctor came; it was a night of struggle, and this morning the baby arrived. Monsieur Paul,"—she leaned out on her chair to me—"you remember all the dolls Marie had dressed last winter? Dolls in the long babyclothes? They were given to the children of the peasants at Christmas, and afterwards trampled into—what you call it?—the borheens! Well, when the baby came this morning, Marie's baby, we had no garment for it. We had to borrow from the woman at the lodge."

The tragedy of the baby-linen was beyond my male ken. My mind went back to other details.

"What became of the message, the cablegram? I asked.

"Ah!" exclaimed Lady Newell, "that was the punishment, the blow, the bringer of all the woe, the arrow aimed at poor Marie. It flew how many thousand miles, and it struck home true, a poisoned dart!"

"You say it was on her lap when you found her unconscious?"

"It was on poor Marie's lap."

"Did you read the message, Lady Newell?"

"I am Marie's friend. I knew everything of her. I am a woman. What do you think? I read the message."

"Is it a great secret?"

"*Oui, oui*, a very great secret."

"May one ask if it came from her husband?"

"One may ask if it came from her husband, monsieur. It did. From the Kish."

I drummed my fingers on the writing-desk. Lady Newell rose, taking a paper from some secret place in the laces of her sleeve. She limped to the desk.

"I put the message away. What a scandal if the servants found it on her lap and read it! No-body has seen it—none must see it—except you."

"And may I read it?"

"I think you had better read it."

She lay the thin wafer of paper on the desk before me, and on folding it out I read this cablegram—

To Mrs. Massy, Deerpark, Ballyrea, County Galway, Ireland. Have instructed my solicitors to file petition of divorce against you naming your paramour and lover Paul Jennings as co-respondent.

K. Massy.

I read the words slowly and carefully twice over, noting the villainous phrasing. I was dimly conscious that Lady Newell had limped down the room, getting me between herself and the light of the window so that she might study the effect of the news on me. I endeavoured to read it for the third time, but the words swam. Something burning hot had jumped into my eyes. Dull knocks sounded over my temples and through my whole body; down into the very depths of my bowels a sensation which I had never experienced before seized me. A knowledge that some wrong had been done, a mean revolting wrong, gripped me like a paralysis. I felt ravaged to the soul.

"Well, Monsieur Paul, what do you think?" Lady Newell asked.

"It is a lie, a vile lie," I said, a hatred for the very document itself sweeping me. "And he knows it to be a lie."

She shrugged her shoulders, moving back again to the window.

"Yes, a liar, a cowardly liar!" I cried, jumping up. I could see the figure of the woman sit back on the chair by the window. The blood was pumping in hot squirts into my head.

"You are impossible," she said. "You cannot see that it is not the Kish alone."

"Not the Kish?" I cried with asperity. "There is his name. If it is not he, who is it?"

"Somebody with him. Somebody of the American culture. Somebody to whom he has been relating the manner of your life here and who has scented scandal and money in the situation.

"Some blackmailer!" I cried.

"Ah! that is the word," exclaimed Lady Newell.

"How I have strained for it the whole morning, racking my poor brain! Blackmailer! What a lovely word! You know, then, the Kish was refused money?"

"I do."

"This was the reply, the return blow, the prompt from his American friends."

"How do you know that?"

"Because the Kish is too much of Connacht to think of divorce. It is more of the American culture, and the French culture, too. Their minds run that way. Kish is of Connacht, like the rest of you, and you have not the civilization, the talent, for the divorce. You are too much of the savage, the primitive, giving and taking in marriage, bringing up—what you call it?—long families, grubbing about in the ground for food, living like the animals! You have the harsh religious mind, like my old servant, Suzanne, from Brittany, who was always saying, 'Lord have mercy on us, Lord have mercy on us!' She would sit in the sun under the cherry trees in blossom shivering at thoughts of the grave. She was in her coffin years before she died! Ah, there is an American mind at the back of the Kish!"

I moved away from the desk to the fire-place. Extraordinary! I had no sooner stepped on the hearthrug than an oppressive sense of the very physical presence of Kish Massy came to me. I could hear his breathing, the little heated puffs of his nostrils. I could smell the scent of the sweat of his fat body. It was the sensation which had come to me the evening I read hatred in the corner of the oblong eye. I spat into the fireless grate.

"*He's* the blackmailer, *he's* the liar, whatever way you reason," I cried. "He is the man, the husband, who put his name to that vile message, who sped the poisoned dart. The venom of his soul is in the conception. By God, I would like to choke him, to squeeze the last breath out of his body."

I strode over to the book-shelves. But Lady Newell was following up her own train of thought. She said, "His American friends saw all the possibilities of a divorce; they reckoned up the value of Deerpark in— what you call it?—hush money. I know these Americans. They come to us in flocks to France. They saw the possibilities of the case."

Saw the possibilities of the case! Like a red flame on my heated brain they blew upon me, vivid as a nightmare. I could see the court, the judge, the witnesses, the barristers, the listeners. I could hear counsel for the petitioner telling the world of the life of intrigue, of debauchery, in Deerpark. I could hear him polish me up as the seducer of another man's wife. I could see myself being spied upon by servants. I could hear my visits and doings in the mansion of the wife dated, labelled, ticked off, legally interpreted. I could see my behaviour, sifted and skilfully worked up to the day of horror when I had been discovered by the husband himself in the woman's bedroom endeavouring to bully her into the making of a will to disinherit her own husband! I had made the husband's life such a hell upon earth that he had to fly his own home, compelling him in sheer self-protection to drag the whole painful story before the court! . . . The possibilities of a divorce story lay to the hand of counsel! By the time he had finished with me nothing would remain except for some loafer of the court, who had beaten his own wife the night before, to spit upon me as I walked out the door. Kish Massy the wronged would get his decree of divorce *a mensa et thora*. My God, what an irony! Mary Heffernan divorced from Kish Massy's table and bed! I laughed harshly . . . Then his figure loomed again in my mind's eye as I had seen him snorting at me on the hearthrug. My hand was on a book and I hurled it across the room. It clattered into the grate. Another and another volume followed, ornaments crashed into the fender, the books sang through the air. I emptied out the length of a shelf and then only stopped, the sweat pouring from my temples.

All the time Lady Newell sat by the window, silent, immovable.

"He's a liar!" I cried, turning to her again. Some instinct that she was against me, that she might even defend him, came to me, galling me to the liver.

She shrugged her shoulders.

"You know him to be a liar and yet you sit there saying nothing, looking at me as if this was not damnation!" I shouted.

Her lips smiled. I strode over to her.

"You know what else he is besides," I said in a low voice.

She looked up at me cooly.

"Well?" she asked.

"You knew him to be what he was in conscience, in intent, in heart!" I said. "You yourself had him watched. The housekeeper knew him for what he was. The very cat smelt murder on his heels."

"Bah!" she cried. Something of guttural contempt in the word was like another stab at me.

"Your contempt is all for me," I cried. "You will stand in with the Kish. You too are turning your eyes to the future master of Deerpark, to the usurper!"

She sprang to her feet. Something in her appearance, something that was as a racial fire within her, checked me. I was conscious of something in the blood and temper of the woman which matched my own passion even in its white heat. I felt that at last this being with her rouged cheeks and golden wig had been stirred, her spirit fired. Her splendid self-control was gone and instead something of the hysteria stored up during her night in the sick room was getting the better of her.

"Bah!" she cried again, the breath quickening. "All your thoughts, all your words, are of yourself, or of him, the Kish. What do I care for the Kish, for you? Nothing! What about Marie? Is there nothing of her in your mind, in your heart?"

The words cut me like a whip. They cut me in their

vehemence and in their truth. What about Marie indeed? Had I not been thinking of myself only? Had I not always been thinking of myself? And if the arrow which had been fired had brought me the pain I had known, what had it not brought to the woman at whom it had been aimed, who had gone down under the blow? Had I indeed anything in my heart worthy of that woman? I shrank at the sudden prospect of all of woe, of pain, of misery, that had come to her.

"Marie was above you all; so much above you all!" cried Lady Newell. "Yet she was the one who was at the pleasure of mean little spirits! Bah! I hate you all!"

I stood speechless before that suddenly aggressive, quivering woman, seeing more in her eyes, her gestures, the thrills of her body, than she could ever make vocal by words. She moved from the chair to the corner of the desk, tottering a little without her stick.

"You don't understand," I said, moving to the centre of the room. She swerved about to me at once.

"What is it to me what you say, what you feel, what you suffer?" she exclaimed. "Nothing! Leave Marie to her pain! *Mon Dieu*! her pain! Who can tell me of that, of what it was—I who had her arms about my body in her agony in the night? Was it not my agony, too?"

I shrank from her, for back to my mind came the look in the doctor's face as he murmured, "God! what that gentle soul went through last night!" Back to my mind, too, came the conversation of the servants behind the *portière.* There was terror for me in the vehement, passionate woman who confronted me.

"What does it matter now who has done the wrong, who has sped the dart? Nothing! All is levelled, all is made inconsequent. All your struggles and deceits and threats—all your talk of divorce, of reprisals—all these are as the dry leaves on the path, blown aside by the wind, put out of the way, forgotten. For that is in the house which makes us all as nothing. Death is in the house!"

I made a movement, like a man who instinctively puts up his hand to shield himself from some vicious blow.

"Oh, you don't believe; you would not have that!" she cried. "But I tell you that Death is in this house. Where have I seen it? In the terror of her eyes, in the green froth at the corners of her mouth, in the grey of her gums, in the hands fumbling on the quilt, hands searching, groping, for something that will never be found. Ah! I tell you Marie has been tried beyond her strength."

"I won't believe it," I cried. "You are overstrung, morbid."

Lady Newell leaned toward me, speaking rapidly—

"Briscoe came but now. Marie looked up at her and did not know who it was came to her. She did not know the woman who has been her slave all her life. She was so weary the eyes closed, she went off into a little sleep, one of the little sleeps that make easy the last journey.

And Briscoe—who could see Briscoe and forget? A black figure, a symbol of the Fates, over the bed, grim watcher over the comings and goings of the race, her head hunched low between her shoulders, her body swaying and swaying! Ah! there was sorrow! And then the head raised, thrown back, the long arms going out over the bed in a great gesture of woe! How these peasants can pray, how they can beseech God and storm heaven! She sang, Briscoe sang, . . . *'Ochone, Mary Heffernan! Ochone, Mary Heffernan!'* There was tragedy in the notes, there was woe! And the words were words for a woman dead, and the cry for a Sept that was no more. Listen! I had been there all night. I had gone with Marie through the storm of the night's agony and never flinched. But now I fled the room, and from the door as I went I saw Briscoe's black figure sink at the foot of the white bed like a drowning woman. Ah! there was sorrow, there was tragedy!"

"My God, my God!" I cried. I was feeling like a man who grows groggy from receiving blows in the face.

"That is it," cried Lady Newell, "mutter to your God and let all your weak prayers be for yourself. What have you ever done for Marie; what have you ever brought to her that has not been a pain?"

"You know nothing of our lives, nothing of our bond, our friendship," I cried.

"Friendship! Bond! Bah! What is the friendship you

speak of but a name for treachery? What is your bond but something in which you have wrapped up your secret? Do not speak of her now. Leave her to her pain! She had not for you the passionate darkness of Betty Carolan! When you speak of her again let it be over the mill-race!"

She was so passionate that she tottered from the desk to a chair, gripping it by the back.

"Friendship is your name for deceit," she cried. "Oh! I hate your sort—you with your half-passion, you who would and wouldn't, you with skill in attentions that cost you nothing, you who hoard up your own passions, the meanest of misers, you who crush a rose on a woman's breast and kiss the petals! Bah! I hate you all!"

I made an attempt to speak. She cut me short. Her venom was appalling.

"Death is in the house!" she cried. "I tell you Death is in the house. Last night with her arms about me, in her hour of agony——"

She stopped suddenly. Somebody was coming down the corridor outside. She made a movement of recovery, tottering back to the writing-desk, gripping it with hands that shook. A breeze from the window blew the flimsy slip of cablegram along the blotting-pad and the movement, catching my eye, filled me with panic lest it should be discovered.

I strode across the room, reaching out for it, my fingers itching to tear the hateful thing to shreds. The footsteps stopped outside.

"No, no, do not destroy it," Lady Newell exclaimed, suddenly gripping my wrists as I reached for the cablegram. The strength of her grip amazed me. She was wiry in a physical sense beyond belief. But the hatred of that message, the terror that it should be discovered, filled me with a blind passion. I jerked her hands from my wrists. She still clung on, our hands swaying upward, a foolish struggle taking place a yard from the desk. A final wrench was more powerful than I intended. She lost her grip, tottering back, and in the confusion her wig was pushed from her head, falling down behind her back. A little cry broke from her as her foot, in its backward sweep, trod on the wig. She swayed so dangerously that I put out my hand to steady her. She quaked under my touch, her body shrinking, and I stepped back appalled. Where Lady Newell had stood a moment before there now cowered an apparition, a nightmare—an old woman with a head bald and shining, gruesome in its whiteness above the distinct line of the rouge high on the forehead, anæmic grey hairs which one might count struggling across the pallid skull. A cry again broke from her, a little cry of muffled despair, such a cry as a woman might utter who was wronged, and in another moment the door opened and Dr. O'Sullivan stood there.

The old woman shrank back, cowering and unnerved.

"I'm sorry," said Dr. O'Sullivan. "I came to tell you———"

"Marie is dead!" The words broke from the shrinking creature.

The doctor bowed his head at the door.

"It's all over," he said. "Mrs. Massy is at peace."

Mechanically I tore up the cablegram and the little shreds of paper fluttered to the ground.

CHAPTER TEN

I

THE dream which Kish Massy had dreamed by
the dining-room fire of Deerpark on a bright
April day came to pass on a sullen, sunless
morning in November. He was not there as chief
mourner—there was no chief mourner—but a vivid funeral procession wound its way through the brown hills
to the churchyard at Gorrybeg. There, for the last time,
the Heffernan vault yawned, taking in the last of the
clan, the mother and the babe. For the child had only
survived the mother by an hour.

I was one of the small band of people who afterwards
straggled back to Deerpark to hear the will read. We sat
silent and gloomy in the silent and gloomy house while
Mr. O'Moore's sweet voice read the will, dated the previous May, and by which Kish Massy was made the pos-
sessor of all that belonged to his wife—all except three

minor bequests: £300 to her dear friend, Lady Agatha Newell, £200 to Dr. Noel Mitchel, the bishop, for religious and charitable purposes, and £100 to her faithful servant, Margaret Briscoe.

When the brief ceremony was ended I handed over to Mr. O'Moore, as the representative of Kish Massy, my keys and a statement of my accounts and walked out of the house for what I believed to be the last time.

Outside the hall door I shook hands with Colonel Burke and Captain Manning.

"I was saying to the Colonel that it is a strange turn in the fortunes of Deerpark," said Captain Manning as he got up on his car. "She intended changing that will—she told me so. It was one of the first things to be done as soon as she got back from Ballinacoorty! And now—"

The Captain flecked the horse with his whip and drove off.

"Pooh soul, she got a shawp knock," said Colonel Burke. "I expect Agwatha will winter in Fwance."

Thereafter my interests shifted. I became engrossed in the business of flour and meal milling and in the development of my own personal farm, long neglected.

Old Hugh Carolan was failing and as he failed he became more and more reconciled to the idea of a son-in-law.

The June following Betty and myself were married. One of the first gifts to reach us was a basket of live lobsters from Ballinacoorty with the compliments of Mr. and Mrs. John Mulcahy!

Deerpark was receding from my life. It lived only in the flickering stories which came to us of Kish Massy. He was still in New York. Indefinite but insistent reports were bruited that he had got married again. His new wife was, they said, a Miss Dorothy Vernon, the daughter of a New York lawyer. But it was fully a year after the death of his first wife before the servants in Deerpark were officially and definitely informed that Mr. Kish Massy and Mrs. Vernon Massy were coming to take up residence in Ireland.

II

Betty and myself had just taken our places in the pew we occupied every Sunday. People were filling into the seats before and behind us. Suddenly the air became charged with a most insidious perfume. I sniffed it suspiciously. What had it reminded me of? Where had I gotten it before? I was so interested that Betty looked up at me quizzically.

"What's the matter?" she whispered. "You look like a man who scents his dinner burning."

The next moment a little sensational wave had passed over the congregation, one of those little electrical currents which everybody affects to ignore and everybody helps to generate. We had the sensation, known only to compact and local congregations, that strangers had come amongst us. The sensation leapt from mind to mind like a taper lighting up the candles on an altar. The whiff of perfume excited me particularly. Presently our sensation was confirmed. For up the church came a trio which drew all eyes. It was Kish Massy, Mrs. Vernon Massy, and Mr. Smith Vernon, her father, the New York lawyer. They marched up to a front pew. Mrs. Vernon Massy's dress swished close to me as they went by, almost drowning my senses with the curious perfume.

Kish Massy had become young, that second youngness which comes through certain compulsions and not by process of nature, like second childhoods. His piquant youngness was expressed in a definite reduction of the girth and in the cut of the clothes to emphasize this reduction. He had that red clearness of skin which proclaims a discovery of the bath late in life. His characteristic frog walk had been subjected to a discipline which was not altogether a success but which, nevertheless, accomplished abbreviations in his comportment. But his second youth was expressed above all in a courageous dying of the hair. Not one of the former wiry grey members remained. They were now all a gleaming lamp-black. And the spring-time movement of his person was emphasized by the softness of his steps, for he wore galoshes. He looked like a man who had all guilty knowledge of stables sweated out through the pores of his skin by a heroic scheme of Turkish baths.

Beside him walked his second wife. She was as tall as himself. She walked with a loose stride. At the same time her figure was erect, that erectness which all American women possess, unconsciously, no doubt, inspired by the statue of Liberty in New York harbour. She looked a product of the gymnasium. Nay, she might even belong to a circus. She was arrayed in a green costume, a large green and white hat, which became her very well. She looked about twenty-seven years of age. "She's good-looking," I thought as I saw her face. Her expression was open, the eyes direct, frank, her bearing independent. She gave one the sense of enterprise, of a woman who would arrange her own affairs, who belonged to a race whose civilization was fresh. And she exhaled that disturbing perfume.

"I have it," I said to myself suddenly. "The pale blue envelopes! She's the real estate business in which Kish Massy had made investments before he had married Miss Heffernan!" A great many half-forgotten little incidents came back to my mind, now more illuminating. I smiled a little grimly.

Papa Vernon walked discreetly a pace behind Kish Massy and his lady. He was a keen, eager, tall man, taking peculiar high steps with remarkably long narrow feet encased in patent leather shoes.

His jaw was also long, sharp, pushful, honed and polished, adjusted and sharpened at the whetstone of life, a life, I should say, that revolved at a pretty rate. I had an uneasy feeling at sight of Papa Vernon. He looked too capable a man to have come to our hillsides merely for the good of his health.

"They're not Catholics," I thought as Papa Vernon and his daughter took their seats in the pew with Kish Massy. They had not genuflected to the altar. They stared about them with frankly curious eyes. Mrs. Vernon Massy took careful stock of the congregation. The women in shawls and cloaks especially attracted her notice. She gave them up for a contemplation of the candles on the altar. Papa Vernon plained his long keen jaw up at the Stations of the Cross on the walls, his eyes going from one picture to the other with a gaze that held some mixture of cynical curiosity. He stooped over and said something to his daughter and she joined him in a survey of the sacred pictures. They half turned their backs upon the altar. Another little electrical wave passed over the congregation. Kish Massy sat between them, his gleaming black head steady and stubborn.

The priest came to the altar and commenced the recital of the prayers before Mass. The members of the congregation knelt down and blessed themselves. Mrs. Vernon Massy made no attempt to do so. Papa Vernon was more enterprising. He made the attempt. I noticed that the hand went from the forehead to the left shoulder, then to the right shoulder and finally to the breast. I remembered that I had seen a very pious-looking actor in the part of Friar Laurence in a performance of *Romeo and Juliet* once bless himself exactly like that. Papa Vernon was, then, a stage Catholic! And if he were a stage Catholic, how many other stage things might he not be?

After Mass the new party from Deerpark drove away in the family carriage. Hot on their heels came another equipage along the Ballyrea road. It contained the Earl of Elmtree.

III

"I won't."

"You will."

"But I say I won't."

"But I say you will."

Betty and myself were having a little tiff; it was not the first. We were coming along the road on our bicycles. My lamp threw a yellow streak of light on the road, for it was dark. The question which had arisen was one as to whether, when we arrived on our way homewards at the entrance gates to Deerpark, we should there dismount and secretly view all that might be viewed from the road of a dance which was there in progress. Betty wanted to dismount; I wanted to go straight ahead home, ignoring the revelry at Deerpark.

When we reached the Deerpark gates we dismounted.

The house was a blaze of light. Most of the windows

were thrown open. The music of a string band playing a Straus waltz came alluringly on the night air. In the left wing the dancing was in progress. The couples went flitting past the windows in the waltz. We stood staring at them for some time. This dance was the culminating event of an unusually big house party at Deerpark.

For something over three years now the Vernon Massys had been in residence there, entertaining on a lavish scale. There had been gossip, of course. There had been things said. There was, for instance, that trip to the Continent the summer before last. Then there was the season that Lord Elmtree had his yacht off the Galway coast, the flights up and down to it, the queer comings and goings of the social vampires whom the place attracted. Captain Manning had been horrified at certain financial transactions carried out by Kish Massy; there had been a wholesale selling of shares in order to make new investments in America. Papa Vernon, who had returned to the States, was understood to be the new financial expert to Kish Massy. Captain Manning felt wounded to the soul when even the brewery shares were sold out in favour of an American phonograph syndicate.

"I always said it, and now it is confirmed," said the Captain. "A fellow who gets on grand with horses is never of account at anything else. Take his hand off a halter and he's a fool."

The waltz music from Deerpark was sweet and allur-

ing. The old house never looked so gay. Betty and myself gazed up at it in silence.

Suddenly a woman laughed quite near in the shrubberies. It was an amused, short laugh. A man's voice
spoke in an undertone. Then there was silence. The
band went on playing the waltz. The revolving figures
flit across the lighted windows. To the hall door came a
figure, standing there in bold relief against the bright
light inside. The figure was unmistakable. It was Kish
Massy. He stood on the steps, then moved about, looking uneasy and undecided. He seemed like one who had
come out to seek something, nervous and anxious, baffled and disturbed. He mopped his face with his handkerchief and went in again.

Across from the shrubberies two figures moved, silent and shadowy. They crossed to a sort of kiosk, one of
the new glories of Deerpark, which had been erected in
the lawn, its body painted vermilion, its cupola a daz-
zling white. The tall shadowy figures disappeared into
the kiosk.

Betty and myself mounted our bicycles and pedalled
along the road.

"Very nice band," I said laconically after a time.

"Very," Betty agreed. Then after a pause, "She's
nearly as tall as he is."

"Who is nearly as tall as he is?" I asked.

"Mrs. Vernon Massy."

"And who is he?"

"Lord Elmtree."

"How do you know?"

"I noticed it as they came out of the shrubbery and crossed to the kiosk."

Next morning the visitors left Deerpark. There was, it was said, a more premature stampede than expected in consequence of some unpleasantness. Mr. Kish Massy had had a quarrel with Lord Elmtree. There was a good deal of confusion in the house. And when it quietened down it was discovered that everybody had gone, including Mrs. Vernon Massy.

A telegram came for Mr. Massy later in the day. It was hinted that it came from his wife announcing her flight with the Earl. The effect on Mr. Massy followed strictly on precedent. He at once made for the sideboard. He did not even pause to put in soda water.

He kept to it at a pace which broke all previous records. And people said he was egged on by the knowledge that he was financially ruined.

"Talk about the Heffernans!" scoffed Broderick the butler. "None of them ever had that man's capacity. He's a wonder!"

CHAPTER ELEVEN

I

I WAS aroused from my slumbers in the middle of the night by a heavy thumping on the front door. I donned some clothes, lighted a candle and descended. When I opened the door I could discern in the light of the candle Augustine Massy's pallid face in its frame of black beard. I looked at him and he looked at me.

"Good morning," I said as he appeared reluctant to speak.

"Good morning, Mr. Jennings," he replied. "I called to ask if you know anything about Kish."

I was never so conscious of Augustine Massy's extraordinary impassivity, his sense of neutrality towards life. When he asked me, at four o'clock in the morning, if I knew anything about his brother Kish I felt inclined to put the candle to his beard in the hope of rousing him.

"I'm afraid I know little about Kish," I replied.

"Of his present whereabouts, Mr. Jennings? Do you know anything of his whereabouts? His present whereabouts are unknown."

"Of his whereabouts I know nothing," I replied. "It is possibly the only thing I don't know about him."

"Well, he's missing."

"Missing?"

"He's missing right enough, Mr. Jennings."

"How long?"

"Some hours it must be now. He escaped about one."

"Escaped?"

"Yes, bedad. Out of the house, out of Deerpark, out of his bed."

A draught nearly put the candle out. The hot grease was running down all one side, burning my fingers. And I was not equipped for a nocturnal conversation at the hall door. I requested Augustine Massy to step in, and he did so.

We sat down in the chill of a room lighted by the guttering candle. Augustine Massy's black beard looked like a splash of ink in the general gloom.

"I might say," he began, speaking in a sepulchral tone," that my brother has been down for some time with an attack of *delirium tremens.* Broderick was up with him last night, and I took my turn tonight. A few nights ago it took four men and the pantry boy to hold him down."

"And you say he has escaped?"

"I do. And so he has. I thought he was grand and quiet so I sat by the fire, and what with the dint of the heat the sleep overcome myself. When the fire went out I wakened up, shivering with cold; and just, Mr. Jennings, as I stooped for the coal-scuttle I noticed the door opened and a fearful draught from it. Then I glanced at the bed. All the clothes were streeling down on the floor. I walked over and I saw, right enough, that the bird had flown."

Augustine Massy's white languid hand stroked the black beard as if he had done very well and did not purpose doing anything more.

"Did you search the house for him?" I asked.

"I roused the servants," he replied. "We got lights and we searched the house, and neither colour nor clue of Kish could we find. We said we'd rouse the neighbors and do the best we could to get on his tracks."

"What's the matter?" a voice suddenly called from the head of the stairs. It was Betty, also roused from her sleep.

"It's all right," I said. But the next moment the baby woke up and the house was no longer silent.

"There's nothing wrong with that fellow's lungs, anyway," said Augustine Massy.

"No," I said, "that fellow's lungs are all right."

I explained to Betty what had happened, completed my attire, and decided to join in the search for Kish Massy.

II

August Massy and myself issued from the house into the bright moonlight of an October morning.

"The question is," I said, "where are we to head for?"

"That's the thing," agreed Augustine Massy. His tone was thoroughly disinterested. He gave me the feeling that we were merely walking down the road for a casual stroll and this feeling irritated me.

A voice sang out somewhere in the fields. It was a feeble voice, but we wheeled about at once. For some moments we saw nothing. I leapt up on the ditch. The country was extraordinarily peaceful in the flood of soft light. The voice came to us again, more decisive. Then in the distance, in a clump of stunted thorns, I saw a figure flit from bush to bush. It was certainly the figure of a man, but a man in an attire which was indefinite.

"It's himself!" exclaimed Augustine Massy, but there was no trace of excitement in the exclamation. "It's very like the talk of him since he took bad. He's always shouting about climbing up an elm tree if it was to cost him his life."

The distant figure disappeared.

"Come along," I cried, and jumping from the ditch into the field set out in a run in the direction of the bushes. It was as certain as anything in life that Augustine Massy if left to himself would walk up very leisurely, or else sit on the ditch for hours droning out his casual observations. At it was he had to follow me as well as he could. We beat about the clump of bushes. A hare sat up on his haunches, his ears alert, and in another moment cut down the hill. But no other sign of life was visible.

"He's gone," said Augustine Massy. Resignation was no name for his tone.

The quarries were some hundreds of yards above us. At my suggestion we bent out steps there. An instinct to avoid all initiative was powerful in Augustine Massy's psychology.

The yawning openings of the earth at the quarries were appallingly suggestive when connected with the mission which had brought us there. What a place for a delirious patient! We looked helplessly about us, peered down into the depths, but all was at peace.

"I wonder did he fall into the quarries," said Augustine Massy. He might as well have said, "I wonder did he put on his hat."

I offered no opinion, and we made a round of the pit-heads. The moon threw its pale beams on the seams in the earth. We struggled up and down over the mounds of splinters. Here and there boulders of rock jutted out in the depths below, throwing long black patches of shadow across the bottom of the quarries. There was a silence which impressed, emphasized as it was by the trickle of water down the declivities. Once or twice we ventured down the rude passages hewn into the quarries, the coarse gravel slipping in little landslides under our feet. While we groped along one of these passages Augustine Massy had what I firmly believe to be the only inspiration of his blameless life. I saw his lean sombre form reach out over a shoulder of rock, his black beard and pallid face hanging over the abyss like a death's head, and his hollow booming voice called out with little command and no hope: 'Kish! Kish! Kish!''

The name rumbled in the quarry beneath us; it passed like a complaining spirit from one cavity to the other and, booming more faintly hollowly as it travelled, died away somewhere in an exhausted "Kish!''

We awaited the result of this experiment, standing tense in the chilly passage. But the earth gave back no account of Kish Massy. The drip of the eternal water on the ledges of rock was like the ticking of a great many clocks. A sense of desolation and despair came to me. A rat squealed, hopped on to the passage before us, another followed, they fought like a pair of dogs in the moonlight, an owl circled overhead, the rats tumbled under a bolder, the owl sailed away and all was again still, except for the watery ticking of all the quarry clocks. Without a word we turned on our heels and scrambled up for the opening.

"He mustn't be here after all," said Augustine Massy, looking about him in a hopeless way. "Maybe he's gone home again by this. Or maybe the others got him." His own eyes wandered in the direction of Deerpark. He was tired of the search.

We stood together, undecided and baffled. A faint sound came to us, unexpected and extraordinarily familiar. I heard it before my companion.

"Listen," I cried.

Imperfectly and brokenly, a very wraith of sound, it came to us, Kish Massy's voice in his little out-of-tune song!

"It's himself surely," said Augustine Massy. "He's always at it: *The Bells of Shandon*."

We followed as well as we could the thin elusive trail of sound. It brought us back in the direction of the mouth of the quarries. There we stood, very much puzzled. We had a clear view of the sloping side of the quarry beneath us, the moon shining directly upon it. There was no trace of a human figure on these slopes, nor along the edge of the pitheads in front of us. And yet the voice was nearer, more distinct. It was uncanny.

"Well, that's not a bad one! Will you look where he is?"

I turned to Augustine Massy as he droned out the words. His white hand was pointing up at the moon as far as I could follow it. For a wild moment I wondered if this second Massy had also lost his health. Then my eye came nearer to earth.

I saw the sight.

My eye ranged along the sloping shaft of a crane

which reached out from the bank over the quarry. Silhouetted against the moonlit sky was the figure of Kish Massy in his night-shirt seated right at the end of the jib of the crane! The spectacle almost made me reel. And although the air of the famous song was difficult to recognize, I could hear the words, tremulously distinct—

> "With symbals
> glorious,
> Swinging uproarious
> In the gorgeous turrets
> Of Notre-Dame!"

I was incapable of intelligent action, or indeed thought, as I beheld that figure seated precariously over a clear and final drop into the bowels of the earth.

"I wonder how did he get up?" Augustine Massy speculated calmly.

The bloodlessness of the fellow roused me. "Hadn't you better wonder how you'd get him down?" I snapped.

But Augustine Massy paid no attention to my manner. "He was a terrible active customer always," he said, "and no beating him at climbing. I always said he'd do something remarkable in the way of climbing." There was a grand patronage in the words, a sustained detachment.

I approached the crane cautiously. Augustine Massy strolled after me. And as we did so the horror of the position became more patent. There was a clear drop into an ugly patchwork of jagged rock.

"There is only one thing for it," I said. "We must swing round the crane so that the jib may reach over the bank and not over the quarry."

"That would not be a bad idea," Augustine Massy agreed. "I suppose he would not slidder down the shaft for us himself. I say, Kish, come down out of that, man alive! It's no place at all for you. You'll get your death of cold."

The figure made some movement on its aerial perch at the words—some endeavour to turn round at his brother's behest. The movement was fatal. His body lolled a little to one side, then slipped.

The weird moonlit scene swam before my eyes as the horror of the thing broke upon me. Kish Massy had, indeed, been my enemy. Between us there had been hatred. But whatever was human in the man's ugly bizarre life warmed in my mind as I saw his helpless body slip for a sheer plunge into the pit and into eternity. My eyelids instinctively sealed my eyes. I waited, tensely and grimly, to hear above the tinkling of the water the hollow distant thud which would tell its own tale of nameless horror. No thud sounded. Instead Augustine Massy's impassive monotone struck my ears again.

"That's not a bad one neither," he said. "His night-shirt got caught on the hook and I thinking he was slipping."

I opened my eyes and looked up at the crane, that shaft of death poised in the grey neutral light of the heavens. I could have shouted in a hysteria of laughter, danced a fantastic dance about the pit head. For suspended between the pale heaven and the black earth was the fat naked body of Kish Massy, swinging from the great hook of the chain of the crane. The shirt was twisted about the shoulders and neck in a crude bulk; through this crude bulk the hook had struck, an act of Fate which saved the slipping body from the maw of the chasm beneath.

When I looked first I thought the spectacle a monstrous parody on a hooked fish. In a slow methodical movement the body revolved half-way round and back again. I could see the gleam of the moonlight on one great haunch now, another again.

The illusion of the hooked fish passed. He was more like some outlandish carcase getting basted upon a spit before a fire, a sight to ravish the minds of all cannibals. If Kish Massy had seen anything more appalling in the hours of his delirium than this horror over the green marble quarries, with the half-hidden things in the rocky delved earth beneath him, I do not wonder that he ran stark mad out of his bed. The only memory of his former existence which seemed in the least familiar was the occasional short jab of the left arm, a gesture which added to his farcically tragic plight.

"My God!" I breathed.

I turned to his brother. The fellow had struck an easy attitude, one leg crossed over the other, his right elbow in the palm of his left hand, his long languid white fingers caressing his black beard, a contemplative expression on his face, his unemotional eyes raised to the spectre which the moon and the stars of heaven also gazed upon.

"I tell you what," he said at last, "it was a good job for Kish he could never bear pyjamas."

A faint rent of clothing up where the body revolved brought my mind back to the possibility of a fresh calamity.

"The shirt is giving," said Augustine Massy. "I heard it giving, tearing upon the hook." If the shirt was giving, tearing upon the hook, the plunge into the quarries was still clear and imminent for Kish Massy. I sprang to the crane, and began to press about the arm on its revolving disk, so that the body, if it did drop, would fall on the bank and not into the abyss. Augustine Massy came to my aid rather leisurely. I saw the body swaying in the air as the crane swung round, for the chain with its hook was only a few feet from the top of the jib. There was another rent of the garment and the heavy body dropped a few inches as it gave. but in a few moments the greatest horror of the position had passed. The arm the crane no longer loomed over the mouth of the quarry.

"Now, quick, get him down," I called out, and grasping the handles of the wheel we started to lower with all speed, the feeling coming to me that I was supplying most of the motive power. The crane had not been oiled, or indeed used at all, for some time past. The rusty chain creaked painfully as it unwound itself from the drum, and the teeth of the drum itself grated in the gearing. But the figure slowly descended, swaying a little to and fro, and in one of the rapid glances I had of it I noticed that the jabbing of the left arm had ceased. At last the feet touched the earth and we ran to afford all the succour we could to the miserable figure. I almost sprang back again as my hand touched the body. No slab of marble which had ever come out of the quarries was so cold as that body. The face, suddenly near to me, I beheld with horror. The protruding, glassy, immense eyes stared up at the moon in a glacial stare. The skin was blue-black. There were wounds and bruises on the body. A scar marked the line of the back where the hook had caught him as he fell. The wisps of hair hung dank and piebald from the head. The sweats of the fever through which he had passed had caused the dye to partly ooze from the hair. Lines of dissipation had eaten into the flesh under the eyes and about the mouth. With all the haste that I could, I cut with my penknife the entanglements of the nightshirt about the throat, where it was gathered as strong and as tight as a rope. When this had been done the shreds of the shirt hung about the body in a hundred fragments. I had the thought that the warrior-bard Oisin must have looked something like this when he had fought with a scourge all the devils in hell.

We laid him down on his back on the ground as gently as we could.

With that we heard the shuffle and voices of a body of searchers. We hailed them. They came plodding slowly to us, an old man coughing incessantly. Some carried lanterns. Some wore overcoats with great capes. But all were old men, and I had the feeling that old men always turn up for a thing of this sort, some instinct for the morbid inspiring them. They made a dramatic grouping about the prostrate body, ominous, silent, playing their lanterns over the prostrate figure, which looked more gruesome than ever in the yellow streaks of the light. They craned their old necks over him, the profile of one little old man with a hooked beak looking like a bird of prey.

"Praise the Lord!' said one, moving his lantern about the figure.

"The Cross of Christ upon us!" said another, hitching his coat on his stooped shoulders.

"He's a fearful and a dreadful sight," mumbled a third.

And all the time the man with the hacking cough peered blindly down at the figure and in the end put out a sinister old claw to feel him.

"His blood is frozen," he said, made the sign of the Cross, and then was shaken with the cough again.

We unearthed a hand-barrow from a tool-shed—not unlike a stretcher—and used for carrying slabs of stone. We took the overcoats from some of the old men and wrapped them about the body on the stretcher. Then we set out for Deerpark. The lantern bearers preceeded the stretcher, behind came the relief hands. The body was heavy, the ground was uneven and difficult; we stumbled and staggered slowly down the fields, the old man with the cough barking and wheezing constantly, the little fellow with the beaked nose so bent that his face hung horizontally over the earth.

"Praise the Lord!" he mumbled every now and then as we stumbled along.

At last we turned up the drive to Deerpark, brushing the laurels of the shrubberies. In the trees overhead a squirrel made some magnificent springs along the branches, clearly visible against the pale sky. Somewhere at the back of the house an owl was hooting. The shuffle of our feet was more sharp on the sand, but nobody spoke, not even the old man bent double, but the coughing was continuous. We staggered up the steps, straining and puffing, then somebody thudded heavily on the knocker.

The door was opened by the quaking hand of Broderick, and we passed in, a solid black shuffling body grouped about the stretcher. We crossed the hall and mounted the broad stairs and thence to the bedroom, where we lifted the unconscious form on to the bed.

The old man with the cough had seated himself on the first step of the stairway, unable to mount, and his coughs made echoes over the place. Augustine Massy had also detached himself from the group, going away in the direction of the kitchen to warm himself at the fire.

About the bed in the room the old men panted, their half-sceptical, half-grim faces sinister in the yellow light. A conversation, feeble as age itself, took place as to what was best to be done. Brandy was to be poured in between his teeth, hot blankets wrapped about his body, the doctor was to be sent for. While they talked and hobbled about the bed of the stricken man I knew quite well that the soul of Kish Massy had quitted its earthly habitation. Already he belonged to the dissolving elements of the earth.

I walked down through the gloom of that grim house, my arms aching, and as I descended the steps from the hall door my eyes caught a patch of the eastern sky, where a shaft of tremulous warm light was already proclaiming the coming of another day.